A BLACKSMITH'S GUIDE TO DRAGON REARING

DRAGONS OF SAFE HAVEN

BOOK TWO

JULIA HUNI

A Blacksmith's Guide to Dragon Rearing

Cover designed by Mariah Sinclair Designs

Editing by Paula Lester at Polaris Editing

Julia Huni

Visit my website at juliahuni.com

IPH Media

20260331.2

In Memory of

Col David P Mott

May your food be French, your powder be light, and your beer be better than just good.

Map Key

1. Dairy Farm
2. Tannery
3. Butcher
4. Bookshop
5. Mercantile
6. Tea Shop
7. Town Hall
8. Cafe
9. Crab and Tankard
10. Silver Acorn Inn
11. Chandler
12. Bakery
13. Blacksmith
14. Stable

The town of
Safe Haven
FarPoint
Valebra
1
2
3
4
5
6
7
8
9
10
11
12
13
14
Safe Haven Bay
← key

CHAPTER ONE

BEFORE THE HATCHING

The stench of old fish, the slippery footing, and the drip of water drowned Nevan's romantic dreams faster than a water bath cooled forge-hot steel. The steady glow of the enchanted stone in his palm highlighted the sheen of sweat on Franisa's pinched face as she edged carefully down the rocky slope, and her fierce grip on his arm signaled her trepidation. Obviously, she found his adventure nerve-racking rather than enticing.

When he had invited Franisa to see the dragon eggs, he'd thought this might be his opportunity to inspire warmer feelings in the baker. They had known each other from childhood—growing up across the square from her family's bakery ensured that. But Franisa was five years older than him, so she'd always viewed him as a child. He'd still been a teen when she married Keldan. And he was just a blacksmith's apprentice when her husband had died, leaving her with two small children.

But now, five years later, Nevan was much more than an apprentice. He was a potential dragon rider. Sir William Ordell had chosen him from all the men of the island, to help him tame the wild sea dragons and form the island's first fire brigade. In the last few months, he'd worked to become indispensable to the old dragon rider, even before he'd heard the man's plan. William might be grumpy, but something drew Nevan to him.

Having grown up on Safe Haven, Nevan had dreamed of taming the sea dragons—like every other child on the island. And now, through his growing friendship with the old man, his dream might just come true. He still wasn't sure how any of that was going to work, but he trusted William's vision. The retired guild master from Verduun understood dragons. If anyone could domesticate them, it was William.

"How much farther?" The normally cheerful brunette gripping his arm pushed damp hair away from her face. "I have to be back at the bakery before the children leave Cala's bookstore."

"Just around the corner. See the purple?" He closed his hand over the glow stone the retired war witch Cala Stormbringer had enchanted for him. Faint violet light illuminated the stone walls of the tunnel, glowing brighter at the bottom of the slope where the way turned.

They paused at the corner, and Nevan shrugged off his backpack. He pulled a covered jar from its padded wrapping and handed it to Franisa. "This is honey. The dragons like it."

"You didn't say anything about dragons." She took the clay jar in both hands, but her voice shook. "I thought there were just eggs down here."

"No, the queens are here too. They don't leave the eggs unattended." He shrugged the bag's straps over his shoulders. "That's why we have the honey. So they let us near the eggs."

Franisa looked at the jar again. "Is this enough? Dragons are big, aren't they?"

"It's as much as I could get on short notice." And the limited funds in his purse. Normally Koni brought honey from his hives, but this excursion wasn't exactly an official one. No one had said he *couldn't* bring a friend down to see the dragon eggs, but he wasn't sure how William would react to a woman down here. Verduunians had some odd ideas about females. And his Ma's stories about life with the Verduunian army lined up with William's notions.

"You go first." Franisa pushed the honey at Nevan, then pulled the jar back to her chest. "Or maybe I should keep this. They know you already. I don't want them to eat me!"

"Sea dragons don't eat humans. Or giants." As far as he knew. His introduction to them a few weeks before had convinced him they preferred honey or goat haunch, but that didn't mean they wouldn't be willing to branch out if they got really hungry. Maybe bringing a bite-sized human down here was a bad idea. Especially one that smelled as sweet as Franisa.

Too late now. "Let's go together." He took Franisa's arm and pulled her around the tight corner into the hatching ground.

Franisa gasped. They stood in an alcove in the wall of the cavern, about four feet above the main floor. The vibrant purple glow of dozens of eggs illuminated the entire cave, including two huge queens sleeping curled around the clutch. And the grizzled human sitting on the floor of the alcove talking to the third, enormous, very awake dragon.

"William!" Surprise and unease sharpened Nevan's voice, causing his exclamation to echo across the cavern. The dragon's head swung toward him, her tongue flicking around his face, then swiveling to inspect Franisa.

The woman shrieked and dropped the jar of honey. It broke on the stone, the sticky stuff splattering the alcove and everyone in it. The sleeping queens' heads jolted up, their tongues darting out to smell the air. With powerful hind legs, the other two dragons launched across the cavern, necks outstretched in their effort to outdistance each other and slurp up the sticky treat.

As all three dragons advanced, Franisa shrieked again and darted back into the tunnel.

William buried his face in his hands, his shoulders shaking. Nevan looked at the dragon rider, then turned to peer toward the passageway. A queens' huge head blocked the narrow opening through which the woman had disappeared. Should he try to push past the dragon and catch up with her?

"Let her go." William lifted his head, his face contorted with an obviously difficult attempt to banish mirth and project displeasure.

"Den bees don't belong in the hatching ground."

"Den bees?"

"Nest Nellies. Guild bunnies. Women who chase dragon riders." William's distaste came through loud and clear.

Nevan opened his mouth to argue, then snapped it shut. Franisa definitely wasn't a "den bee" and now he'd probably ruined any chance of making her see him as more than the little boy across the square.

EIGHT MONTHS LATER

THE SALTY SEA AIR BLEW THROUGH NEVAN'S THICK CURLS, pushing the damp tendrils away from his face as he and Starlight raced above the sea. Although he knew better, he itched to reach down and touch the frothy waves.

The thrill of flight stole his breath away. Pairing with Starlight, the runt of the sea dragon clutch, had changed his life. No longer a blacksmith's apprentice or itinerant handy man, Nevan had become one of the first three dragon riders of Safe Haven, besting even the elven mayor. People in the town treated him differently now. They showed him respect he'd never received before. And when he was on Starlight's back, he felt he could do anything.

As if in response to his thought, Starlight banked, the tip of her right wing slicing through the surf. "Careful. We don't want a repeat of yesterday."

The little dragon chirped cheerfully in response and straightened out. When she'd dipped her wing too deeply the previous day, they'd spiraled into the sea. He'd gotten a few bruises, but the dragon hadn't sustained any injury. He'd certainly learned a lesson, but he wasn't sure Starlight shared his newfound caution.

Starlight tilted up, flaring her wings to slow her speed. Nevan's legs slipped on the dragon's shoulders, and he tightened his knees. "Hey! You're going to drop me!"

With a mischievous flick of her tail, she tapped the top of his head, then shimmied. His wet fingers slid away from her slick hide. He grappled but couldn't get a grip, slipping down her back. Foreseeing the obvious conclusion, he took a deep breath as he fell into the warm ocean with a splash. The dragon circled over him, bugling in triumph, then settled to the water, flipping her wings like a duck. She twisted her neck around to flash a cheerful draconic smile.

He put a hand on her side, using her buoyancy to keep himself afloat. Not that it was necessary—his giant heritage made him surprisingly lightweight despite his size. He tipped his head back and let his feet bob to the surface, floating on his back. "I definitely need to get those flying straps."

A cold breeze whipped little whitecaps up around them as they floated. Although Safe Haven's near-equatorial location meant winter didn't include snow and sleet, the winds blew colder and sunset came earlier. The sea stayed warm, but the wind cut into Nevan's face and chilled his fingers. He paddled closer to Starlight and flung a leg over her back. "Let's go home. It's cold."

With her powerful wings, Starlight launched from the surface of the sea, rising at an ever-increasing angle. She lifted into the sky, catching an updraft from the heated stone of the cliff, then wheeled around to land on a wide ledge about two-thirds of the way up the rocky promontory.

The three dragon riders of Safe Haven officially lived at FarPoint tower. William had purchased it last year and, with Nevan's help, restored the house he and Cala now occupied. Their dragons slept in the renovated stable, a comfortable space with enough room for six dragons and riders. Nevan was the only rider currently living there, but if William's plans came to fruition, he'd need to move out when the next—larger—class paired with their newly hatched dragons.

None of them were sure exactly when that would happen. Unlike the long-domesticated war dragons of William's native Verduun, the sea dragons hadn't been studied much. The three of them speculated often, but they'd have to wait and see when the dragon queens would lay another clutch.

In the meantime, Nevan had decided to build a home for himself and Starlight in the caves below the tower. He'd found a suitable space and started making it habitable. Starlight seemed to like the nest. Den? Lair? Nevan had been trying to come up with a good name for the dragons' home, but so far none of the words seemed to fit. The Verduunian dragons lived in a guild house, but no matter how nice he made the cave, that phrase wouldn't be suitable.

Nevan slid off Starlight's wet back and landed on the flat stone ledge. It was wide enough for the man and the dragon, with space to spare. A shallow cave stretched the length of the ledge. He had to duck to get inside, but it opened into a nicely vaulted room. Sunlight penetrated to the back of the cave in the winter, but in the summer, the overhang would protect the space from overheating. It was deep enough to hold a bed for him and a warm hollow for Starlight. He'd installed vertical beams to support a wall across the front, with plans to insert the largest windows he could afford and a big door to allow the dragon access. Then he'd put in a wood stove for the cooler winter months and perhaps run a fresh water supply.

Standing in the weak sunlight, he stripped off his wet clothing and put on the extra shirt and pants he'd stashed after the previous day's dunking. He hadn't thought he'd need them so soon. He didn't have a spare pair of boots, so he'd have to go barefoot until they dried. Luckily, his giant blood kept his feet warm even when the rest of him was chilled. But maybe he'd prioritize installing the wood stove. It would be nice to have a little extra warmth on these chillier winter days.

Behind him, Starlight curled up in her stony hollow, basking in the mild sun. With a fond smile for his partner, he picked up his tools to continue building their future home.

CHAPTER TWO

Rhythmic kneading of the dough calmed Franisa. Push and fold, turn and dust with flour. Repeat. Breathe in the scents of yeast and cinnamon and butter. Breathe out the frustration of single motherhood. Her father-in-law had pulled her nine-year-old son out of school yesterday, without her approval or knowledge.

The muscles in her shoulders and back tightened again. She pummeled the dough with her fists, sending a fine cloud of flour across the worktable. That arrogant, rude… she couldn't think of words bad enough to describe her father-in-law. Mainly because she didn't tend to have those kinds of thoughts about anyone. Franisa Hearthwell saw the best in everyone.

But in recent months, she'd begun learning to read, painstakingly memorizing letters and words. She knew how much harder it was for an adult—her children seemed to pick it up effortlessly. She wanted both of them to stay in school until they were good at it, not merely able to puzzle out the price list in the pub. Her father-in-law believed education was for humans and that Enrich would be better served to learn a trade.

"But he's only nine!" She slammed her fist into the dough again. "And three quarters human!" The back door creaked, and a cool winter breeze wrapped Franisa's skirts around her legs and sent a shiver up her spine.

"Enrich?" Cala Stormbringer stood in the doorway, holding a basket. The retired witch's long wavy brown hair was pulled back in a braid, with a few gray wisps curling around her face. She wore full pants and a long tunic, with a flowing cloak around her shoulders. Early pre-dawn light gave Cala a spectral appearance. The witch cocked her head as she stepped over the threshold into the lamplight. "You're kneading already? Am I that late?"

"No. I couldn't sleep." Franisa folded the dough under to form a smooth ball, dropped it into an oiled bowl, and rolled it around so the shiny side faced up. She flipped a clean cotton towel over the bowl and moved it to the proofing shelf above the oven. "I started early."

Hanging her wrap on the hook behind the door, Cala looked around the room, her brow rising as she spotted the seven covered bowls on the shelf. "You've been busy. What is Gnollis complaining about now?"

Scraper in hand, Franisa froze. "How did you know he..." She broke off with a groan. As she scraped the flour and dough from the thick maple worktop, she told her friend about the argument. "He took Enrich out of school. Again! It's not that I don't want him to learn a trade. Maybe not mining, but something. But he needs to finish school first. Reading is hard! Enrich needs to learn it now, when he has time and a teacher to help him. Not when he's old and has to feed a family." She gestured at her own chest, sending a dusting of flour down her front.

Cala laughed. "Twenty-eight isn't old. But you're right that it's harder for adults. Where is Enrich now?"

"Asleep in his bed, I hope." Franisa glanced up at the thick timbers that supported the second floor of the bakery. "Although the children should be waking soon. And he's going to school today if I have to walk him there myself."

"Since I clearly missed the kneading portion of our morning, maybe I can walk him to the schoolhouse. I've noticed your father-in-law exhibits a certain... discomfort around me."

"Ha!" Franisa wiped the surface down and took a small wooden bowl from the shelf beneath. "He's terrified of 'the war witch.' He thinks you'll turn him into a newt. In fact, until you moved out to the lighthouse, he refused to come to town." She sighed. "I don't suppose you could move back?"

Cala chuckled again. "Sorry, no."

"I'm kidding. I know you and William are very happy at FarPoint. I just need to find someone else for him to be afraid of." Franisa took a cup of flour to the crock of sourdough starter beside the oven. She added it, poured in some water, stirred, then replaced the lid.

The witch rolled up her sleeves. "What can I help with?"

"You can mix the spices and sugar for the rolls. The first batch should be ready to shape soon." Franisa dusted her hands on her apron. "I'm going to wake the children."

Leaving Cala in the kitchen, Franisa climbed the steep steps to the upper level of the bakery. She had lived over the shop her entire life, working in the bakery with her parents from an early age. She'd memorized all of their recipes and learned enough figuring to calculate measurements and manage the funds. But her father didn't think girls needed a formal education, so she hadn't learned to read.

Safe Haven's temperate climate meant the winters didn't get too cold, and the heat of the ovens kept the living quarters warm and cozy. She opened the door at the top of the stairs and walked down the narrow hall to the central living space. After her husband had died, she'd moved to the small bedroom tucked beside the stairs. Enrich and Eloise shared the large bedroom at the front of the building. When they got older, she might have to rethink the arrangement, but for now it worked.

She opened the door and stuck her head through. "Time to get up, sleepyheads! The sun is coming up!"

Enrich groaned and stuck his head under his pillow. Eloise, only five, popped up in her bed and hopped out. "Is it time to make the sea shell rolls?"

"Almost. Cala is mixing the sugar and spices."

"Yippie!" Eloise whipped her nightgown over her head and pulled her clothing from the pegs by the door.

Franisa left her struggling into her shirt and crossed to the other bed. "Enrich. Time to get up."

"I don't feel well." His voice was muffled by the pillow. "I can't go to school today."

"If you can't go to school, you can't work with Gran-da."

He wiggled deeper under the covers. "That's too bad."

She flipped the pillow away and put a hand on his forehead. "You aren't feverish. Shall I have Cala come up and check?"

Enrich threw back the covers and leapt out of bed. "No! I'm not that sick!"

Although Cala had been a war witch, specializing in floods and hurricanes, she had also learned basic healing and first aid at the academy. And despite a lack of experience, she seemed to have an instinctive grasp of how to deal with children. Although she had become the town's beloved storyteller, her healer persona had left an impression on any child claiming false symptoms. Franisa wasn't entirely sure what had transpired when Cala had diagnosed Enrich's previous "illness," but whatever she'd told him had magically cured him.

"Why don't you want to go to school?" Franisa sat on the edge of the bed.

"I—I want to go to school." Enrich squirmed out of his night shirt.

"He doesn't want to work with Gran-da." Eloise flung the words over her shoulder as she raced out of the room, her bare feet slapping on the wooden floorboards.

Franisa rose and grasped her son's shoulder. Gently turning him to face her, she pulled his shirt down over his body. "You don't?"

Enrich ducked his head. "Eloise doesn't know what she's talking about."

"Really?" Franisa handed the boy his pants then leaned down to look into his face. "You can tell me."

Enrich took his time stepping into the canvas pants and pulling them up over his skinny hips. He tied the waist and buckled the belt he'd left threaded through the loops. A quick glance at his mother sent his gaze to the floor again. "It's fine."

"Enrich." Franisa put her hands on both shoulders and pushed him down onto the bed. She sat beside him. "Why don't you like working with Gran-da?"

He turned his face away. "I don't like going into the mine."

"He takes you into the mine?" Franisa reared back in alarm. "He said they didn't allow children down there! I thought they had to be twelve or thirteen..."

"He said I'm strong enough to help. Dwarf children aren't as big as me." His shoulders slumped.

"Just because you're bigger! Doesn't he realize you'll soon be too tall to work in the mines?" Gnollis had promised Enrich would work with the dwarf children who brought food to the break shack, emptied the ore carts, and learned to repair the equipment.

She hadn't been thrilled with the idea even with those stipulations, but she figured it would give Enrich a chance to try out the trade and see if it was something he wanted to pursue, since he'd made it abundantly clear he wasn't interested in the bakery. And honestly, fighting with her father-in-law had always made her a little sick to her stomach. The man ruled his family with an iron fist, despite his small stature.

She'd never understood what had induced Philomena, her mother-in-law, to marry him. Dwarf-human couples were unusual, even on the island of Safe Haven. But Philomena claimed it had been true love. And it must have been, because Gnollis had been besotted enough to let Philomena raise their son to be a "lazy, spoiled brat." But every "mistake" he'd made with Keldan, he seemed determined to correct with Enrich.

If only Keldan were still alive, Franisa might have been able to resist her father-in-law's demands. She snorted a laugh under her breath. Keldan had never stood up to his father, letting his mother fight all his battles.

"Your gran-da and I are going to have some words."

"He won't listen to you. You're just a girl."

His dismissive tone tightened Franisa's shoulders. "I may be 'just a girl,' but I am still your mother. And he has no right to force you to do something dangerous just because you're bigger. And no business trying to make you into a dwarf." Although, maybe she should talk to Philomena. The woman might be willing to step in on her grandson's behalf.

"Go to school. I will tell the schoolmaster you are not to leave the classroom, even if your gran-da says otherwise." She patted his shoulder.

He rose, his shoulders slumped. "It won't matter. Yurgen is scared of Gran-da."

"Maybe I can ask Cala to talk to him."

Hope dawned on Enrich's face. "That would work! He won't risk crossing a witch."

Sighing, Franisa rose and followed her son out of the room. Asking her friend to terrify her father-in-law was not the way she wanted to live her life. But if it would keep Enrich out of the mine, she'd do it. She'd do anything to keep him safe.

When they got downstairs, they found Eloise and Cala working together at the bench, the little girl chattering constantly. Cala spread the softened butter across a rectangle of rolled-out dough while Eloise sprinkled sugar spiced with cinnamon and cardamom atop another one. Aislin, the pixie who lived in the bookstore, flitted around the room sweeping up the sugar when Eloise got too overzealous.

"—and then the littlest dragon popped up out of the ocean and spitted water all over Nevan!" Eloise giggled hard, holding her sides.

"Mind the sugar." Cala pointed at Eloise's latest spill.

"But Aislin likes cleaning." The girl and pixie nodded together.

"Mama doesn't like buying extra sugar," Franisa said as she stepped into the room. "And don't get me started on the price of spices." She turned to her son. "Fill up the woodpile, then you'll get breakfast."

"Yes, ma'am." Enrich shrugged into the thick woolen coat hanging beside Cala's. The hem came down to his knees, but Franisa had rolled the sleeves so he could wear it.

As the door shut behind him, she turned to Eloise. "You forgot to make the bed."

"Oops!" Eloise flung one more spoonful of sugar on the dough and jumped down from the step stool. "Come on, Aislin!" The little pixie flittered out of the room on her heels.

With the children out of the room, Franisa confided her problem to Cala. "I never wanted him to work with the dwarves, but his gran-da insisted. And since he promised he wouldn't go in the mine, I thought... Now I don't know what to do."

Cala finished spreading the butter, her brow furrowed. Finally, she put the knife aside and picked up Eloise's abandoned spoon. "You should speak with Koni. Surely, he doesn't condone child labor."

Franisa drew in a deep breath and let it out in a long sigh, then started rolling Eloise's dough. "Gnollis is so touchy about what he calls 'outside interference.' He says it was the school that turned Keldan into a 'lazy bum'—his words, not mine. He won't admit he and Philomena had any culpability."

"You haven't told me much about Keldan." Cala kept her eyes on the bread dough, spreading the sugar much more carefully than Eloise.

Franisa started to reply, but the back door burst open. Enrich stomped in, his wooden shoes clattering against the stone floor. The two women worked in silence while the boy stacked an armload of wood in the cubby beside the oven and departed.

When the door shut, Franisa sighed. "He was as unlike his father as it's possible to be. He loved nothing better than sitting by a fire and reading a book. In fact, he tried to convince your aunt she should sell the bookstore to him, but we didn't have the gold to buy it. I think he hoped she'd give it to him."

She cast a quick glance at Cala, but the witch kept her gaze on the sugar. Franisa picked up a knife and began cutting the rolls. "Everyone here says he was lazy, but really, he was a dreamer. I guess sometimes those are the same thing. And he was definitely spoilt. Philomena would give him anything he asked for. I've never understood how she convinced Gnollis to part with his treasure, but she gave Keldan gifts all the time. Usually books. Sometimes I think she kept your aunt in business. They didn't really get involved with our children until long after Keldan was killed. They still don't have a use for Eloise." She stabbed the knife into the dough more viciously than necessary.

"What happened to Keldan?" Cala asked as she started rolling her own lump of dough.

Franisa sighed. "It was a freak accident. You know we don't get a lot of storms out here, but that night a wild one hit the island. Your aunt said later she thought it might have been a spell gone wrong—" She broke off, her cheeks heating. Only the Borgonne employed weather casters, and at that time Cala had been the high war witch. If a weather spell had gone wrong, it would have ultimately been Cala's fault.

Cala stepped back to pull a baking pan from the cupboard against the wall. She set it on the bench and began moving Franisa's cut rolls into the pan. "That was what, five years ago? Early spring?"

At Franisa's nod, the witch went on. "We had a... an incident about that time. A poorly trained wizard tried to pull a storm that was beyond his power. Usually that isn't a problem. Either the storm doesn't move or they manage to bring in a minor rain instead of a deluge. But in that case, the storm hadn't completely coalesced."

Cala stopped and made a gesture with her hands as if pushing two things into each other. "Wentir was strong enough to pull most of it, then lost control halfway to Verduun. The storm split apart. His mentor should have dispersed the remains, but she... She'd gone on a bender after a bad breakup. By the time I was made aware of it—I thought we caught it before it hit land. I'm so sorry!"

"It didn't hit the island." Franisa turned a sad smile on her friend, then began cutting the second roll of dough. "Keldan had a hideout in the outer islands. Another thing his mother gave him. There was a little cottage, and he had a sailboat. He'd take a pile of books, half the food in the larder, and disappear for days at a time. After the storm, Koni sent some of the fishermen out to check for survivors. They found the cottage destroyed. And Keldan was under the rubble."

The door opened again, and Enrich came in with another load of wood. "That's all that will fit, Ma." He slammed the door and began unbuttoning his enormous coat. "When will the rolls be ready?"

"If you want to wait, you can take a fresh one when you leave for school." Franisa pulled a bowl from the proofing shelves and put the tray in its place. "Yesterday's are over there if you want to eat now." She nodded at the day-old basket.

"How about both?" Enrich slipped out of his wooden shoes and padded across the warm bakery to grab a roll.

"Did you finish your chores?" Franisa asked.

Eloise skipped down the steps, the pixie trailing sparkles in her wake. "We did!"

Enrich shoved the roll into his mouth and picked up the basket. "I have to deliver this to the town hall, then I'm done."

"Wait! I want one before you go!" Eloise scampered across the room.

Enrich darted through the curtain that separated the bakery from the shop at the front. "You'll have to catch me first!"

"No running in the bakery!" Casting an exasperated look at Cala, Franisa hurried after the children.

CHAPTER THREE

The little bell over the bakery door rang as it opened. Late morning sun slanted through the windows, casting warm stripes across the pale wooden floor. A slender older man sauntered in. He wore his wispy hair on the long side—a style that did not hide the balding spot at the back—and a carpenter's belt with carefully polished tools hung at his hips. He smiled at Franisa, showing off ragged teeth beneath his straggly moustache.

"*Oravai*, Rolph." Franisa greeted him with a polite smile from behind the counter, grateful the yeast and spices of the bakery masked Rolph's odd, singed odor. She couldn't quite place it, but the scent was acrid and unpleasant. It was a good thing Eloise wasn't here—she tended to notice smells. Loudly. "Do you have my delivery?"

"Yes, of course, my dear, but no hurry." Rolph looked her over in a way that made her skin crawl. Once she'd married Keldan and had children, most of the men in the village stopped looking her way, but Rolph was an unwelcome exception.

But the man was an expert carpenter, and he offered Franisa an excellent price on the work she wanted done. A year ago, she'd commissioned him to rebuild the failing worktable in the kitchen, and he'd done the work quickly and well. Although she tried to make it clear their arrangement was a business transaction, he'd continued to come to the bakery, offering to fix whatever needed repair for little or no cost.

No *monetary* cost. He enjoyed making remarks that made her blush.

He paused by the glass-topped counter and indicated one of the cardamom sea shell rolls with a stained finger. "I'd like one of those, if you don't mind. And some tea to go with it."

"I'm happy to wrap up a roll for you, but this isn't a tea shop. Mistress Thistlewick serves my rolls, if you'd like to sit a spell." She waited with the tongs in her hand.

"Surely you can make an exception? I've done a great deal of thirsty work for a reasonable fee. Is a little consideration too much to ask?" He came around the end of the counter. "I can sit in your kitchen while you work so I won't give your customers any ideas."

She backed into the doorway leading to the kitchen, putting one hand on either side of the opening to block his way. "Let's conclude our business first."

He rolled his eyes a bit then plastered on a smarmy smile. "Of course, my dear. Gwardil is delivering it as we speak." He turned and made his leisurely way to the front door.

Taking a deep breath of the bakery's fragrant spiciness to calm her frustration, Franisa yanked one of the sea shell rolls out of the tray, deposited it on a piece of cloth, and tied the bundle with swift, smooth movements. Then she followed him out the door, the package held casually by her side. She wouldn't give him any reason to return to the shop.

In the square in front of the bakery, Gwardil had parked his wagon. The two-wheeled affair held a large box, about four feet long and two feet square. Winnie the donkey stood between the traces, her head cocked back and her bright eyes watching the dwarf. No one on the island seemed to know which of the pair was in charge, but Franisa would bet on Winnie.

Gwardil pushed his peaked cap back on his head, exposing his bushy eyebrows. "Here ya go." He leaned down to place a chock against the cart's wheel, blocking it in place.

"We go through this every time, little man. I pay you to *move* the furniture. That includes taking it off the cart." Rolph's eyes narrowed as he stared down at the dwarf. "Chop chop."

A tiny smirk twitched the thick gray and brown beard that covered Gwardil's face and chest. Although he no longer worked in the mines, he wore it in the traditional style, with little carved wooden trinkets braided into the unruly strands. They clinked together as he placed the second chock and came around the end of the cart.

The bells on Winnie's harness jingled as she shifted in place, trying to turn her head farther. Franisa moved to the beast's head, scratching behind her ears. Although she was certain the donkey was smarter than the dwarf—and possibly more intelligent than most of the island's populace—she'd learned years ago that the animal enjoyed human touch. She also relished the sugar cube Franisa had dropped in her apron pocket this morning in anticipation of the delivery.

While she stroked the donkey's soft neck, Gwardil unlatched the gate at the back of the wagon. A click of his tongue brought up Winnie's head, and she backed away a few steps, forcing the wagon to tilt on its single axle. The large wooden box slid to the end of the bed. Gwardil put his shoulder against the bottom and slowed its drop, carefully lowering that end to the cobblestones of the square.

He put his hand under the other end of the box, still perched on the wagon. Another click of his tongue sent Winnie forward a couple of paces. The wagon returned to horizontal, and Gwardil caught the box as it slid off the end. He lowered it to the ground, then nipped forward to grab the chocks. Tossing them into the back as he climbed on, he clucked to the donkey. The bells jingled again, and the pair trundled across the square.

"Hey, this isn't where I wanted it!" Rolph hollered at their backs.

Gwardil waved a hand without looking back, and Winnie brayed loudly.

Rolph growled under his breath. "I *will* find another carter."

Franisa bit back a retort. Rolph wouldn't find another because he was unwilling to pay more than a pittance for the work.

The scrawny man carefully shifted the box to a place of pride under the windows beside the bakery door, muttering about ungrateful workers and unfulfilled contracts the whole time. When he'd gotten it into place, he opened the hinged top and withdrew a couple of pieces. "I'll get the back and arms on, and we'll be in business."

Franisa nodded dutifully. "Thank you." She considered going back into the bakery, but she didn't want to give the creepy old man any reason to follow her inside.

He muttered some more while he worked, attaching the pieces and polishing the finished bench with a stained rag. "There you are, my dear. A bench with a box built into the base. Quite an innovative design, if I do say so myself."

Was he trying to take credit for her idea? "Thank you," she said, keeping her expression neutral. She lifted the heavy wooden seat and inspected the hook that would allow her to latch it open. The interior was divided into six smaller, open-topped boxes. Another box with a coin slot was latched to the underside of the lid. She could leave orders for customers here, and they would put payment into the box to be collected later. "It turned out just as I envisioned."

Rolph hooked his thumbs into his belt and gave her a condescending smile. "Your original idea was clever, but it required a great deal of refinement to achieve. I'm rather proud of the results."

She reached into her apron pocket and pulled out a small bag of coins. "Here is the amount we agreed upon. And your sea shell roll." She held out the money and pastry. "As always, I appreciate your skilled work."

His eyes narrowed as he pocketed the coins, and he moved closer. "I thought we were going to have a cup of tea with these?" He reached out and slid a stained finger down her arm in a way that made her itch to pummel him with her rolling pin. "We've been working together for many months but had little time to really get to know each other."

Franisa took a step back, her legs bumping into the new bench.

"Unfortunately, I'm quite busy. Running a bakery alone takes most of my time."

He crowded closer. Franisa leaned back and landed on the bench with a thump. Although she'd never cared for the man, and his attitude toward her had always made her cautious, she'd never felt physically threatened by him. His slender frame inspired little fear in a woman accustomed to heaving bags of flour and kneading massive bowls of dough. But with him looming over her, she felt a little quiver of trepidation.

"Mama!" Eloise skipped across the square, swinging a small basket from one hand. An older girl—Sala, the half-elven daughter of the town mayor—held her other hand, and Enrich trailed behind with Sala's twin brother Int. "What's that?"

The little cavalcade of children swarmed around the adults and the newly installed bench, throwing out questions and comments. With a sour grimace, Rolph took a couple of steps back, giving Franisa room to rise and demonstrate the usefulness of her new acquisition.

After everyone had a chance to lift the seat, test the hook, and investigate the latch to the coin box, Franisa shooed them away. "There are left over sea shell rolls inside if anyone is hungry."

The children cheered, the boys jostling to reach the door first. Franisa held it open for them, turning to look back at the carpenter. "Thank you again for your fine work."

His leer returned as the last of the children disappeared inside. "I'm sure this will improve your bottom line. Not that it needs improving." He rested a proprietary hand on the back of the little bench while dropping his gaze to her hip.

Gritting her teeth, Franisa nodded pleasantly. "I don't know about that, but it certainly will allow me a little more freedom."

Eloise appeared in the doorway, a chunk of gooey sea shell roll clutched in her hand, a little of the caramelized filling dripping down her fingers. Even the day-old rolls oozed a mouthwatering breath of cardamom, cinnamon, and vanilla. The little girl licked some icing from the top and nodded at Rolph. "Why's he still here?"

Franisa stifled a chuckle, wishing she could be so direct. "We're just concluding our business. Thank you, *again*, for the bench, Rolph. You do fine work."

Rolph's lips pressed together in displeasure. "Thank you for the commission."

Shoving the last of the pastry into her mouth, Eloise moved closer to her mother and sniffed. "What's that smell?" She sniffed again. And again.

"Probably the fresh oil on the wood. That's what makes it shiny and weather-proof." Franisa turned her body a little to shield the girl from the man's glare. "It has a strong scent."

The girl leaned closer to the bench and sniffed again, then took a step toward Rolph. "No, it's him. He smells burnt."

"Eloise!" Franisa bit her lip. Eloise's penchant for smelling things—and people—had embarrassed her before, but nothing she said to the girl seemed to stem her often unflattering habit. "We've discussed this. We don't smell people. And if we do, we don't comment on it."

"That was quite rude," Rolph snapped.

She turned toward the carpenter, a natural instinct to defend her daughter overriding her embarrassment at the girl's manners. "I'm so sorry." She tried to imbue some semblance of apology into her tone, but it came out cool and dismissive. "I will take her inside so we can discuss her behavior. Good day." She swept the girl back into the bakery and pulled the door closed behind her. Then she flipped the little sign and bolted the door, grateful for the reprieve.

CHAPTER FOUR

Starlight landed on the stone wall at the tip of Far Point. The tower, originally built to warn sailors of dangers that didn't actually exist, dominated the end of a high rocky peninsula jutting out into the Queleria Sea. A two-story thatched house extended from one side of the tower with the stable on the other and a garden in the rear. A six-foot wall protected the garden, which encompassed all but a tiny stone triangle at the very tip of the promontory.

Finn, the dragon master's mount, liked to perch on the top of the tower, and Nari, Cala's partner, always landed safely in the walled courtyard beside the stable, but Starlight preferred the garden wall. The first few times she'd landed there, Nevan had slid precariously down her side, heart in his throat, to the tiny platform of stone that overlooked the hundred-foot drop to the beach. After a couple of landings, it occurred to him he could simply climb down into the garden on the other side and let himself out through the gate.

He unbuckled his flying straps—he wasn't going to get dumped in the drink again. Klausi, the leather master, had helped him design straps that ran around Starlight's neck and upper body on either side of her front legs, connecting with two more straps along her back. Rings hung from the upper strap, allowing him to buckle his own belt to hers. Since he'd started using them, he hadn't ended up in the sea. At least, not on his own. Sometimes the mischievous dragon dove in with him still on her back, just for fun.

Nevan patted Starlight's haunch then slid down into the garden he and William had repaired when the dragon master first arrived in Safe Haven almost a year before. Most of the plants were dormant, but the flame bush still glowed red against the gray stone of the wall. Nevan tiptoed down the path to the gate. Although both of FarPoint's human occupants had assured him they preferred he dismount on this side of the wall, he still felt like an intruder sneaking past the big windows and double doors that led to the main house.

When he pulled it open, the arched wooden gate creaked loudly, and he winced even though it was mid-afternoon rather than late night or early morning. A quick, guilty glance at the windows assured him no one was watching, and he ducked under the low lintel, pulling the door shut behind him.

He made his way around the thatch-roofed house to the far side where the dragon lair stood. Hands on hips, he looked through the wide arched doorway—more than tall enough for his nearly seven-foot height. Was "lair" the right word? It had a negative connotation in his mind. William had told him the dragon accommodations in Verduun were sometimes called a nest, but that was too bird-ish for his taste.

He entered the courtyard, ducking his head despite the more than adequate height. He might be only half giant, and the smallest of his family, but banging his head on enough human-sized doorways had ingrained the habit.

The former stable sat to his left, attached to the tower and house via a corridor that ran past a storage room and newly installed water closet. The twelve-foot wall behind him protected the courtyard from visitors—not that a lot of villagers came out this far—and the winds that occasionally swept across the peninsula. A lower wall ran along the sheer cliffside, butting up to the garden wall on which Starlight perched.

The tall double door to the lair stood open, allowing the weak winter sunlight and stiff breeze to air out the space. Three dragons in an enclosed area tended to get pungent.

His dragon's head slewed around when he entered the yard, but she didn't leave her post atop the garden wall. The Safe Haven dragons had no need for a sentry, but the dragons didn't care. One or more of them was nearly always "on duty" from their preferred perch. Today, however, neither of the others were visible.

Nevan wandered into the lair and grabbed a broom. As he swept out the dirt and debris carried in on the dragons' feet and hides, he thought again about a name for the building. Sea dragons naturally nested in the caverns beneath, but the three who had paired with humans preferred to stay closer. Hence the stable turned lair. He and Starlight had a cozy home in the back corner, close to the big porcelain stove. Heat emanated from the tiles, but when he opened the fire door, he saw only coals. He added a log—just to keep the fire alight—and shut it.

His own cubicle—formerly a large horse stall—was hidden behind a thick curtain. He pulled the heavy brocade open and swept out the sand Starlight had tracked in. He'd put a low bed in the corner—large enough to accommodate his big frame and a good part of Starlight's as well. A sturdy dresser held his clothing, and a small desk sat under the high horizontal windows. The low ceiling helped keep in the heat, but it also trapped the musky dragon scent.

Leaning over the desk, he opened the windows to allow some circulation. The other stalls were empty. Since Cala and William lived in the main house, and no one else had paired with a dragon, he and Starlight had the big lair to themselves, except at night when Nari and Finn often curled up in a stall near the door.

"Nevan?" Cala called from the courtyard doorway. "Are you in here?"

"Here!" He moved back into the common space, sweeping his little pile of dust with him. "I don't suppose your bookstore pixie has any friends who'd like to live with the dragons? I hate cleaning, but I like things tidy."

Cala laughed as he intended. She had a deep, throaty chuckle, and hearing it always brightened his day. "I've asked her three times. Still no."

"Ah, well. It's lucky we live on a stony outcropping instead of a muddy swamp." He moved past her, pushing his little pile of sand out the door. "I don't know how they manage to bring it all the way up from the beach."

"It's a mystery. William is back. Do you have time for a discussion?" Cala gestured toward the door.

"Does this 'discussion' include treats?" Nevan leaned the broom in the corner behind the house.

"It didn't, but if you want to make a quick flight into town, it could. Charge to the guild, of course." Cala's lips twitched. "Franisa made sea shell rolls this morning."

Nevan's cheeks heated, and he looked away. He'd had a tiny crush on the baker for years, and somehow Cala had figured it out. Thankfully, she never mentioned it, but she never passed up a chance to throw him in Franisa's direction either.

"You didn't bring any with you?"

Cala stopped trying to hide her smile. "I left before the first batch came out of the oven. I thought *you* might want to pick them up. It's a short flight."

"We just got back from a long one." Nevan looked toward his partner, his embarrassment fading as he switched the subject. "She's getting stronger every day, but I don't know if another trip so soon…"

Starlight jumped from her perch on the point, sweeping her wings once to loft herself into the courtyard. She peered eagerly at Nevan, clearly ready to go again.

Cala slapped a hand against the dragon's flank. "I think you have your answer. Good girl."

Nevan shrugged and jingled the straps still attached to his belt. "One batch of sea shell rolls, coming up."

Stepping back, Cala shaded her eyes to look toward the sea. "Take your time. It looks to be a fine day."

The cold winter breeze kept his cheeks from heating again, and

Nevan nodded, hoping the blush hadn't returned. Was Cala trying to nudge him toward her friend?

Once he was aboard and strapped on, Starlight hopped to the low wall and flung herself off the side. She caught a thermal almost at once, soaring up before they'd fallen more than a few feet.

Nevan laughed and patted the dragon's shoulder. "You're getting so good at this."

A smug sense of agreement flooded his mind. Starlight was becoming proficient at communicating too. The three dragon riders had spent countless hours discussing their capabilities. William said the big fire dragons used images to communicate, but the more independent sea dragons had proven many times they didn't always follow their bigger cousins' precedents. Although Nevan often attempted to visualize locations and instructions for his partner, he had never received any images from her. Just feelings.

Starlight wheeled to the right, gliding over the stony peninsula on which FarPoint stood. At this altitude, the rolling hills between the stony outcropping and the town resembled gentle green waves. Off to the left, the island grew steeper, the lush trees giving way to the stony lip of SeaView Ridge.

The island was part of the remains of a volcanic caldera. Land sloped from the high inner cliffs down to the sandy outer beaches. The town of Safe Haven sat along a natural harbor along the outer south-eastern side. Far Point protruded from there to the south and west, forming the tail end of the long, crescent shaped island. Farther to the north, the town of Valebra clung to the side of the inner cliff.

The rest of the islands were mainly uninhabited. He'd heard tales of a hermit on one of the northern isles, and a few of the fishermen had small cabins farther west. But most folks lived on Safe Haven where they could purchase goods and hear the local gossip.

Starlight rode the breeze down to the town, circling to find a good landing place. Finn had landed on the church steeple a few weeks ago, which resulted in an angry complaint from the priest. Nevan had known and feared Friar Anselm since childhood and even with a dragon at his side had no desire to confront the man.

"How about the paddock?" He leaned over Starlight's neck, pointing at the fenced field behind the blacksmith's forge. He wasn't sure how Starlight knew what to do—did she hear his words or see through his eyes or simply look where he was pointing? But she never failed to land where he asked. Except when she wanted to tease him, like when she'd dropped him in the ocean a few days back.

The little dragon flared her wings and landed neatly in the center of the open space. The horses shied away from her, stampeding to the far side of the field where they huddled in the corner by the fence, their eyes wide, their bodies trembling. Maybe landing there hadn't been such a good idea. His father would have his hide if they terrorized his customers' mounts. He quickly unlatched his belt and slid down the dragon's side. "Go fly around. You can pick me up in a bit. Somewhere else."

Starlight nuzzled his shoulder, then bunched her muscles and leapt into the sky. She flew off to the left, avoiding the frightened horses. Sea dragons didn't eat large mammals, so why they inspired terror, he didn't know. Maybe it was the novelty. Wild dragons rarely ventured over the human occupied areas of the island, preferring the previously uninhabited FarPoint and the smaller, empty islets of the caldera.

Making a quick detour across the field, Nevan took a moment to reassure the horses. He offered them the dried fruit he kept in his pocket for Starlight and patted their smooth necks. By the time the fruit was gone, the animals had calmed, so he climbed over the fence. The dirt road leading to Valebra gave way to cobbles at the corner of the large, low building. He stomped his feet, trying to dislodge the mud he'd accumulated in the horse paddock, then stepped back as a wagon rattled down the street toward him.

Brenet the butcher drove the wagon, with his son sitting on the bench seat beside him. They waved but didn't stop. "Morning, Nevan!" the boy called.

"Morning, Romulus." Nevan returned the salute. "Brenet."

The elder orc's grin revealed a broken tusk and several jagged teeth. Nevan had heard some folks found them intimidating, but Brenet had lived in the village as long as he could remember, and he knew a heart of gold hid beneath the orc's rough appearance.

The forge stood on one side of a large cobblestone square. An ancient stone basin in the center held a pump, providing water for the village. Indoor plumbing had been added to most of the buildings many decades ago, but the pump remained and had proved useful when the butcher's shop had caught fire last year. That fire had led William to attempt domestication of the sea dragons, so although it had resulted in some losses for Brenet's family, Nevan couldn't help but be grateful for the event.

The large front doors of the forge stood open, and rhythmic clanging echoed from within. Nevan's father was the blacksmith, and when Nevan had paired with Starlight, his youngest half-brother had taken his place as apprentice.

As if drawn by the thought, Gebhard sprinted out of the dark cavern of the forge. "Nevan! Are you coming to dinner tonight?"

The teen looked a lot like Nevan, with thick curly dark hair, a cheerful, round face, and dark eyes. But despite his age, Gebhard towered over Nevan by at least a foot, and the boy was quickly filling out. Working in the forge had developed his upper body, and the leather vest he wore put his bulging biceps on display.

Nevan drew in a deep breath and let it out slowly. He loved his family but had always felt a little misplaced. His human mother had died when he was very young, and while his giant stepmother had raised him as her own, his comparatively petite stature forever marked him as different. Becoming part of the dragon guild had given him a new family—one where he was the largest, not the smallest. And for some reason, that made him feel more comfortable with the older human dragon riders.

But he'd been so busy with Starlight he'd failed to spend any time with his family. Maybe now was a good time to remedy that. "I'll see if I can get away."

Gebhard's eyes sparkled, and he threw his arms around Nevan, squeezing hard enough to make Nevan grunt.

"Oops, sorry!" Gebhard let him go with a grin.

Nevan rolled his eyes. "Go ahead, say it."

Gebhard patted him on the head. "Don't want to damage the little guy. Hey, where's Starlight?" He looked eagerly around the square.

Nevan pointed up. The dragon soared high above them, almost indistinguishable from the birds enjoying the morning breezes. Nevan frowned. Maybe some of those birds actually were dragons too?

Gebhard's face fell. "I was hoping to see her. Will you take me for a ride some day?"

Trying to hide a grin, Nevan raised a skeptical brow. "I'm not sure. She's a little dragon, and your bulk might be too much for her."

Gebhard shoved Nevan playfully, nearly knocking his brother down. "Ha! Good one. I don't weigh that much."

"More than me, I'd wager." Nevan measured their comparative heights with his hand. "But she's getting stronger, so maybe someday."

"Oi! Gebby!" their father shouted from inside the forge. "Stop bothering the dragon rider and get back in here. I need more water!"

With a sheepish grin, Gebhard picked up the massive pail he'd dropped to hug Nevan and headed for the pump. "I'll see you at six! I'm telling Ma, so don't let her down."

Nevan drew in an indignant breath but then realized he probably had let her down by not visiting earlier. "I'll be there." He turned to face the bakery.

It stood across the square from the blacksmith. Before he paired with Starlight, Nevan had spent more time than he cared to remember watching the bakery. Franisa was a few years older than him, but he'd taken a fancy to her at a young age, and it hadn't abated over the years. Her gentle attitude and sweet disposition called to him.

The front door of the bakery opened, the bell hanging over it jingling merrily. The ancient and intimidating Goodwife Terman emerged, with her crony, Goodwife Wrenright on her heels. Nevan leaped forward to hold the door for the two older women. Terman, the taller and crankier of the pair, gave him a swift, habitually disapproving look. Then her expression changed to one he'd never seen on her face—a smile.

"Dragon rider! How nice to see you!" Terman gave a genial nod.

Behind her, Wrenright did a comical double take, then bobbed a little curtsey. "Dragon rider."

Nevan tried to respond the way he'd seen William do. "Ladies. Oravai."

Terman smirked a little, and Wrenright fluttered her eyelashes. The two women were easily old enough to be Nevan's grandmother, so their almost flirty attitude threw him off guard. What had he done to invite this? Swallowing hard, he pulled the door as far as it would go and slid between the now stationary women and the building to escape inside. "Have a pleasant day."

The door swung, nearly clipping Wrenright's heels. Terman's exasperated, "Well, I never!" reached his ears before it closed completely, shutting the women out.

Franisa's laugh brought him around, his cheeks heating. She stood behind the counter, holding a domed glass lid in one hand and a pair of wooden tongs in the other. "You have a fan club, Nevan." A metal tray of frosted sweet rolls rested on the polished wooden surface, and Franisa used the tongs to place them on a large plate. After piling them high, she replaced the glass cover over the plate. "What can I get for you?"

Nevan gulped, his cheeks still pink. After these many years, he'd learned to interact with her without sounding like a besotted idiot, but it required effort. He took refuge in the old women's behavior. "Why were they being so... odd?"

"You're a dragon rider, now. One of the elite." Franisa's sweet smile sent a warm shiver down Nevan's spine. "Did you want some of these?" She pointed the tongs at the plate.

"Yes, please. Three would be welcome." He shifted from foot to foot. "Why do they care if I partnered with Starlight?"

Franisa shrugged as she stacked three of the rolls on a square of fabric. "Goodwife Terman likes to think she's the most influential person in town. Being friendly with the dragon riders is good for her reputation."

"I guess I'd rather have her fawning over me than reprimanding me. She used to call me clumsy and ignorant."

"That's unkind." Franisa's eyes narrowed. "And untrue. She is not a nice woman."

"Who's not nice, Mama?" Five-year-old Eloise popped out from behind the curtain separating the bakery from the shop.

"Eavesdropping is not nice." Franisa tapped her daughter on the nose. "And I misspoke. She's not a bad person, but her behavior is unkind."

"You mean Goodwife Terman." Eloise nodded emphatically. "She's mean. And she smells gray. Like camper."

"Camphor. But pointing out how someone smells is also bad manners, remember?" Franisa tied the corners of the napkin to hold the rolls, then pushed them across the counter toward Nevan. "Should I charge these to the guild account?"

"How did you know?" He picked up the package by the knot.

"Cala said she was going to send you to get some." Franisa smiled pleasantly as she pulled a leather-bound book from beneath the counter. "Do you need anything else?"

"No." He started to turn away, then swiveled back. "Actually, can I get a loaf of bread? And can I pick it up later? I want to take it to my ma. For dinner. I mean, she's making dinner, but I want to bring bread." He flushed at his awkwardness.

"That's so sweet!" Franisa looked down at her daughter. "Take note, child. Bring your old mother gifts when you visit."

Eloise giggled. "But you *make* the bread!"

"And you aren't old!" The words burst from Nevan's mouth a little louder than he'd intended.

The baker looked up from her ledger with a wry grin. "Thank you. But I feel it sometimes." She flipped through the heavy pages until she found one with a little dragon drawn in the top corner, then ran her index finger to the bottom of the short column of figures. "Three sea shell rolls is nine coppers." She wrote the number in the column and closed the book. "And the bread will be two, but you can pay me when you pick it up."

Nevan stopped patting his pockets—he'd forgotten to bring any coins. Since joining the guild, he rarely had to spend his own. He flushed. "Thank you. How late will you be open?"

"Only until two. But if you come later, I'll leave the loaf in the box. And there's a place for payment. Eloise will show you. Thank you for coming in, Nevan." She slid the ledger back under the counter.

The little girl skipped around the counter and grabbed Nevan's hand. "Come on, I'll show you!"

He had to stoop a little as she pulled him across the small shop and out into the square. As the heavy wooden door swung shut, he looked back, but Franisa had disappeared.

Eloise dropped his hand and patted the bench beside the front door. The bottom of the seat was framed in like a box. "This is the new pickup box. Mama puts the breads in here." She wrapped her little hands around the front edge of the seat and tried to lift.

"I've got it." Nevan easily swung the hinged seat upward. The bottom of the bench had been divided into six interior boxes, and a small receptacle was attached to the underside of the seat with a slot in the front.

"Careful, it's heavy! There's a hook." Eloise pointed at an S-shaped metal bracket hanging from the corner of the seat back, then tapped a small hole in the seat. "That goes here, to hold it open." She pointed at the coin box. "That's where you pay. Then your bread is in here. Mama will put a dragon on your bag."

"A dragon?" Nevan tested the hook, looping it through the corresponding hole. It held the heavy wood easily. "This is a neat solution. Who built it?"

"Rolph, the carpenter." Eloise wrinkled her nose, and her tone turned disgruntled. "He's always here. Making things. Fixing stuff. Eating the *brødtorte*!" Clearly the last crime was of gravest import to the child.

Nevan nodded solemnly. "That is... concerning." He unhooked the seat, then lowered it back into place, wondering if the carpenter was courting Franisa. He was older, but some women liked that, or so he'd heard. And not only did Rolph have a thriving business, but he also owned a fine house in the village that had been in his family for generations. A little stab of jealousy went through him. As a dragon rider, he had little to offer any woman, let alone a successful bakery owner. He pushed the envy down and tried to keep his voice even. “Sharing the *brødtorte* is hard.”

The girl jumped up on the seat, which was a little too high for her, and leaned back, her legs sticking out by his knees, as if prepared for a long gossip. “And he smells burnt!”

CHAPTER FIVE

Franisa returned from the kitchen to find Nevan had left the bundle of sea shell rolls on the counter. Since Eloise hadn't returned, it was a good bet the dragon rider hadn't left yet. She lifted the improvised bag by the knot and pushed the front door open.

Warmth washed through her at the sight of Nevan and Eloise sitting together in front of the bakery. Eloise sat close to the giant, huddling behind his bulk as a stiff winter breeze blew in from the sea. Franisa couldn't hear her chatter, but the child's flashing eyes and sharp tone indicated she was incensed about something.

As she paused to draw breath, Nevan's deep voice cut in. "It's very kind of you to share the *brødtorte* with him. I'm sure he'd be very sad if you didn't. I know I would."

Eloise poked a finger at Nevan and smiled. "I would share with you. You're nice. And you smell like dragons." She leaned closer and drew in a deep breath.

"Eloise!" Franisa stepped into the sunlight. Nevan's head snapped around, a guilty look on his face. He really shouldn't encourage the girl to gossip, but she had a soft spot for anyone who was kind to her children. "How many times do I have to tell you? Smelling people is not good manners. And you forgot your rolls, Nevan."

The giant jumped up from the bench, his face red. "I, uh, I don't mind if she smells me. Dragons smell nice." He took the bundle of rolls. "Thank you. Cala would have made me come back for these. Not that I'd mind. It's not that far, and—"

Laughing, Franisa raised a hand to stem his bashful rambling. "You're always welcome, of course. But better if you don't have to run the same errand twice. I assume Eloise showed you the pickup box before she started gossiping?" She cast a motherly glare at her daughter.

"I wasn't gossiping. I was telling him about the bench." The girl slid off the front of the seat, jumping to the ground beside the dragon rider. "And I said Rolph eats too much *brødtorte* and smells burnt. It's not gossiping if it's true!"

"Actually, it is." She beckoned to the little girl. "There's no reason Nevan needs to know what other people eat or smell like, so it's gossip. In you go. Find Aislin and go play in the back yard."

The little girl reached up to tug on Nevan's hand. "Do you want to play with us? We're making a pixie village!"

The giant smiled gently. "I would like that, but I have to take these back to FarPoint. Maybe another time?"

Eloise nodded happily. "Yes. And next time, bring your dragon. She can play with us too." She skipped to the front door.

"I'm not sure she'll fit in your yard…"

"It's okay. We can go to the field behind the stables. They gots lotsa room for dragons." Eloise grunted as she pulled the front door open far enough to slip through. "Bye bye!'

Franisa turned back to Nevan as the door thudded behind her daughter. "Don't encourage her. She thinks everyone has time to play."

"I usually do. The dragons don't take a lot of time." He glanced up at the sun and remembered he was supposed to meet with William and Cala. "But today I have to get back. Thanks for bringing me the rolls." He lifted them in salute, hesitated for a long moment, then headed across the square.

"Of course. And your bread will be waiting." She patted the back of the bench when he turned back to wave, then watched him walk away, surprised at the mild sense of disappointment that she wouldn't be here when he returned. He really was a very nice boy. Or man, rather. Now that he was a dragon rider, she'd have to get used to the idea that he'd grown up.

There were only five years between them, but as a child, that had seemed a huge gulf. Now, as a single mother, she felt every one of her twenty-eight years, some more heavily than others. She returned to the bakery with a sigh. With the baking done, it was time to inventory her supplies and plan for the morrow.

At least she didn't have to clean much anymore. Aislin, Eloise's pixie friend, adored cleaning. And she encouraged the children to help. Enrich wasn't a fan and escaped as soon as he could, but Eloise happily trailed behind the fairy, dusting, sweeping, and wiping down the tabletops. She wasn't very good at washing dishes yet, but Aislin took care of any food the girl missed.

Franisa cast a quick look over the sparkling kitchen and headed into the larder. She pulled a slate from its hook beside the door and picked up a piece of chalk. Time to make a list.

When the bell over the door rang, she set aside her slate, now covered with simple drawings and numbers, and headed into the shop. Her father-in-law stood in front of the counter, only his pointed hat visible over the top.

"What can I do for you, Gnollis?" Franisa made sure her tone was respectful. She might not like the man, but she couldn't insult him to his face. During the lean years, when Keldan had spent virtually every penny the bakery brought in, Gnollis had ensured she and her children didn't starve. She'd never forget that. And neither would he.

She came around the end of the counter so she could see the dwarf. He stood almost four feet high—tall for a dwarf, she'd learned. Deep wrinkles around his eyes gave him the appearance of a dried-out apple core. He wore little trinkets braided into his thick, white beard—the circular symbol of the One, the crossed pickaxe and shovel of the mining guild, and a few items she didn't want to get close enough to puzzle out.

"The schoolmaster wouldn't let me take the boy. He needs to learn a trade!" The dwarf crossed his arms and stuck his chin out belligerently.

Franisa let out a soft sigh of relief. Cala's chat with the headmaster must have borne fruit. "He's only nine. And you promised he wouldn't go in the mines!"

"He's bigger than most of the miners. Of course he should help with the heavy work."

"Gnollis, he's a child. And he's not nearly as strong as even the smallest of the guild members. You're endangering him—"

"I don't endanger my kin!" The dwarf's eyes lit up, glinting red with anger. "And I won't have you telling me how to run my mine!" He stomped his foot, then pivoted smartly. "As long as he's my kin, he's my responsibility. And I'll do as I see fit! You tell that war witch to stop meddling in my business!"

Before she could respond, he stomped out the door.

Sagging against the counter, Franisa reviewed her options. Obviously, the headmaster had grown a backbone, but she wondered how often she'd need to ask Cala to reinforce his newfound courage. And what would happen if she did? Gnollis wasn't going to let her defy him. He'd figure out another way to get Enrich away from her.

According to dwarf law, Gnollis was completely within his rights. Dwarven children started working at the mines early, and few of them ever went to school. Keldan had been the exception, and Gnollis wasn't going to let that happen again.

Maybe it was time to enlist Philomena's help. Her mother-in-law terrified her more than Gnollis, but the woman clearly knew how to sway the dwarf.

With a decisive nod, she took a clean cloth from the drawer to wrap up some more rolls. She'd close the bakery early, send the children to the bookstore, and visit her mother-in-law.

CHAPTER SIX

Clutching his sea shell rolls by the knotted fabric, Nevan hurried away from the bakery, taking care not to look through the forge's open doors. He didn't want to get drawn into a conversation with his father or brother. He'd already spent too much time talking with Eloise and didn't want to keep the guild master waiting any longer. Once past the corner, he slowed a bit, emerging into the thin sunlight at a brisk walk.

Soaring high overhead, Starlight spotted Nevan beside the horse paddock. Before he could warn her away, the little dragon dove at the field, swooping low over the horses who had spread out again, sending them in a stampede toward the stables. With a happy bugle, she tipped her wings and settled gracefully on the top rail of the long fence.

"That wasn't nice!" Nevan gave the mischievous dragon a stern glare, similar to the one Franisa had bestowed on Eloise. He tried to emulate her tone. "We don't scare the horses."

He got a burst of surprise and a tinge of shame from the dragon, but she flipped her wings and lifted her chin, like a child who knows they've done wrong but isn't willing to admit it. He crossed his arms and stared her down. The dragon shifted back and forth on the fence, then turned her head away, chirping at a bird as if she hadn't a care in the world. Nevan tapped her shoulder, and when she looked his way, he grabbed her head on either side of the big jaws.

"Not nice. Don't scare horses." He tried to project the image of petting a horse, but visualizing things was never his strong suit.

He must have gotten the idea across because the dragon's gaze dropped and her shoulders slumped. A wave of contrition washed over him. He gave her jaw another gentle squeeze, then released her. "Let's head home, now." He looked at the rails of the fence. Although giants were oddly light for their size, he wasn't sure the fence would support both him and the dragon. "Hop down here, will you?"

As the dragon jumped off the fence, someone whispered his name. *"Nev'n."*

He looked around, but no one was nearby. It was probably his brother playing a prank. Or the communication device! Mentally berating himself, he reached into his pocket and pulled out the enchanted disk. It was larger than the biggest of coins—nearly as big as a normal human's palm—and carved with runes on either side. The smooth, rounded edges slid easily in his hand, the wood silky against his fingers. He held it close to his mouth, even though Cala had told him that wasn't necessary. "Hello?"

Nothing. Maybe he had imagined the voice. He started to slide the artifact into his pocket. The disk vibrated, and he nearly dropped it in surprise. Fumbling, he held it to his ear then to his lips again. "Hello?"

"Nevan?" Cala's voice issued from somewhere. Not directly from the disk, but somehow inside his head. The sensation was uncanny. He'd had the disk only a few days and used it only once before because it unnerved him.

"I'm coming back to FarPoint," Nevan said into the disk.

"That's fine. We're here when you get back. No rush."

"I—did you call to me?" He frowned and looked around the field again, but no one else was in sight.

"No. You called me." Cala chuckled. "Magical devices take a bit of practice to get used to. I'm glad you tried it out."

He peered closely at the medallion, but it looked exactly the same as always. "I'll try to do better."

"That's perfect. See you soon." The disk vibrated again, this time a single short jitter that made him think the magic had terminated.

He turned the disk over in his fingers. Aside from the vibration, there was no indication when it was working and when it wasn't. With a shrug, he slid it into his pocket and climbed onto the dragon's back. He looped the leather straps through the metal rings and with a satisfying snap, pulled them tight. Then he leaned forward to slap the dragon's neck. "Let's go."

With a strong downward sweep of her translucent wings and a thrust of her powerful legs, Starlight shoved away from the ground. She preferred to soar lazily off the top of the cliff at FarPoint, but because sea dragons spent so much of their time in the water, they were able to launch quickly from the sea or solid ground. William said they achieved altitude much faster than the bigger war dragons.

They climbed high into the sky, the village dropping away until it looked like a child's toy. Starlight angled toward the higher edge of the island, where she could spend hours gliding on the thermals, but Nevan used his legs to nudge the dragon farther south. She obediently turned, making a direct flight toward FarPoint. The tiny tower grew quickly as they approached, until she landed gently on the garden wall.

Nevan unfastened the straps, leaving them hanging from his belt rather than Starlight's harness. When he visited the bakery, Nevan had left the straps on the dragon, but now, since he'd be busy for a while, he wanted her free of extraneous gear.

As he slid down into the garden, Cala hailed him from the open door. "Come on inside!"

Nevan waved his acknowledgement, trod across the stone path, then sat on the little bench beside the door to remove his boots. These had been specially designed by William and Klausi, the leather smith, with clever straps to secure them tightly at the ankles and calves.

Cala stepped out to take the cloth-wrapped rolls while he undid the boots. "You could have come inside to do that." She tipped her head at another bench inside the room and the two pairs of boots tucked beneath.

"They're muddy." He set them under the bench and rose. He hoped he hadn't left a mess in Franisa's bakery. He'd been so flustered by the flirty old women he hadn't checked his shoes properly before entering. Flushing, he stood in the garden a moment longer to let the sea air cool his cheeks.

He entered the house, carefully closing the door behind him. It shut with a solid thud, cutting out the sound of the sea and the cool, salty breeze. A fire in the tiled stove provided warmth, and the thick braided rug protected his stocking feet from the stone floor.

William sat at the large wooden table in the center of the room. The older man had curly, graying hair and a stern, clean-shaven chin. His magical prosthetic protruded from the bottom of his pant leg, and his other foot was encased in a knit slipper. Beyond him, Cala stood beside the kitchen dresser, placing the rolls on a plate. She carried them to the table and sat beside her husband.

Nevan took his customary seat across from William. Since they'd begun this dragon riding adventure, he'd eaten many meals at this table. William and Cala both encouraged him to think of the main floor of the house as his own home. Since he'd been living at FarPoint longer than Cala had, and had helped William rebuild the abandoned structure, the transition hadn't been too difficult, but now that William and Cala were married, he felt a bit like a third wheel. Having the stable to himself gave him some of the independence he wanted.

He took a mug of tea from Cala and added a scoop of honey. For a few moments, they ate and drank in silence. Then William pushed a piece of paper across the table to Nevan. "What do you think?"

Nevan set his tea aside and leaned over to squint at the writing. He'd learned to read as a child but hadn't had much use for the skill since he'd apprenticed to his father. And William wrote in the Verduunian style, which was difficult to decipher. He puzzled through the first few words then looked up. "A training schedule?"

"Yes." William tapped the paper. "The whole purpose of this venture was to build a fire brigade. Now that we've learned to fly, we need to learn to fight fires. And we need to teach the dragons to follow directions." The older man raised his brows at Nevan.

Of the three dragons, Starlight exhibited the most mischievous streak. Neither Nari nor Finn had dumped their rider in the sea or stampeded horses for fun. Although Nari did enjoy chasing the sea birds across the beach. But in general, they seemed to accede to their riders' wishes better than Starlight did.

"I'm working on it, William. But she doesn't seem to know what I want. She's really good at places. Today I told her to go to the field behind the blacksmith, and that's exactly where she took me. And coming home, she followed my instructions when I turned her away from SeaView Ridge. But when I try to visualize what I want her to do… she just doesn't understand."

"Do you really think she doesn't understand?" Cala put a hand on Nevan's arm, her touch gentle, as if she could soften her words. "Or is she simply not interested in following instructions? Maybe you need to be a bit more stern."

He thought about her reaction to his reprimand at the horse paddock. "Forceful isn't really my strong suit." Despite his comparatively larger size, Cala and William exuded far more authority than he. Much of that could be attributed to their earlier professions. Cala had been the High War Witch of the Borgonne for decades until her magic began to fade, and William had commanded the famed dragon guild of Verduun.

But Nevan, the runt of a giant family, had always been gentle, meek, humble. Starlight's quiet personality had seemed like a good fit —until she started exhibiting her impish streak.

"You'll get it. Dragons need human guidance if they're going to be part of the team. You're doing a great job." William picked up his tea and nodded at the paper again. "We'll keep working on it. And I believe these exercises will help. What do you think?"

Nevan blinked in surprise at William's question. "Are you really asking me?"

"Of course." William sat back in his chair and folded his arms. "I've come to realize the sea dragons may be cousins to the dragons of Verduun, but they're different in many ways. A good leader surrounds himself with people who are smarter than him—in at least one area.

You know a lot more about the sea dragons than the rest of us. So what do you think?"

With an encouraging nod from Cala, Nevan drew the paper closer and read it a second time. He tapped a line. "I like these. But here on Safe Haven, we've always fought fires with a bucket brigade. If we want to employ a new method, maybe we need someone who's smarter than us in that area." He cast a sly grin at William.

The old dragon man sat upright, poking a finger first at Nevan, then at Cala. "Yes! You are correct. Safe Haven doesn't have a fire brigade. I wonder who I can get from Verduun..." His gaze went to the far wall, lost in thought.

Nevan turned to Cala. "How did you do it in the Borgonne?"

Cala waved both hands. "That won't be much help. Calling storms to put out fires was one of my defensive responsibilities." She pointed at her husband with a wry smile. "He started them, and I put them out." She mimed dumping a bucket on a fire.

Nevan scratched his chin, his fingers rasping in the thick stubble. His giant genes meant he had to shave every day—twice if he wanted to be clean shaven in the evening. Most giants grew a full beard for this reason, but that always made him itchy. "I suppose the dragons could carry a big bucket in their talons."

"That doesn't really take advantage of their unique abilities." Cala pursed her lips as if blowing.

"No... but there's no reason they couldn't do both." At her raised brow, he went on slowly, feeling out the idea as he spoke. "We could get Klausi to craft a big, leather bucket. When there's a fire, we scoop up some water, dump that on the fire, then the dragons spout on whatever is left?"

Cala snapped her fingers. "And the buckets could be used to bring a large amount of water to the site, so we wouldn't have to fly so far to... re-fuel."

William rose. "Those are excellent ideas. Write them down. I need to draft a letter to Master Kent of the fire guild. He might have additional ideas for us." He tapped his chin thoughtfully. "Might be better to invite him to visit rather than ask him via mail. Faster. More secure. I'll talk to Koni."

Cala raised her communications disk, and Koni's voice rumbled inside Nevan's head. "Did someone say my name?"

"You could hear us?" Nevan asked, aghast. Did the disk allow the elf to eavesdrop constantly?

"No. Serendipity." Koni laughed merrily. "I called to ask Cala about something, and I heard William mention me."

William explained what he wanted: a secure way to contact his friend, a part of the Verduun Fire Brigade. "It's too bad more people don't have these magic medallions."

"I've seen that reality. It's not as good as you might think," Koni said. "But I can help you with a slower means to contact him. Write a letter, and I'll ensure it gets to him and only him."

"I was hoping you would say that. Did you need anything else?"

"Not from you. But I do need to ask your dear wife some arcane questions about magic."

"That's my cue to depart." William rose with a little laugh and kissed Cala on the cheek. "Come, Nevan, let's try out a few of these exercises."

CHAPTER SEVEN

After leaving Nevan's loaf of bread in the bench, Franisa put her bundle of sweet rolls in a basket and headed out. The walk to the dwarven village took a little over an hour, so she set a rapid pace. Today was a bookstore day for the children, and Cala wouldn't send them home until the shop closed at five, so she should have plenty of time to speak with Philomena as long as she didn't dally.

The cobblestone road from the square in front of the bakery turned to dirt just beyond the stables beside the blacksmith's forge. Despite her anxiety over visiting her mother-in-law, she enjoyed the crisp air and gentle sunshine. A faint tinge of woodsmoke was not unpleasant; it reminded her of evenings by the fire when she was a child.

After she'd married Keldan and taken management of the bakery, she hadn't had time for lazy evenings. When she wasn't baking or cleaning, she'd taken on some mending to add a little money to her coffers. She'd never let Keldan know she'd been paid for that stitching —the coins she'd earned had gone straight into her private rainy-day fund... which she'd promptly spent each time he'd raided the bakery's funds to buy more books.

When she reached the turn leading to the dwarven village, she paused to rest. A flock of little birds chattered in the lush greenery around her. A crow landed on the weathered signpost that pointed onward to Valebra, cawing loudly before launching into the sky. As she turned off the main road, she gave an almost violent shake of her head. Some of those early years had been grim, and she didn't need to think about them now.

Or maybe she did. The memories might make her angry enough to face Philomena. By the time the path meandered into the dwarven village, she'd wound herself into an anxious knot of anger, self-doubt, and panic.

Village was a strong word. Most dwarves seemed to prefer to live in abandoned mines. Little buildings—barely big enough to cover the top of a ladder—with doors no higher than her waist, stood at irregular intervals on either side of the path. Some of them were painted pretty colors and decorated with currently empty flower boxes, but most of them looked like abandoned garden sheds.

In the center of the village, a human-sized dwelling loomed over the others. The half-timbered building looked very much like the structures in town, with white-washed plaster between heavy dark beams, thick paned windows, and a thatched roof. On the left, a bow window jutted out into the front garden, its wavy green glass glinting in the afternoon sunlight. Taking a deep breath, she walked down the stone path between the winter-dormant shrubs and empty, Dorfmundish urns to the bright green door.

With another steadying breath, she knocked, using more force than she intended. In her ears, the thuds seemed to roll through the village, alerting everyone in town to her presence. She kept her back straight and her gaze on the door, pretending she hadn't a care in the world.

The door swung inward, and Philomena stared up at her. The older woman was short, under five-feet tall in her stockings, but she exuded a commanding presence. Stiffening her spine, Franisa indicated her basket. "I've brought you some sweets, Mother. May I come in?"

Her mother-in-law gave her a swift once-over, then stepped back to grant her entry. "To what do I owe this... honor?"

How did her simple words make Franisa feel so inferior? As she'd told her daughter many times, good manners were a gift to be shared, and petty comments only hurt the one making them. But under her mother-in-law's critical eyes, she found it hard to remember that sage advice.

Franisa lifted her chin. "I have a matter I wish to discuss with you." Slipping her shoes off by the door, she removed her wrapped bundle from the basket, which she placed beside her shoes. She carried the rolls to the large dining room table at the back of the room and set them on the polished wood.

Even after ten years, she didn't know much about her mother-in-law. The woman was originally from Dorfmund but had fallen in love with Gnollis when he traveled there, setting up trade deals with gold and gem dealers in the wealthier country. They had married and returned to his home after a brief courtship. Franisa had often tried to imagine what the human had seen in the dwarf but failed every time. Maybe it was his wealth rather than his person? She would probably never know. Her mother-in-law had never opened up to her.

But Philomena had managed to convince the dwarf to open his coffers and provide her with a comfortable, human-style home, as well as servants to care for it. Franisa had to imagine it was a love match, at least on the dwarf's side.

Philomena gestured to the sitting area near the bow window and sat in the throne-like chair closest to the fire. She lifted a little handbell from the table beside it and rang. As Franisa nervously perched on the edge of the hard chair across from her mother-in-law, a pixie burst into the room in a flutter of glittering dust.

"Tea, please." Philomena glanced at Franisa then returned her gaze to the pixie. "And put those rolls in the kitchen. They will make an adequate breakfast."

The tiny green-clad woman bowed, then zipped to the cloth-wrapped rolls. She grasped the knot in both hands, her wings beating fast enough to stir up a breeze, and lifted the package, which was easily five times her weight. The pixie and her massive burden bobbed away through the doorway in the back of the room.

"I didn't know you had a pixie!" The words popped out before she could censor them. She had no reason to be informed of Philomena's household and certainly hadn't visited except when absolutely necessary.

Philomena nodded regally. "She joined the staff a few months ago."

Franisa ached to ask more questions. In her experience, pixies didn't seek employment but were attached to a location. Aislin lived in the bookstore and had for years—centuries even. The little pixie had never explained why she began to help in the bakery, and Cala had merely said she enjoyed "playing" with Eloise. Who would this pixie be playing with?

But Franisa had bigger fish to fry. Steeling her nerve, she leaned closer to her mother-in-law. "I need your help."

A gleam of what might have been triumph flashed in Philomena's eyes, but it was gone before Franisa could be sure. The older woman sat back in her chair and waved a lazy hand. "You may proceed."

Franisa gritted her teeth at the comment clearly designed to make her grovel, like a peasant before a queen. Well, if it would keep Enrich safe, she would grovel. "I hope—I beg you to speak with Gnollis about Enrich. About working here."

"Your son should be grateful for the opportunity. It is difficult for humans to break into dwarven society."

Franisa blinked. Was that a hint of vulnerability? Had Philomena found it difficult to join the ranks of the dwarves she seemed to rule over? Pushing that thought to the back of her mind, she went on. "I am grateful Gnollis has introduced him to the rest of the clan. But he promised Enrich would stay with the children. Outside the mine!"

This time it was Philomena who blinked. "He's taking Enrich into the mine?"

"Because he's so much bigger than the other children. But he's not strong enough—or mature enough—to work in such a dangerous place."

Philomena looked away, her brows drawn down. "I hadn't realized..." She coughed, and her tone came out a little defensive. "I cannot help you. Gnollis rules the mine. It is not my place to tell him how to run it."

"But you wouldn't let Keldan work in the mines!" Franisa leaned across the space between them, extending a hand. "He listens to you. The only way I can keep Enrich away from him is—"

"What?" Philomena's head snapped around, and she pinned a cold, hard stare on her daughter-in-law.

Franisa withdrew her hand, keeping her gaze on her lap. "I asked Cala to speak with the school. And to escort Enrich there. But—"

"Ha! I knew he was afraid of the witch!"

Shocked by her mother-in-law's gleeful exclamation, she glanced up. Philomena's cheeks went pink in a display of embarrassment Franisa had never witnessed. The older woman tried to cover it up by ringing the bell again and snapping, "Where is our tea?"

The pixie fluttered into the room again, pushing the tea tray through the air in front of her. It drifted down onto the table, knocking the bell off the edge. A flutter of glittering pixie dust settled over the tray then the pixie and dust popped out of existence.

Grumbling under her breath, Philomena poured two cups of tea. As usual, she added milk and a healthy spoonful of honey to each cup, then dropped a shortbread cookie on the saucer and handed it to Franisa, managing to slosh tea over the rim as their hands met. Philomena pinched her lips together and lifted her chin, as if disgusted by Franisa's clumsiness—even though she had been the one to spill the tea.

Franisa took a polite sip, hiding her wince at the sweet, lukewarm beverage. She preferred her tea hot and black, with no sweetener. As Philomena well knew. She set the cup on the side table, the soggy biscuit untasted. "Will you help me?"

The older woman looked Franisa over, her gaze lingering on the faint dusting of flour on her sleeve and her carefully mended pocket. "No. I told you, Gnollis rules the mine. It's a pity you never remarried. Then you'd have a man to negotiate on your behalf." She made it sound like Franisa had tried and failed to attract a second husband.

Gritting her teeth, Franisa tried to think of something pleasant to say. Raising two children virtually on her own left her little time to dally with a man. Gnollis and Philomena had made no effort to help her after Keldan's death and had only shown an interest in Enrich when he grew large enough to work.

Giving up on diplomacy, Franisa surged to her feet. "Fine. If that's what it takes... Thank you for—no, never mind. I don't feel the need to thank you for your passive aggressive hospitality. I won't trouble you again." She turned on her heel and stalked to the door.

"How dare you—!"

Whirling, Franisa cut her mother-in-law off—something she had never done before. "I would dare anything for my child. You, of all people, should understand that. You coddled your own son—against the wishes of your own husband. Why would you for an instant believe I wouldn't do anything to protect mine?" Heart pounding at her own temerity, she slipped her feet into her shoes, grabbed her basket, and stalked out the door.

CHAPTER EIGHT

By the time he finished training with William, Nevan was exhausted. He thought about sending word to his family that he would not be available for dinner, but since they had no magic amulets, and he had no homing pigeon, that would require going into town. If he was going to do that, he may as well stay for supper.

Making use of the new water closet he and William had installed, he cleaned up. As he returned to his cubicle, he passed Starlight snoozing by the stove. After adding another log to the firebox, he donned a fresh shirt and his best leather vest.

"Starlight?" he whispered.

The dragon stirred but didn't rouse. He hated to wake her, but he'd gotten used to flying and hadn't left enough time to walk down to the village.

"Ho there, Nevan!" Koni Erden, mayor of Safe Haven, stood in the doorway. The elf wore a brocade vest over a white shirt, with knee-length pants, tall boots, and a soft hat with a feather. A gold-trimmed cape hung from his shoulders.

Nevan whistled softly as he crossed the room then lowered his voice. "Hello, Koni. Why so fancy?"

Koni looked down at his attire. "What, this old thing?" He paused expectantly, but when Nevan gave him a puzzled frown, he went on. "I have some mayoral duties down at the Silver Acorn. Visiting dignitaries, if you can believe it. And I popped out here to get William's letter for the Verduunian fire chief. But you know I can't resist saying hello to our dragons." He peered past Nevan into the darkened stable. "William said he wore you two out."

Nevan scrubbed his fingers through his thick hair and sighed. "I didn't realize firefighting was going to be so much work. I mean, sure when you're actually doing it..." He mimed throwing a bucket of water. "But the training..."

With an understanding nod, the elf turned away. "I don't want to wake the hard-working dragon. And I must be in town before sunset."

Following Koni into the courtyard, Nevan glanced at the horizon. "Sunset? You're going to be late."

A sly, self-satisfied smile flitted across Koni's face. "No. *You* would be late, but I have my ways. Give Starlight my best." He lifted a hand and turned to take the path down the narrow, rocky peninsula toward town.

"Wait. Can you take others along *these ways*?" Nevan hurried after Koni. "Others like me?"

"Do you have an appointment? A tryst perhaps?" Koni raised his brows suggestively. "A lovely young baker lady breathlessly awaiting your arrival?"

Nevan's cheeks burned. "No! What do you— No." Even the mayor knew of his infatuation? Taking a deep breath, he tried to look dignified. "No, I've got dinner with my family."

"Ah. You do not want to be late for that. Come along." Koni strode swiftly down the dusty path across the stone. "There's a saying, 'your failure to plan does not constitute an emergency on my part,' but since it costs me nothing to help you out..."

"I've never heard that before." Nevan lengthened his stride to keep up with the elf. Although Nevan had at least a foot on him, Koni moved with an astounding speed that somehow still looked like a lazy stroll.

"Another reality. They get a bit jumbled sometimes." Koni waved his fingers at his head.

Nevan had heard Koni talk about "another reality" before, though the elf never bothered to explain what that meant. He often presented a flamboyant and mysterious persona, and Nevan didn't like to pry, but tonight it seemed as if he were inviting questions. "What does that mean?"

Koni cast a mischievous smile at the giant, his eyes glinting in the lamplight. "Someday, I'll tell you. Thank you for accompanying me on my journey." He stopped and gestured down the lane.

Stumbling over the cobblestones he hadn't noticed, Nevan looked around in amazement. They stood at the edge of town, where their dirt track met paved road. "How—"

Spreading his arms wide, Koni backed into the square where Cala's bookshop stood. "That I will not explain! I must maintain my sense of mystery."

"How did you know I was thinking that?" Nevan rubbed his temple. "Can you read my mind?"

The elf laughed. "Not really. I work hard to be mysterious. I'd be disappointed if you *weren't* thinking that." He bowed, arms still outstretched, and turned, his cape swirling around him. "Have a lovely evening, Nevan! Give my greetings to your parents," he called as he disappeared down the street that led to the port.

Scratching his head, Nevan crossed the square in the other direction and ducked into the dark street leading to the smithy. Gas lamps burned in each of the town's squares, but the streets between were unlit. Nevan had never worried about walking through town after sunset. The village was a safe place—Koni saw to that. Besides, no one in their right mind would attack a giant. Even in the dark.

As if challenging his thought, arms closed around him, one cutting across his neck, the other around his waist. They tightened, lifting him off the ground.

Nevan grabbed the arm at his throat, pulling down to keep his airway free. "Gebby!"

Laughing hard, his brother Gebhard dropped him. "How'd you know it was me?"

"The smell." He chuckled at Gebhard's indignant gasp, then leaned his elbow into his brother's side, pushing him away. Or trying, but the boy was anchored to the ground like a rock. "There aren't a lot of giants in Safe Haven."

"There are sailors." Gebhard elbowed Nevan, sending the smaller man reeling into the chandler's shop.

"They stay down by the port. Or in the Crab and Tankard. They aren't going to attack a random guy—they all know Koni would banish their ship." He pointed across the square. "I'm going to pick up the bread I ordered from the bakery. Tell Ma I'll be right in."

"Better hurry! Dinner is almost ready!" Gebhard trotted around the fountain toward the forge. "Tell your crush I said hello!"

"She's not—" He broke off—Gebby was already out of earshot. Cheeks burning, Nevan went to the bench and lifted the lid. He dropped his coins in the little box and took the only item inside. Carefully replacing the heavy seat, Nevan held the cotton-wrapped loaf up to the light. A little card with a dragon on it was tied to the drawstring closing the bag. He paused to breathe in the toasty, yeasty scent of the bread, then walked around the other side of the fountain, nearly running over a smaller figure.

"Oh!" Franisa grabbed the front of Nevan's vest for balance then let go. "Sorry."

He looked down at her in surprise. In the shadow thrown by his shoulders, he couldn't see her face, but her voice sounded stuffy, as if she had a head cold. Or had been crying. "Are you well?"

She drew in a deep breath and settled her shoulders, stepping back. "I am far from well, but there is nothing you can do about it." Her tone came out hard and tired.

"Are you sure? You don't have to do everything on your own." His heart beat fast, anger at whatever, or whomever, had distressed her overwhelming his embarrassment—surely she'd heard Gebby's taunt. "If I can help, I will."

She let out a short, hard laugh. "Unless you want to marry me, there's nothing you can do."

CHAPTER NINE

In the silence, Franisa berated herself internally. What had possessed her to blurt that out? Especially after Gebhard had taunted Nevan about his infatuation. "I'm sorry, that was—never mind."

"You want to marry me?" Nevan stuttered.

"No, of course not." The giant recoiled at her sharp denial, and she put a hand on his arm. She knew he'd been sweet on her when they were children. Despite his size, he was a sensitive soul, and she didn't want to hurt his feelings. "I don't mean… It's not you. I don't really want to marry at all."

That wasn't actually true. Although Keldan had been a less-than-perfect partner, he'd shared daily life with her. They'd enjoyed many wide and varied conversations, thanks to his voracious reading. Even after all these years, she missed their tea-time conversations. And he had given her two wonderful children.

Since his death, she'd learned to survive, even thrive on her own. But she was tired of doing everything by herself. And a husband would undoubtedly have more success in keeping Enrich out of the mines.

Nevan cocked his head. "If you don't want to marry, why did you ask?"

"It's a… misunderstanding with Keldan's parents. Gnollis won't—" She broke off, not wanting to air the family's dirty laundry.

"Ah. Dwarves don't let their women make decisions. My ma told me that. She couldn't believe it when we moved here."

"I wish my ma…" Franisa's mother had been nearly as subservient to her husband as most dwarven women, a trait Franisa had never appreciated or understood. Thanks to Cala's Aunt Milli, and the other strong women in the village, Franisa had learned to see males and females as partners, not master and servant. And although his own father obviously didn't practice what he preached—or maybe *because* he didn't—Keldan had never treated her as less than an equal. Or maybe he simply preferred having a wife who managed everything so he could focus on his books.

She took a step away from Nevan's solicitous bulk. "It's not something you need to worry about."

"Friends help friends." Nevan turned as she moved past him. "If I can help you, I will."

She shook her head. "Thank you. You're a good friend. Which reminds me, thank you for spending some time with Eloise. She really likes you."

"She likes how I smell." Nevan laughed, the deep chuckle warming her to her toes. "Apparently dragons smell better than burnt."

"Burnt?" She took another step toward the bakery, and Nevan turned with her, putting his face into the lamplight.

He blushed. "She said something about Rolph, the carpenter. I don't think burning wood smells bad, myself, but…"

"She is very interested in scents. Last week, she told me Goodwife Wrenright smelled yellow, which according to her is a mix of turmeric and—" She broke off, remembering the other scent Eloise had identified. "Well, let's just say yellow is an appropriate color for that smell too."

Nevan laughed again.

A door across the square opened. "Nevan! Where are you?" Gebhard yelled.

The giant started guiltily. "I'm sorry, I must go. But I will help you however I can."

"Don't worry about me." Franisa made shooing motions at him. "I'll work it out. Enjoy your dinner. Wish your mother good evening for me."

"How'd you know—" He looked at the loaf of bread in his hands. "Oh, yeah. Oravai." He turned and trudged across the cobbles, disappearing through the giant-sized portal cut into one of the massive doors across the front of the forge.

Franisa let herself into the bakery and barred the door. Nevan's comforting presence had banished her melancholy for those few minutes, but it returned in full force. The lamp in the square cast wavery rectangles of light through the thick glass of the mullioned windows, allowing her to reach the curtain dividing the shop from the bakery without stumbling. Once in the back, she made her way by touch to the back door. She hung her cloak on the peg beside it, then trailed her hand along the wall to the staircase beyond the pantry.

When she reached the top, she took a deep breath and pasted a smile on her face, then pushed the door open and entered the warm light of her home. The children glanced up from their game on the floor but continued bickering happily over the knucklebones.

"Time to clean up," she told them.

"What were you doing, Mama?" Eloise jumped up from the floor, leaving her brother to pick up the game pieces.

"I was just clearing my head." She stirred the stew bubbling gently on the tile stove, then went to the dresser to take out some bowls. "Put these on the table, will you? Enrich, can you run down and get a barley loaf? I forgot to bring one up."

The boy set the handful of bones in their bowl on the windowsill and crossed to the door. He pulled it ajar. "It's dark down there." A shiver ran through his body.

"You aren't afraid of the dark, are you?" She watched him carefully as he asked.

"Dark? No. It's just—" He sighed and pulled the door wider.

Franisa took a candle stub from the dresser and tossed it to him.

With a nervous smile, he stuck a matchstick into the top of the lamp and lit the candle. Then he disappeared down the stairs.

LATER THAT NIGHT, AFTER ELOISE WAS ASLEEP, FRANISA WENT into the children's room and sat on the edge of her son's bed. "Are you awake?"

"Yes." The boy rolled to his back. Enough light came through the front windows to allow her to see his face. He yawned, but he didn't look sleepy.

"Why didn't you want to go downstairs tonight?" She kept her voice low, even though Eloise, like most small children, could sleep through anything.

"It's nothing."

"Enrich, has your gran-da—does he tell you men aren't afraid of anything?"

The boy hesitated. "He's right. Men are brave."

"Being brave doesn't mean not being afraid. It means doing something even when you *are* afraid. If you weren't afraid, it would be easy, not brave."

Enrich grunted, but she couldn't tell if he was agreeing or not.

"Going downstairs, even if you were afraid of the dark, was brave."

"I'm not afraid of the dark!" He sat up suddenly. "I'm just... Going down the dark stairs is like the mine." The last words came out so softly she almost didn't hear them.

"And the mine is scary."

"Yes." Enrich sat up suddenly, throwing his arms around her and squeezing his face against her chest. "I don't want to go down there again!"

As she held her sobbing child against her body, Franisa's resolve stiffened. She let him cry himself out, then she held him away by his shoulders. "You don't have to go down there again. Ever. I will do whatever it takes to make that happen."

~

FRANISA CREPT DOWN TO THE KITCHEN. THE DARKNESS OF very early morning seemed to press against the windows, and she shivered. She didn't normally mind being up before dawn. In fact, she usually enjoyed the quiet of early morning. But after tossing and turning for hours, she'd finally given up on sleep. The quiet of the village seemed to mock her. She poked the fire to life, adding another log, then started the first batch of bread dough.

As the faint pink haze of dawn lightened the horizon, Franisa sat on a high stool behind the shop counter, sipping her tea. The hair that had escaped her bun curled around her ears, tickling her cheeks. From this vantage, she could see past the blacksmith, down the alley to the dark fields barely beginning to lighten beyond. The streetlight still glimmered in the square, casting a long wavering form as a woman approached the bakery. Cala, coming to help with the baking.

The witch bypassed the front door, heading down the side alley to the kitchen yard. Franisa slipped off her stool to meet her friend in the warm, cinnamon and cardamom scented room.

A brief gust of winter breeze cooled the steamy space as Cala slipped through the opening and swiftly shut the door. She looked around the kitchen in dismay. "Am I late again?"

"Maybe the walk from FarPoint takes longer than you think." Franisa handed her friend a cup of tea. "But I started early—too early. I—I need your help."

Cala set the thick ceramic mug on the counter and faced her friend. "Anything." She wrinkled her nose. "Anything I can manage. I can't call a storm anymore. Or hex anyone."

Franisa sniffed and snickered. "That's a shame. A hex would be the easy answer. But Philomena would probably figure it out, then she'd hire a stronger witch to hex me back."

"Gnollis?"

Franisa handed Cala two plates and nodded at the closest pan of sea shell rolls. "This conversation requires sustenance." She took both cups and led the way into the cooler front room. "Come and relax after your walk."

"I didn't walk." Cala set a warm roll in front of her and perched on the second stool.

"I saw you crossing the square." Franisa nodded at the front windows of the shop.

Cala smiled. "I flew. Nari left me in the field behind the blacksmith. Nevan said the horses would be inside this early, so it's safe enough to land there." She sipped her tea. "Why am I hexing Gnollis?"

"No hexes." Franisa waved both hands. "That would definitely come back to haunt me."

"I was never any good at them anyway. Even at the peak of my powers. A strong hex requires a... negative emotional connection." Cala noticed her friend's confusion and went on. "You have to really hate someone. Or something. And transfer that bitterness and contempt into the hex. Loathing isn't my strong suit."

Franisa reached across to squeeze the witch's hand. "I am not surprised. But no, I just need to keep Enrich away from Gnollis until I figure out a more permanent solution."

"If you don't mind him missing school, he can come out to FarPoint with me. When we aren't training, Nevan is doing some more construction. He'll pick up some skills and some figuring. I could help him with reading too. And, of course, I'm still coming to the bookstore twice a week."

"I—I don't want to impose."

"Nonsense. Nevan can use the assistance. He's started working on a more permanent residence, so he can move out of the stables when the next class of dragon riders moves in." Cala chuckled. "Planning ahead. But he likes to stay busy."

"The next class? When will that be?"

"No idea. We still aren't sure how often the dragon queens clutch." Cala picked up her fork and cut a bite of the roll. "Delicious, as always."

"That's what keeps them coming back." Franisa slipped off her stool. "I'll wrap some for you to take with you. And wake Enrich."

Leaving her cooling tea and roll on the counter, she hurried into the kitchen and up the stairs. As she opened the door at the top, Aislin popped into the room from wherever pixies lived when they weren't in the real world. Sparkling dust swirled around her, disappearing before it reached the floor. "Aislin will wake the children, Mistress Franisa!" The pixie's high, cheerful voice chimed musically, harmonizing with the church bell now tolling.

Leaving the pixie to her task, Franisa trotted back down the steps to wrap some rolls for the dragon riders. Cala met her in the kitchen, the large wooden peel in her hands. "I think the bread smells about right. Did you put them in on the half hour?"

"Yes." Franisa drew in a deep breath, then nodded in approval. "You're getting quite good at this."

Opening the big oven, Cala ducked away from the cloud of escaping steam. Then she slipped the long, flat wooden blade under the first loaf and pulled it out. With a quick flip, she exposed the browned underside of the rounded oblong and tapped a finger against the bottom. "Hollow means it's done!"

Nodding at her friend's enthusiasm, Franisa helped her extract the six loaves, then slid another half dozen across the blackened stone floor of the oven. By the time they were done, the children had thundered down the stairs. She set them to their morning chores while she cut some of the previous day's bread to make breakfast.

After Enrich headed outside to get a load of firewood, Cala turned to her friend. "Taking him out to FarPoint is only a temporary solution. He's too young to pair with a dragon—even if we had a hatching soon."

"I know." Franisa blushed. "I'm working on a more permanent plan."

Cala's eyes narrowed, her eagle gaze flicking to Franisa's cheeks. "Permanent?"

The heat in her face intensified. "Philomena thinks I should marry again. A new husband would have authority in Gnollis's eyes. Keldan's children will always be part of Gnollis's clan, but he respects a man's right to run his household as he sees fit. Which includes any children under that man's roof, no matter their parentage."

Cala's jaw tightened. "A man can say no, but a woman can't?"

Franisa's heart warmed at the anger in Cala's voice. "In the dwarven world, yes."

"Except Philomena?"

"I don't really understand that relationship." Franisa turned away to scrape some spilled frosting from her worktop. "As far as I can tell, Philomena can do no wrong in Gnollis's eyes. I tried to enlist her help, but she declined. I get the impression she thinks she's helping me by not helping."

"You're too kind to that woman." Cala wrung the water out of a cloth and slapped it on the counter to scrub away the last traces of sugar and milk. "If she told Gnollis no, he wouldn't dare to take Enrich. I almost feel I could hex them. If I had that kind of power left." She flexed her hand experimentally.

Franisa touched her shoulder. "I don't want you doing that for me. Cultivating hatred isn't good for the soul. I just need to find a willing husband. That shouldn't be too hard. Rolph has shown some interest. And he could use an apprentice..."

Even as she said the words, her stomach curdled with distaste. In the abstract, Rolph was a solid choice, but in person he made her cringe. Not that feelings were significant in a marriage. Her first union had taught her that. Their initial indifference had blossomed into mutual understanding and tranquility. But she'd always hoped a second one would be on her own terms, with someone she actually felt something for, not dictated by an external force.

"Rolph? The carpenter?" Cala's lips pressed together in disapproval. "I don't think—"

"He smells burnt." Nose wrinkling in dismay, Eloise skipped into the room with the pixie on her heels. "I don't like burnt."

Cala's head cocked to one side and sniffed. "I always liked burning wood. It reminds me of climbing up a well-used spell tower..."

"Oooh, a spell tower!" Eloise gripped a fold of Cala's pant leg.

The witch had taken to wearing trousers when she'd paired with her dragon, but she favored a wide cut that almost looked like a skirt. She glanced down at the child, then at Franisa, and raised a brow.

With a gentle shrug, Franisa went back to stacking the cooled loaves in a basket. When Cala had originally appeared in the village, she'd immediately made friends with the children, offering reading lessons and book loans from her aunt's old bookstore. Franisa had initially worried about the stories the older woman might tell of her service in the Borgonne army, but she'd soon learned Cala preferred to put those days behind her. The few stories she told were well edited for their audience.

"Casting weather spells works better if you are closer to the source." Cala gestured at the ceiling. "The army would build towers for us to climb on, and sometimes they get hit by stray lightning. Especially when you're training a new mage. So, to me, burnt wood smells like new power. The smell still gives me a little hope."

"Mister Rolph doesn't smell like hope. He smells like sadness." Eloise pursed her lips primly.

"Maybe it isn't burnt wood you're smelling?" Cala poked the little girl gently.

With a giggle, Eloise squirmed away. "Mama said carpenters smell of sawdust."

"I never sniffed the man." Franisa shook her head. "We've discussed this before. It's not good manners."

"I know, but I can't help it. I just breathe and..." The child puffed out her cheeks and crossed her eyes, her hand gripping her throat. Then she dissolved into giggles again.

"Eloise, go wash your hands." Franisa pointed at Cala's pant leg. "You got butter on Cala!"

"Aislin can fix!" The little pixie had been puttering around the room, whisking spilled flour away, but at Franisa's exclamation, she flitted to the witch. With a complicated waving of her tiny feather duster, a cloud of sparkles appeared. They settled on the greasy stain on Cala's clothing, obscuring it completely. The pixie stared at the spot, her brow furrowed in concentration, then waved the duster again. The sparkles fell away, leaving clean fabric.

Cala smirked and flicked her hand at her leg. "That spot is cleaner than the rest of this outfit."

"You needs to let me clean alls the clothes." Aislin's little face wrinkled in consternation. "It doesn't look good if a pixie's people is messy."

"You can clean these tomorrow. They'll probably be even dirtier by then." Cala swiped at the clean patch again then glanced out the window at the brightening sunlight. "I must get back. William has a full schedule for the fire brigade today!"

Franisa stilled. Did that mean Nevan wouldn't have time for Enrich? She'd need to find a different solution for the boy.

As if hearing Franisa's thoughts, Cala turned to the door. "Where is Enrich?"

"He should have been back by now." Franisa hurried to the door. "He was just getting the firewood." Early morning sunlight spilled into the little yard, illuminating the tiny stream running across it, the huge stack of wood against the back fence, and the winter-dead garden. But there was no sign of the boy.

CHAPTER TEN

Nevan yanked his boots on, shuffling across the stone floor of the stable toward the wide-open door. Heat from the stove warmed his back, but the clear morning had dawned unusually cool, and a brisk breeze flattened his shirt against his chest. He paused by the door to pull a heavy winter cloak from the peg, then pulled the door shut as he exited the building.

"Starlight!" He blew a sharp whistle, then bent to buckle the straps on his boots. The little dragon dropped into the courtyard before he'd gotten the second one done. "Good girl!"

"Nevan!" The dragon rubbed her head against his side, burrowing under the cloak draped over his arm.

He took a step back and stared at the dragon. "Did you just *talk* to me?"

Starlight's head butted against him again. *"Nevan."*

Dumbfounded, Nevan leaned against the wall of the stable, his jaw slack. Dragons didn't speak. Like their bigger cousins the war dragons, sea drakes responded to visualizations. Or at least Finn and Nari had. Although Starlight always empathized with his mood, and usually knew where he wanted to go, she hadn't seemed to understand his attempts to visualize instructions.

"Nevan. Fly." The dragon sidled sideways to present her flank.

"Uh, yes." He finished buckling his boot, then shrugged into his cloak. The communication medallion in his pocket vibrated and he fumbled it out. "Yes?"

"Nevan." Cala's voice echoed through his head, much like Starlight's. "Enrich is missing. We need help. Come to the bakery." The device vibrated again before he could answer.

Enrich was missing? Putting his foot on Starlight's haunch, he sprang up to settle astride her shoulders. As her muscular body bunched beneath him, he touched her neck.

The dragon froze, almost quivering with anticipation. They'd worked hard on the wait command, and Nevan could tell she didn't like it. But he wasn't going to fall off again—he'd be little help to Franisa lying on the ground with a broken neck. He buckled his belt to Starlight's harness, his fingers clumsy in his haste, then tapped her neck twice. "Go. To the smithy." He tried to project an image of his former home from the air.

Instantly, Starlight launched into the sky, leaping over the low wall and catching the upswelling thermal from the sea below. They wheeled to the right and soared low over the cliff top, heading inland.

The disc in his pocket vibrated again, but he didn't dare remove it. If he dropped it from this height, he'd never find the enchanted medallion again. And Koni had made very clear the time and difficulty involved in creating a new one. As they flew, he wondered briefly if there was a way to attach the device to his belt, like the straps that kept him physically linked to his dragon. Would a leather pouch interfere with the device's magical capabilities? He'd have to ask Cala or Koni.

They banked over the town, diving toward the field behind the forge, arriving incredibly fast. Did the dragons have the ability to use the elven roads Koni walked? Or did they have their own magical routes? Or had he merely been distracted, watching for any sign of the boy?

Starlight flared her wings, dropping quickly to the corner of the field closest to the smithy. With a grateful slap against her neck, Nevan unbuckled the harness then slipped down the dragon's side. She was probably small enough to land in the square in front of the forge, but the fountain in the center might impede her ability to take off. "Stay here, Starlight."

"Nevan." The dragon pushed him toward the fence with her nose. *"Here."*

He stared at her in amazement. She gave him another push, as if reminding him of the urgency of the matter. With a swift caress to her head, he turned to scramble over the fence.

He burst into the little square and tore across the cobblestones around the fountain, nearly running into his brother Gebhard scooping water from the basin with his ten-gallon bucket. "Nevan! What's the hurry?"

"Franisa's son is missing!" He scrambled around his giant sibling and continued toward the bakery.

"Enrich? No, he's not." Gebhard grabbed his arm as he hurtled past.

Nevan tried to pull free. "Yes. Cala called me."

"He's in the smithy." Gebhard released him.

Suddenly free, Nevan stumbled then regained his balance. Relief washed over him. "He is?"

With a nod, Gebhard slipped a bucket handle over each of the hooks protruding from the wooden yoke across his shoulders and stood, grunting under the massive weight. "Yeah. He said he wants to apprentice to Da."

"And you didn't think to tell Franisa?" Nevan flung a hand at the bakery.

"Figured she'd sent him." Gebhard tried to shrug, and the water in the buckets sloshed. "Probably not a great idea. He's tiny. Even tinier than you." He flashed his big, square teeth in a cross between a grin and a grimace, then stomped toward the front doors of the smithy, his buckets splashing as he moved.

"Thanks. I'll... I'll be over in a moment." Nevan sucked in a deep breath and hurried across the square toward the bakery. A lamp glowed in the front window, even though the shop wouldn't open for a couple of hours. In the distance, he could hear a woman's voice calling Enrich's name. He pulled at the handle, but the door was locked.

Detouring around the side, he made his way down the narrow street to the back garden. The gate stood wide, but the door was closed, so he knocked. "Franisa? We've found him."

The door opened, revealing Eloise and the pixie. "Nevan!" Eloise jumped to grab his hand, squeezing his fingers in excitement. "You're here!"

"Where's your mother?" He resisted the girl's attempt to drag him into the bakery.

"She's with Cala. They're looking." Her eyes went wide. "Enrich is gone!"

"I found him." Nevan reached into his pocket, his fingers sliding around the smooth wooden communications disk. No one had said the devices were secret, and Franisa needed to know her son wasn't missing, but he felt conspicuous using it in front of an audience. He withdrew the medallion and pressed his thumb against the carving. "Cala?"

"She's with Mama." Eloise's bright eyes locked onto the disk. "What is that?"

"Nevan? Are you here?" Cala's voice sounded in his mind, similar to Starlight's words earlier.

Did the dragon have a connection to the medallion? He'd have to ask Cala. Later. "I found Enrich. He's at the smithy."

A brief, muted buzz followed, like a conversation held too quietly to be heard, then Cala spoke again. "We're coming back." The sound cut out.

Eloise pulled at his hand again. "I heard Cala!"

"You did?" He crouched down to look at the child. "Just now?"

"Yes. She said she's comin' back. How did her voice get in my head?"

He held up the device. "This is a…" Was there a name for it? "Elven magic."

"Oooh." Eloise reached out slowly to touch the wood with a careful finger. "I want one."

"Sorry. They're just for dragon riders." He stood and slid the disk back into his pocket.

"I want to be a dragon rider." Eloise gave his hand another tug. "Girls can ride dragons too."

"Of course. Cala is paired with Nari." He turned to scan the lane, then pointed. "There she is. You stay here." Pulling his hand from Eloise's grip, he hurried toward Franisa. "He's at the smithy. With Gebhard."

The baker spun around, angling around the fountain in the center of the square. "Enrich!" She marched up to the large front doors of the smithy. One stood ajar, so she set her shoulder between the thick wood and the door jamb and pushed. The heavy door barely moved.

"Allow me." Nevan grasped the edge above Franisa's head and pulled it wide.

With a swift glance back at him, she stormed into the dark maw of the smithy. "Enrich! Where are you?"

The glow of the forge barely lit the inside of the big building, casting faint red shadows across the walls. Gebhard and Enrich stood in a corner, looking at something in the young giant's hands. At his mother's voice, Enrich looked up then moved slowly closer to the giant, as if aware he might be in trouble. "I'm right here." His aggrieved tone didn't hide his trepidation.

"You were supposed to bring wood in for the ovens, not run off to play with Gebhard." Franisa grasped his arm and shook it a bit. "I thought your gran-da had taken you away to the mines again!" Her voice trembled.

Enrich looked away, his face contrite. "We weren't playing. I thought since Nevan isn't a blacksmith anymore, maybe I could be the new apprentice. Gebhard was showing me what he does."

"You don't need an apprenticeship yet! You're only nine." Franisa looked past the boy toward Gebhard. "Is your father here? Did he approve?"

"No, Mistress Hearthwell." Gebhard set aside the plow blade he'd been holding and dusted his hands on his apron. "He's not down yet. I told Enrich I could ask him, but I don't know if he wants another apprentice. And smithing is hard work. It needs big muscles." He cast an apologetic glance at Enrich.

Franisa glared at Gebhard. “He needs to be in school, not learning a trade. He can do that when he’s older. Ten or twelve summers. Not nine.”

“Yes, mistress. I attended school until I had fourteen summers.” He glanced down at the boy. “It’s important to know how to read and figure.”

Enrich wrinkled his nose and looked away. “I know. I wanna, but—”

Franisa slid an arm around Enrich’s shoulders. “Did you think if you were working here you wouldn’t have to work… there?”

The boy nodded, his eyes downcast.

“I told you—you aren’t going back there. Ever.” Franisa gave her son a little squeeze then released him. “Come home with me. We’ll break our fast, then you can go to FarPoint with Cala and Nevan.”

Enrich’s head snapped up, his eyes sparkling. “I can? What about school?”

“You’ll get plenty of schooling with us.” Nevan jerked his head toward the door. “I’ll meet you in the square.” He strode past the boy to his brother. “Thanks for looking out for him.”

Gebhard nodded. “He’s a good kid. Just not big enough for this.” He watched over Nevan’s shoulder, then called out, “Leave the door open!”

Nevan glanced back, but the others had already left. The door stood open far enough to allow some light into the smithy. The large buckets Gebhard had filled at the fountain stood beside the forge, waiting for hot metal to be submerged. The coals glowed brilliant red, and finished metal glinted on racks beside the door. “Let me know if you see Gnollis loitering around, will you? He’s trying to make the boy work in the mines.”

“He told me. Enrich, not Gnollis, obviously.” Gebhard moved over to the stove to add some more fuel. “What’s your interest in them?”

Nevan hoped the heat of the stove would hide the warmth of his cheeks. “They’re neighbors. Friends. We look out for each other.”

“Sure, that’s it. Friends.” With a laugh, Gebhard clapped him on the shoulder, the force seeming to drive Nevan into the ground.

Ignoring his brother's taunting tone, Nevan strode toward the door. "I'll see you later, little brother." Gebhard's laughter followed him out.

When he emerged, he found the others hadn't gotten very far. The two women and the boy stood on the far side of the square in front of the bakery. Cala took a half-step in front of Enrich, and her clear voice rang out. "The boy is not going to the mines, Gnollis."

Nevan hurried around the fountain, skidding to a halt behind the group. The dwarf, looking exceptionally threatening despite his short stature, stood on the doorstep of the bakery. Beyond him, Eloise and Aislin peeked between the loaves of bread in the window display.

"I am the head of the clan!" Spittle flew from Gnollis's lips as he glared at the women. "If I say the boy will work in the mine, he works in the mine!"

"Koni won't stand for child labor." Cala took a step closer, forcing the dwarf back against the door.

The heavy pick in Gnollis's hands shook, but whether from anger or fear of Cala, Nevan couldn't tell. The dwarf squared his shoulders and leaned closer to the witch. "That elf doesn't tell me how to handle dwarf business."

"This isn't dwarf business!" Franisa moved up next to Cala. "Enrich is my child, and I won't have you endangering him!"

"He's a dwarf. That puts him under my authority."

"He's three-quarters human." Franisa's voice trembled, but she held firm. "And he's my son."

"He's my grandson. My responsibility." The dwarf smacked the pick handle into his other hand.

"You never took any interest in him until he was big enough to be useful to you." Franisa looked wildly around the square, as if searching for support. Her gaze settled on Nevan for a brief second, then she turned back to the angry miner. "And now that he has a new father, he's no longer your responsibility." She spit the last word out like a curse.

"New father?" Nevan, Cala, and Gnollis all spoke at once.

Franisa whirled and pulled Nevan to the group, pushing Enrich into his shadow. "Yes. Nevan and I are betrothed."

CHAPTER ELEVEN

"What was I thinking?" Franisa dumped a bowl of dough onto the bench. "I should never have dragged Nevan into this!" After the dwarf left them, she'd retreated to her bakery without a word to the giant. It was the coward's way out, but in her panic, she couldn't think of what to say to him.

Cala had followed her inside a few minutes later, the gentle giant nowhere to be seen. Franisa wasn't sure if she was grateful for the reprieve.

"I'm not sure he minds." Cala's lips twisted in a little smirk.

Franisa punched the dough, deflating the bubbles more violently than necessary. "But I blurted it out in front of Gnollis. There was no way he could disagree!" She glanced under her lashes at her friend, then went back to pounding the dough. "I know he was sweet on me when we were kids. I never should have put him in that position."

"He's still smitten." Cala set the kettle on the stove and took some mugs from the shelf. "And to be honest, I think that's what convinced Gnollis."

Franisa groaned. "I shouldn't have to trap a man into a betrothal to protect my son." She folded the dough and slammed the heel of her hand into it.

Cala touched her arm. "Stop. You don't want to overwork it."

Franisa yanked her hands away from the innocent dough. Flipping a cloth over the mass, she turned away, dusting her hands on her apron. "How do I get him out of this? If I call it off, Gnollis will take Enrich back to the mines. He might even try to take him away completely! I've heard him muttering about how I'm turning him into a pixie. He's trying to 'fix' all the things he thinks he did wrong with Keldan. And he doesn't seem to realize Enrich is only nine. I think it's his size..."

Cala put her hands on Franisa's shoulders, stopping her jerky pacing. "Stop. Breathe. We can figure this out. For now, he's safe. Why don't you come out to FarPoint, and we can—"

"I can't face Nevan right now! After what I did to him—" She pulled away from Cala's grip and whirled to the far side of the room. A distant bell heralded the arrival of a customer. "Besides, I have a bakery to run." She yanked the curtain aside and strode into the shop.

"We have heard felicitations are in order." Goodwife Terman's supercilious tone matched her upturned nose and haughty eyes. "I've been telling Wrenright it was coming. For months."

Franisa flushed, her gaze darting to the smaller woman. "Telling her what?"

"That young Nevan would finally get up the nerve to ask for your hand!" The tiny Wrenright practically cooed with excitement. "Pairing with a dragon has certainly increased his self-confidence."

"He should have done it correctly. Asking your father-in-law first would have been appropriate." Terman picked up a loaf of bread, squeezed it, then returned it to the basket. "But it's about time he stopped mooning over you and did the deed."

Franisa gasped, her lungs seizing as if someone had punched her in the stomach. Deciding to ignore the gossip, she fought to draw in a deep breath and channel some of Nevan's supposed new self-confidence. "Please don't squeeze the bread, Goodwife. No one wants to buy a squashed loaf."

Terman turned the full force of her glare on Franisa. "Well, I never! How am I supposed to check its freshness?"

A spike of anger stiffened her spine. Franisa pointed to a basket near the door. "*Everything* here is fresh except the day-olds. And those are going to the town hall for the community pantry. There is no need to *test* any of it."

The curtain rings rattled as Cala came through with a tray of newly frosted sea shell rolls. She set them on the counter, the cinnamon and cardamom wafting out to fill the room with almost magical warmth.

Or maybe it was actual magic. Terman turned a less judgmental eye on Cala. "Those are clearly newly baked. I'll take two."

Cala deftly stacked two of the rolls on a clean cloth and tied the bundle as Franisa had taught her. She handed it over to the old woman with a raised brow. "Enjoy."

Terman slapped some coins on the wooden countertop and snatched up the rolls, tucking them into her basket. "I'll take a loaf of the rye as well. Something fresh. And not squished."

Cala nodded pleasantly, then scooped up the loaf the older woman had dropped a few moments earlier. "Here you are. Baked this morning."

Terman's gaze darted from Cala to Franisa to the basket, as if searching for some kind of excuse to get a different loaf. Finally, with a condescending sniff, she added it to her basket and sailed toward the door. "Come, Wrenright!"

The smaller woman dropped a few coins on the counter, seized a fresh barley loaf, and with an abrupt nod of thanks, scurried after her companion.

Franisa turned to her friend. "Can you believe her?"

"She's always spoken to me thus." Cala lifted both hands. "Which is why I brought out the rolls."

"Whatever you did to the scent... She's never bought those. Doesn't like to spend on indulgences, she always says."

Cala smiled enigmatically. "I can still manage small magics—especially with pastries as good as yours."

"Thank you. But it wasn't her attitude about the bread. It wouldn't be a Tuesday morning if Goodwife Terman didn't squash a loaf or two. I meant about..." She looked around the room even though she knew they were alone, then lowered her voice to a whisper. "Nevan."

"Aislin won't share your secrets, you know." Cala finished moving the rolls to the covered platter on the counter and replaced the glass lid. "House pixies literally can't."

"I wasn't actually worried about *her*. But she's not *my* house pixie. Are you sure she won't gossip about me?"

"When she started cleaning here, her obligation to keep your secrets commenced." The witch laughed. "It's funny, isn't it? I think of cleaning as a chore, so the idea that doing it obligates her in other ways is completely foreign. But for Aislin, cleaning is a privilege, so in exchange, she incurs certain obligations, like confidentiality."

"As interesting as pixie customs are, stop trying to distract me!" Franisa pushed the loose hair away from her brow. "Does everyone in the village think Nevan wants to..." She made a helpless gesture.

"Everyone *knows* he wants to." Cala laughed gently. "I thought you were incensed about her suggestion he ask Gnollis for your hand." She offered a mug of tea.

Franisa spluttered incoherently for a moment then took the hot beverage, trying to organize her thoughts. "If Nevan and I were really..." She waved again. "That is actually the custom among dwarves. When a woman marries, she becomes part of her husband's clan. That bond doesn't dissolve when the husband dies, which is why I'm in this predicament in the first place!" She gazed up at the ceiling, wondering why the One felt the need to make her life so difficult. "It would be different if my own parents were still alive."

"I don't know why a grown woman needs someone else's permission to do anything." Cala crossed her arms, leaning against the counter. "That's something I never appreciated about the Borgonne until I left. I was—I am!—my own person. I don't need a keeper."

"It's different for you. You have magical powers." Franisa set her tea aside, untasted.

"You do too." Cala flicked a finger at the loaves and rolls. "A less flashy magic, perhaps, but magic all the same. The people of this village wouldn't buy your bread if they could make their own as good. That's power."

Franisa sighed. "It doesn't help me stop Gnollis. He is the leader of the dwarves. If they believe he has control over me and my children, I can't change their minds."

"I think we need Koni." Cala picked up her own tea and pushed through the curtains to the back.

Franisa followed helplessly. "I can't leave the bakery. I need to sell my bread!" The bell over the door rang, and she gestured to the front of the building. "See?"

Cala took her friend's hand and squeezed it. "Go sell your bread. Your children are safe today. And tonight, come out to FarPoint and we'll figure out how to fix this." With one last squeeze, she called to Enrich as she headed for the back door.

BY MIDAFTERNOON, FRANISA HAD SOLD MOST OF HER WARES. She put a loaf designated for the butcher into the bench and closed the lid. Enrich often made deliveries after school, but with Gnollis's interference, that custom had ended. She sighed and went back inside, latching the door behind her.

Taking the leftover bread and rolls to the community pantry was also part of Enrich's morning duties—another task that had been preempted. She loaded the contents of the basket into her drawstring bag and took her coat from the peg. "Eloise!"

The little girl skipped down the stairs. "Are we going to the bookstore?"

"No, darling. Today is Tuesday." When Cala had first moved to the island, the children often went to the bookstore after school. After she paired with the dragon, she spent less time in the store. On Mondays and Thursdays the shop—now a lending library—was open for a few hours in the afternoon. Cala helped the youngsters practice their reading aloud while the smallest children "helped" Aislin clean.

Eloise's sharp gaze took in her mother's cloak and the drawstring bag in her hand. "Are we going to the town hall?"

"Yes." She took her daughter's cloak from its peg and handed it to the child. "Then we're going to FarPoint."

"To see the dragons!" Eloise squealed and clapped her hands.

She nodded. "Yes, you can see the dragons. I have to speak with Cala. And Nevan."

"Is he going to be my new papa?" The words sounded innocent, but Eloise's sly smirk looked like it belonged on a much older face.

Franisa choked. What should she tell the child? She'd put Nevan in an impossible position, but to back out would leave Enrich in danger. And while Cala had insisted the pixie would keep her secrets, she doubted her five-year-old daughter would be as trustworthy. "We aren't sure."

Eloise used her whole body to pull the door open. "You're getting cold feet." She nodded wisely then scampered ahead.

With a surprised laugh, Franisa scooped up the basket of baked goods she'd assembled to take to the dragon riders. "Where did you hear such an expression?" She pulled the door shut behind them and turned the latch.

Eloise shrugged. "Mistress Sarai said it once."

"She was here months ago! I can't believe you remembered." Franisa frowned as they strolled to the square. What could William's sister possibly have been talking about? "And you used it correctly," she muttered under her breath.

Eloise swung around cheerfully. "I gots the gift of gab. That's what Mistress Sarai said." She skipped up the little street toward the square. "Ooh, look! Nevan! Hallo, Nevan!"

The young giant stood at the end of the street, his winter hat clutched in his hands. When he met Franisa's gaze, his face went a brilliant shade of red. Completely unaware of the tension between the adults, Eloise grabbed his hand, hanging from it as if he were a tree. He looked down at the little girl, the red fading as he greeted her. He swung his arm out in an arc, pulling Eloise's feet off the ground. She squealed with pleasure.

"Good afternoon, Nevan." Franisa tried—and failed—to keep her own cheeks from burning as she greeted him. She started to apologize, then thought better of it. Little Eloise not only had the gift of gab—she had the ears of a bat. "Did Cala send you to collect us?"

Eloise let go of Nevan's hand, her feet thudding to the cobblestones. "Are we flying?!" Her little hands balled into fists under her chin, and she danced in place, practically sparkling with excitement.

"No, not today. Sorry." Nevan smiled slightly at her moan of dismay. "Starlight isn't ready to carry passengers yet. We haven't tested that. But you can play with her out at the nest." He reached out to Franisa. "Let me carry that for you."

She handed him the basket destined for FarPoint but held on to the bag of day-old bread. "Can we stop by the town hall? I need to drop this off."

"Do you live in the nest?" Eloise grasped the giant's free hand again. "Why is it a nest? Is it in the caves? How many dragons live there?"

He lifted her from the ground again, swinging her several feet with each step and cutting off her excited questions. "We're still trying to decide what to call it. I'm not sure I like 'nest' but I'm not a fan of 'lair' either. William said they call the guild house a 'den' in Verduun. What do you think?"

As they strolled down the lane toward the town hall, Eloise rattled off an increasingly ridiculous list of names for the dragons' living quarters. Nevan thoughtfully responded to each suggestion as if "dell" or "pod" were good names for the majestic creatures' home. As they passed other residents of the village, many of them cast knowing looks, and a few younger women sighed and fluttered their lashes. Franisa struggled to maintain her sense of calm.

They walked by the Crab and Tankard, calling out a greeting to Elspeth as she swept the steps leading down to the door, then turned on the street leading to the port. As they emerged onto the long pavement that curved around the little bay, a chilly winter wind bit the tips of Franisa's ears and nose and rattled the furled sails of the ships tied to the long piers. They passed the elegant Silver Acorn Inn that sat along the crescent-shaped plaza, then stopped in front of the little building that housed the town's official functions.

A bench similar to the one in front of the bakery sat beside the door of the modest building. Eloise skipped up and attempted to raise the heavy seat but required Nevan's assistance to get it open. Removing the loaves from the drawstring bag, Franisa added them to the stash of salted cod and blemished fruit and vegetables inside.

Nevan lowered the bench seat. "Who is this for?"

"Koni started it a couple of years ago. After the storm that killed Keldan. Lots of fishermen lost their boats and livelihood, and the town wanted a way to help them. Anyone with extra can put it here, and anyone who needs food can take some." She chuckled. "Blacksmiths don't make much in the way of leftover food. And I suspect a family of giants doesn't either, so you wouldn't know."

"Not young male giants. My ma claims we eat the pantry bare." Nevan took Eloise's hand again. "We'd best be going—it's a long walk to FarPoint, and I don't have a unicorn."

"A unicorn?!" Eloise jumped in place. "Who has a unicorn?"

"No one *has* a unicorn," Koni said as he joined them on the town hall's front step.

Franisa clutched a hand to her chest in surprise. Although she knew of Koni, and had spoken with him on several occasions, she held the elven mayor in awe. Cala had mentioned some of his magical abilities, and while she'd grown accustomed to the witch's meager powers, the seemingly all-powerful mayor scared her a bit.

"Are you coming out to FarPoint with us?" Nevan asked as he shook hands with the mayor. "That will make it easier."

"I am. I heard William was making his Verduunian curry, and I won't pass that up. It's one of the few things he cooks well." The elf stretched his arms wide and bowed almost horizontal. "Oravai, Mistress Hearthwell! And Mistress Eloise!"

Franisa's eyes widened. The mayor of Safe Haven knew her daughter's name? "Oravai, Lord Mayor." She bobbed a curtsey.

"Hallo, sir Lord Elf!" Eloise released Nevan's hand to bow in imitation of Koni. "Do you have a unicorn?"

He laughed and crooked an elbow at Franisa. "Please, call me Koni."

"Franisa." She shifted the empty drawstring bag to her other hand and nervously took his arm.

Koni reached for Eloise's free hand. "As I said, no one *owns* a unicorn. They are free creatures of magic and can go where and when they please. Sometimes, if you're very lucky, they will help you." He moved down the cobblestone path, taking them toward the edge of town. "Hold tight to Nevan so the magic doesn't leave him behind."

"Magic?!" Eloise skipped along, letting the men lift her off the ground as Nevan had done earlier. With two of them to swing, her feet barely seemed to touch the cobbles. "We're using magic?"

"It's a long walk to FarPoint, but if you hold my hand, you can take the shortcut." Koni winked at Franisa. "You wouldn't actually get lost if you let go, but it's easier."

"I wondered about that," Nevan said from the other end of the line. "I didn't hold hands with you last time."

"And I was bereft." Koni heaved an obviously false sigh.

Franisa choked out a laugh. "What kind of shortcut are we taking?"

"I have access to the elven routes." Koni said this with a negligent shrug, as if elven routes were a common phenomenon.

Maybe they were, but Franisa had never heard of them before. "What is an elven route?"

"There are faerie lines across the island. I am able to make use of them to travel more quickly." He nodded as they crested a gentle slope, and the tower came into view.

Franisa stumbled to a stop and cast a look over her shoulder. The village they'd been walking through only a few minutes before was invisible behind them. Even the tall church tower was out of sight behind the rolling hills. She dropped Koni's arm, then clutched it again, afraid she'd be left behind. "That was—"

"Magic!" Eloise let go of both men and raced ahead along a path worn in the stone. "I see a dragon!"

"That's Finn." Nevan stretched his long legs to catch up to the little girl. Grasping her around the waist, he swung her up to his shoulder.

She squealed in delight, then gripped his curly hair. “Where’s Starlight?”

Franisa watched the giant stride toward the tower with her daughter on his shoulder, his gentle care warming her to her core. She turned to the elf, speechless, her mouth opening and closing.

With a laugh, Koni poked his elbow out again. “Shall we?”

She took his arm and started forward. “I don’t even—” She broke off and shook her head, unable to articulate the many questions swirling in her mind.

He patted her fingers. “Let’s get up to the house before Nevan eats all the curry.”

CHAPTER TWELVE

Nevan strode along the smooth path worn across the stone of FarPoint. At the end of the outcropping, the tower stretched, tall and slender, into the pale winter sky. Finn, William's dragon, sat atop the tower, wings folded, head swinging in a wide arc as he watched the sea below. From here, he couldn't see Starlight or Nari, but they were likely to be playing with their wild siblings in the sea.

Eloise sat on his shoulder, her tiny, warm body pressed against the side of his head. Her fingers had curled into his hair, pulling a little as he walked, not quite hard enough to be painful. She asked him endless questions about the dragons, giving him no chance to respond, which suited him just fine at the moment.

Since this morning, when Franisa had declared him to be her betrothed, Nevan felt as if he hadn't had a chance to breathe, let alone think. After their encounter with Gnollis, Cala had taken Enrich out to FarPoint along the elven lines Koni used. They were so efficient, they'd almost arrived before he and Starlight could reach the place by air. Then the whole group had practiced some of the drills William had set for the new fire brigade. They'd scooped water from the sea as they skimmed low over the waves, and Starlight had performed spectacularly well. He, on the other hand, had held on tight and hoped he wouldn't end up in the sea.

The flying straps had done their job, and he'd only gotten soaked by the spray, not from being dunked. After a quick meal, a warm bath, and a change of clothes, Cala had dispatched him to collect Franisa and her daughter. And now here they were, approaching the den again. Lair. Nest.

No, still not right, but he couldn't focus on names as his thoughts turned again to the new "relationship" between him and Franisa.

Arranged marriages were not uncommon on FarPoint. In the dwarven community, they were standard, and some of the humans followed the same custom. In fact, he was pretty sure Franisa's marriage to Keldan had been arranged by their parents. Which seemed odd, now. Wouldn't Gnollis have sought a dwarven maid for his only son?

Nevan's own parents were a love match, but they had met and handfasted before moving to Safe Haven. Cala and William had chosen each other, but both of them were well past the usual age for an arranged pairing. And their previous occupations had probably made personal relationships difficult.

He laughed softly to himself. He had little knowledge of what life had been like for either of them in their war-torn countries. Maybe now that he was a member of their team, he'd learn more about Verduun and the Borgonne.

"What's so funny?" Eloise interrupted herself to ask.

"Sorry. I just remembered something Starlight did the other day." As they walked the last few yards to the house, he told her about getting dumped in the sea. The little girl giggled loudly at the story.

The front door to the house burst open, swinging so hard it banged into the whitewashed wall. "Oops!" Enrich jumped out onto the stoop and caught it as it swung back.

"I hope you didn't damage the house!" Franisa hurried past Nevan to inspect the wall behind the door.

Nevan grasped the wiggly little girl on his shoulder and set her on the ground. She ran up the steps, past her brother, and into the building. "Mistress Cala! Master William!"

William appeared in the doorway behind the boy, watching Eloise disappear into his house with a bemused expression. "I'm sure the winds have done worse work with the door, Mistress Franisa. And if there's a hole, it will give the boy something to do on the morrow."

"I'm so sorry." Franisa climbed the two steps and thrust the basket at William. "I've brought bread—sourdough with herbs and cheese baked in. And some rolls for the morning. I would have brought more, but some sailors came and bought all of the sweets."

Lips twitching at her nervous babbling, William took the basket and handed it off to Enrich. "Take that to the kitchen, lad."

"Aye, sir!" Enrich followed his sister into the house with his burden.

William stepped back to allow Franisa entry. "Please, come in. All of you." His brows went up as Koni ascended the steps, and he bowed ironically. "And the mayor! To what do we owe this honor?"

"You won't find it much of an honor when I've drunk you out of house and home!" Koni clasped hands with the dragon rider and followed Franisa into the house.

Nevan nodded to William as he climbed the steps. "I'm sorry to inundate your home with guests."

"Nonsense, Nevan. My home is your home. Quite literally." William waited for Nevan to enter, then pulled the door shut. "You know Cala and I want you to feel that way."

"I know, sir, but..."

William ushered him toward the kitchen. "Perhaps you'll feel more at home in the bakery?" The older man's eyes twinkled.

Nevan swallowed and clutched William's arm, holding him in the entry. "I—"

William leaned close. "Love comes at unexpected times. Best to grasp it with both hands when you have the opportunity." He gently punched the younger man's arm and went into the kitchen.

Nevan stared after his mentor. Is that what William had done? Grasped love when it presented itself? He and Cala seemed so happy together. But love came to both of them. Did he want to be with Franisa if she only thought of him as a means to protect her son? With a sigh, he followed the others into the warm kitchen.

With the addition of Koni, Franisa, and the two children, the large room felt pleasantly full. William handed Koni a tankard of something and directed him to a comfortable upholstered chair beside the big, tiled stove at the end of the room. The dragon rider sat opposite him in a matching chair with a small table between them. Someone had closed the shutters on the landward windows, but those on the seaward side remained open to the walled garden. The bright glow of the early winter sunset painted red, orange, and pink streaks across the sky above the high stone wall, leaving the garden itself in shadow.

Cala lit the gas lamp on the kitchen dresser by the stove, then turned and spotted Nevan. She beckoned to him, holding out the lit match. "Light the overhead, will you?"

When the three of them took their evening meal in the kitchen, they normally only lit the single lamp. But for special occasions, William had hung a circular frame over the big wooden table. Or rather, he'd had Nevan hang the frame. It held four oil lamps with metal shades that directed the soft light downward. Nevan's great height made it easy for him to lift the chimneys and light the wicks.

"You are very useful." Eloise stood at Nevan's side, watching him work.

He snorted a laugh. "Thank you, I guess."

"Like Aislin. Mama says she's a useful nuisance." Eloise paused for a moment. "What's a nuisance?"

"It means sometimes you get in the way." Franisa swept forward to pull the child from under Nevan's feet. "And I never said Aislin was a nuisance. I said she kept the nuisance busy." She poked the girl's stomach with a smile.

Eloise giggled and squirmed away. "I'm not a nuisance!"

Cala looked at the assembled group. "We should have asked Aislin to join us."

Nevan frowned, then followed the older woman's gaze as it settled on first Eloise then Enrich. The boy stood by the window, watching the adults as they settled around the room. Although their "betrothal" had come about to protect the boy, he didn't need to be present for some discussions. And he suspected letting little Eloise know their match was fake would be a certain way to inform the entire village. "Enrich?"

"Yes?"

"Can you take Eloise to visit the dragons?" Nevan gestured across the room at the door. Franisa jerked a little at the suggestion but didn't argue. "Take her through the inside."

Enrich's eyes narrowed, as if he knew they were getting him out of earshot, but he nodded obediently. "Yes, sir. Come on, Weezie."

"Dragons!" Eloise sang out the word and skipped across the room! "I get to see the dragons! Have you already talked to them?" Her accusing tone made the adults smile.

"Of course. I've been here all day." The boy scowled and hurried after his sister. "Wait! You don't know where they are!"

"That was easier than I thought it might be." Cala set two tankards on the table and gestured to the chairs.

"Will they be safe with the dragons? Eloise is... exuberant." Franisa pulled one of the heavy wooden chairs from the table, frowning.

"The sea dragons are quite placid. And they're used to Enrich already. They'll be fine," Cala said. "Gather around for the war council."

"War council?" Franisa echoed.

Nevan grasped the back of her chair to push it in and used a little too much force. Franisa let out an "oof" when her stomach hit the edge of the table.

"Sorry!" He pulled it a few inches away, then hurriedly sat in the one next to her.

"We're going to war with Gnollis, aren't we?" Cala brought a crystal glass and sat on Franisa's other side. She had made Nevan try the red wine when she first bought a case from a trader from the Borgonne, but he preferred the ale William drank. She offered the glass to Franisa. "Do you want some of this?"

The baker shook her head and warded off the glass with both

hands. "No, thank you. Elspeth has tried—" She grimaced and lifted the other tankard. "I'll stick with ale."

Nevan clanged his mug against hers. "Good choice."

Koni and William rose and came to join them. The dragon rider sat across from Nevan, while the elf refilled his stein from the pitcher Cala had placed on the table. He stood at the end and raised his drink. "I understand I'm here to witness and record a handfasting?"

Nevan choked on his ale. Franisa spit hers across the table.

"No?" Koni smirked as William hurried around to pound Nevan's back.

Cala went to the big stone sink to get a cloth. She wiped the spilled ale from the polished wood. "You might want to wait until no one is drinking to make pronouncements like that, Koni." She sat again and made as if to sip her wine then paused with the glass at her lips.

The elf sat. "I thought this was a finalized decision? Announced to the world in the square? That's what Gnollis gave me to believe."

"You've spoken with Gnollis?" Franisa clutched her tankard so tight her knuckles turned white. From his seat at her side, Nevan could only see her shoulders and one ear as she faced the elf, but tension rolled off her in waves. Did she regret her declaration already?

"He came to see me. Probably right after you and Nevan declared your undying love." Koni's eyes sparkled as he darted a look at Nevan. "The man was in a tizzy—he came all the way out to the farm. I made him wait until I was done harvesting the honey. The bees did not care for his agitation."

Franisa dropped her head into her hands. "I am so sorry." She turned to Nevan and gripped his arm. "I didn't mean to... He was so insistent, and Philomena said it was the only way to stop him—"

Nevan gulped and awkwardly patted her fingers. "I understand. It's a good thing Koni wasn't there, or we'd be married by now." He tried to smile.

Cala tapped a finger on the table then pointed at Koni. "What did you tell him?"

"I said you hadn't arranged the ceremony yet but that in the eyes of the law—" He poked a thumb at his own chest and left the statement hanging as he downed some more ale.

"What?" Nevan snapped.

"I told him your declaration of intent was enough for me. That gives Nevan authority over Enrich's future. And that I assumed he'd want the boy to apprentice as a dragon rider."

"Wait just a minute." Cala pushed her chair back, fists clenched. "Are you telling me that here, on Safe Haven, a woman doesn't have control over her own children's futures?"

"I am not saying that." Koni patted the air with both hands. "But you know the law in Safe Haven isn't actually codified." He glanced at Nevan. "It isn't written down. What we believe and live by has been handed down to us by our ancestors. Or rather, your ancestors, since mine don't hail from here. And each community lives by its own rules. For the dwarves, the clan controls the children's future. Franisa's children were adopted into the dwarven clan when her own parents passed on."

"But dwarven children don't go into the mine until they're older. Why is he forcing my son to do it?" Franisa wagged a finger at Koni. "And don't tell me it's because he's big. He's smaller than most human boys his age."

"That's his dwarven genes." At their puzzled frowns, Koni waved a hand. "It means he gets his lack of height from Gnollis. And he's still much bigger than the other dwarven children his age. But I didn't discuss that with him. I told him Enrich's future is now Nevan's concern, not his, and he left."

Franisa covered her face with her hands again. "So now what?"

"Now Enrich goes back to school. And Nevan trains him to be a dragon rider apprentice, whatever that means." Koni grinned mischievously. "He and I can apprentice together."

"You still want to try for the next hatching?" William tapped his tankard against the empty one in front of the elf. "Excellent."

"But we don't know when that is!" Nevan shoved his hand through his thick hair.

"Perfect. The boy isn't old enough to pair with a dragon anyway, so having a nebulous future date for the next hatching works in our favor." Koni slapped his hand against the table in emphasis. "Problem solved."

"Not really." Franisa's hands dropped to her lap. "What happens when Gnollis realizes we aren't…" She trailed off.

Koni shrugged. "That is out of my control. I suggest you make sure he doesn't realize that. In whatever way you deem appropriate."

Nevan swallowed, darting a look at Franisa. He'd dreamed of asking for her hand but never thought it would be like this. Did he want to tie himself to her knowing she might never feel the way he did?

He had seen many arranged marriages become fruitful and loving relationships. But his parents married for love, and he'd never imagined his own story would be any different. He thought he'd find a woman who made his heart leap for joy, woo her, and they'd be together forever.

And for a long time, since he'd first begun feeling attraction to the fairer sex, he'd dreamed that woman would be Franisa. But he'd never been bold enough to make a move. She seemed so capable. Completely consumed by her business and her children, with no interest in a second husband.

Now she needed him. Would that be enough?

CHAPTER THIRTEEN

Flustered by the idea of actually marrying him, Franisa couldn't meet Nevan's eyes. "I can't ask Nevan to—"

"To what?" Koni asked, his eyes glittering with mischief.

"Koni," Cala said repressively. "Why don't we let Nevan and Franisa discuss this. Alone."

William shifted, his chair grating against the stone floor. "Agreed. It's not our concern." He nodded at Franisa. "Not that we aren't concerned about child labor. Enrich seems like a good lad, and I don't want him toiling in the mines. But whether you decide to tie yourself to that lunk or not—" He waved his tankard at Nevan, a little smirk betraying his affection for the giant. "He's a good man. You could do worse."

"But what about him?" Franisa tried to keep her question even rather than a wail. "He doesn't deserve to be stuck with an old woman and another man's children. I've seen how the girls in Safe Haven look at him. He could have his pick."

"What?" Nevan's head came up. "I could? What are you talking about?"

She finally looked at him, exasperated. "Didn't you see them? As we were walking through town. Sighing and smiling and winking?" Could he truly be that clueless?

"They were?" He frowned at her. "Today? In town?"

"Oh my gosh. Yes, today. At the port!" Franisa shimmied her shoulders, flipped her braid over one, and batted her eyelashes at him. "Good even, Nevan," she cooed, then sharpened her voice and nodded curtly. "Mistress Hearthwell."

Koni smothered a laugh and refilled his tankard. "Olivia Brandywine? That's remarkably accurate."

Franisa pointed at Koni. "Yes. And Catriona Muloyi. And Lark Woohame. It was—" she broke off, glancing back at Nevan. "He really didn't notice."

Nevan's face went red. "They've never paid me any heed before."

"You weren't a dragon rider." William chuckled darkly and crossed his arms. "Happened all the time in Verduun. The ladies like a dragon man. We called them den bees." His smirk faded under Cala's mocking glare. "I didn't say I was involved. But they were there, swarming around."

Nevan pushed his chair back. "I'm not sure I like the idea of being pursued because of Starlight. And I don't know how she'd feel about that."

"Dragons don't usually care." William shrugged.

"War dragons might not care." Cala pointed at her husband. "You don't know what sea dragons think."

"Finn seems to like you well enough." His gruff tone didn't hide the humor in his reply.

"A darn good thing, or you'd be living in the stable with him." Cala refilled Koni's tankard and rose.

"This is my house, witch!" William roared.

Nevan stood and tugged on the back of Franisa's chair. "We should go somewhere else. When they get like this…"

"Is he really angry?" she whispered as she rose.

"No. It's how they—" Nevan's face flushed again.

"Flirt." Koni, still holding his tankard, sailed past them toward the door. "My work here is done."

"Hey, don't steal my dishes, elf!" Cala called after him.

Koni drained the tankard and handed it to Franisa. She took it, but he didn't let go. Lifting her eyes, she met his gaze. He lowered his voice. "Nevan is the swiftest, most sure answer. But if that is not to be, I will help you." He released the stein and slipped away.

Franisa stood frozen, the weight of his words holding her in place. There was no doubt in her mind he was right on both counts. But was the "swiftest, most sure answer" the right one?

Setting the tankard on the table, she turned to Nevan. "Can we speak? In private?" She cast a quick glance at Cala and William still mock arguing at the other end of the room.

Nevan nodded and took her arm. "This way." He led her into the entry. The long, narrow room stretched the depth of the house, with the front door on the right and an arch on the left, revealing a curved staircase. Across the room, another door stood ajar, this one leading to a dark hallway. At the far end, Franisa could see light and hear her children's voices.

Turning left, Nevan went through the arch and started up the steps. He paused on a landing beside a window, waiting for her to catch up. "This is private enough. Or we can go on to the top." He pointed upward.

"I haven't been up there since I was a child. Is there anything new?" Still flustered, Franisa grabbed at the distraction, starting up the next set of steps.

"We've made a few changes. For safety and comfort. Glass in the windows, for example." Nevan followed her along the curving staircase, warm and solid at her back. "But it's seventy-two steps."

"I remember. Let's go up." After a long climb, they reached a little round room. A ladder across from the top of the stair led to a trap door. Small windows glazed with thick, green glass let in a little light but offered no view. "Can we?" Franisa pointed at the ladder. "Or at least open a window to look out?"

"Up is better." He climbed a single rung to unlatch the door and push it open. The breeze seemed to catch it, slamming the wood against the roof above. Dust sprinkled down on them. "Sorry." He continued up the steps.

Franisa climbed after him, realizing as she went how much taller he was. She'd always known the half-giant was big, but having to climb five rungs before her fingers grazed the ceiling, when it had taken him only one, cemented it in a way that mere observation hadn't.

All thoughts of size were swept away when she emerged from the hatch. Stars blanketed the sky overhead. The flat roof, separated from the sheer drop by only a low railing, felt much smaller than the room below, although she knew that wasn't the case. As she climbed the upper rungs of the ladder, Nevan reached a hand down to help her out.

Her hand looked like a child's in his palm, but his grip was gentle yet sure. She let him half-lift her up the last step and climbed onto the roof.

The sea spread out below them, gentle waves glinting in the starlight, stretching to the tiny isles along the outer edge of the reef and to the horizon beyond. A sliver of silver moon peeked over the edge of the sea, sending a shimmering road across the calm water toward them.

"This is—" She turned, breathless, to take it all in, and came up against a wall of leathery hide. "Oh!" The memory of her one and only previous encounter with a dragon set her heart pounding.

Nevan put a hand on the dragon head snaking around him to sniff at Franisa. "Finn. Don't scare the lady."

The head paused, then bobbed, as if nodding, at the end of the sinuous neck. The snout moved closer, slowly, tongue darting out. She stepped back, running into Nevan's solid bulk.

He chuckled ruefully. "Sorry. Franisa, this is Finn. He just wants to get a good smell—it's how dragons recognize people. And each other. Maybe that's why Eloise likes them so much." He slapped the dragon's solid neck. "Finn, you big brute, be civilized. I know this is your place, but I didn't think you'd be up here so late."

At a sharp whistle, the dragon's head swung away, turning to look down at the house. A light in the garden revealed William, waving up at them. He put his free hand beside his mouth to call, "Finn! Leave them alone!"

Finn's head swiveled back, and his tongue darted around Franisa's face again, not quite touching her but seeming to taste the air around her. Then he shifted away and dropped off the side of the tower.

Franisa drew in a shaky breath, breathless but less frightened than she might have expected. She'd gotten only a sense of curiosity from Finn, no menace. "That was... unexpected. In a day full of unanticipated events."

"*I* should have expected it. That dragon loves this perch."

"He listened to you." She tilted her head to look up at Nevan, the growing moonlight casting strange shadows on his face from this angle. "Even though he isn't yours?"

"The sea dragons are less, I guess 'possessive' than the war dragons —which is what we usually hear about, since no one has paired with these before. Finn and Nari will usually listen to me. As much as they listen to anyone." He added the last bit softly as he gazed down.

Finn landed on the high seaward wall, his long neck curved down into the garden. William said something to the creature, pushing his head aside with a laugh. The two tussled for a few moments, then William went back into the house. Finn turned on his perch and dove over the side of the cliff, swooping upward as he soared across the sea.

"So, like children?" She tracked the big dragon as he turned and with a few easy wing strokes, skimmed back over the wall, landing in the courtyard beside the stables.

Nevan laughed. "I guess. I don't have much experience with them, either."

"You are amazing with Eloise." Franisa bit her lip, then turned to face Nevan. "And with Enrich. But you have no responsibility for them. I'm sorry I dragged you into this farce. I can figure out some other way to protect them."

Still staring out to sea, Nevan lifted both hands. "I don't mind."

"Nevan." She gripped his sleeve, turning him to face her. "You don't have to marry me. Koni said he will help me find another solution.

Maybe he can adopt us into the elven clan. Or I can get Cala to—" She broke off, not sure how either of them could adopt a grown woman.

"I want to help you." Nevan finally looked at her. "Koni said the declaration of intent was enough. We can schedule the handfasting for next year, and by that time, maybe Gnollis will have forgotten about it. Or Enrich will be too big for the mines. Or you'll find a new solution. Or a new man."

"But don't you want a family of your own? If you're tied to me, even in a pretend betrothal, you can't pursue any of those pretty girls." She reached up to grip his arm, the muscles solid and warm through his thin linen shirt. "I don't want to interfere with your life."

He snorted a derisive laugh. "You aren't. I'm so busy out here with Starlight and William's new training plan I don't have time for girls. And as you pointed out, I'm young. Next year is time enough to look for a wife. If I decide to do that. William waited until his fifties."

"William must not have wanted children." She realized the error of her statement and amended it. "Or he didn't care if the mother of his children was much younger. Although obviously he's not having any with Cala." Cala's odd hot flashes, which ignited her braid on occasion, had made it clear to the world she was beyond child-bearing.

"I'm not sure that would have stopped him." The words seemed to pop out of Nevan's mouth without conscious thought. He ducked his head. "I don't mean Cala. Obviously. But I mean—" He drew in a breath. "From what he's told me of life in Verduun, children are often sired outside marriage around the dragon guild."

"The den bees." Her cheeks warmed as she uttered the phrase. "Raising children with a partner is hard enough. I don't know why anyone would intentionally choose to do it on their own." Not that her partner had helped a lot, but his mere presence had protected her—not least from her father-in-law. Although had she not married Keldan, maybe Gnollis would have no authority over their son. Or maybe he would have all the authority. She wasn't sure how dwarven customs regarded children out of wedlock.

"Then we're agreed. We'll have Koni officially announce our

betrothal with the handfasting scheduled for next summer." Nevan stared out at the sea as he spoke.

"I didn't agree to that!" She put her hands on her hips, staring up at the young giant. How could he so casually tie himself to her?

"Would you prefer autumn?"

"I meant I didn't agree to the betrothal."

"You're right. You didn't agree—you proposed it." He leaned down to look her in the eye. "And you just said no one would intentionally choose to raise children on their own. So I'm here to help. I think fall equinox would be a good date for a handfasting."

Franisa gazed up at the uncharacteristically decisive giant. She gave herself a mental shake. She didn't really know Nevan that well. Maybe her previous impression of his mild character had been incorrect. She kind of liked this new take-charge attitude. But that didn't mean she was going to let him ruin his life for her and her family. "Fine. But only if we're completely honest with each other. Now that the girls in town are paying attention to you, you might want to court one of them. If that happens, you need to let me know so I can break off our engagement."

Nevan regarded her silently for a few minutes, then put out his hand. "Done." From somewhere below, a dragon bugled.

"What was that about?" Franisa put her hand in his large one.

With a quick, warm squeeze, Nevan let go and turned toward the trap door. "They do that sometimes. Shall we go down?"

"Is Starlight as curious about strangers as Finn?" She turned to back down the ladder.

"Oh. I keep forgetting you haven't met her."

She looked up, noting his frown. "We've been busy. All of us. And after my initial introduction to dragon-kind, I wasn't exactly anxious to try again." She laughed self-consciously.

"You mean Finn? Or the hatching cavern last summer?"

She waited for him to join her in the circular room. "The queens. I wasn't exactly a gracious guest. More like terrified." She clutched a hand to her chest. "I'm still not sure I'll ever be comfortable around them."

"The queens were different." He gestured to the stairway, letting her precede him down. "None of us really knew what to expect from them. And they aren't as comfortable around humans—or giants—as our guild dragons. Plus, they had eggs to protect. I'm sure Starlight will love you."

The warmth in his voice made her cheeks flush in response. She knew Nevan had been sweet on her for years, but hearing him speak in that unguarded, clearly affectionate tone about his dragon gave her a squishy feeling, like a big dollop of sweetened cream, whipped to perfection. It made him sound less like her besotted little neighbor and more like a mature, manly adult. "I just hope I don't run away screaming this time."

His big, warm hand squeezed her shoulder. "You won't."

At the bottom of the circular stair, instead of returning to the kitchen, they took the short hallway to the stables. Nevan gestured at a door on the tower-side of the building. "That's the new water closet we installed. It's very nice—hot water from the stove in the stable, even a bathtub. The place didn't have one before."

She paused to peer through the partially open door, but it was too dark to see the interior, so she gestured for him to continue. They passed a small window looking out to the front of the property—the side facing the trail to the village. Then another door on the other side.

"Storage." Nevan opened one at the end of the hall. "And my home."

Two steps took them down into a large, open room. A fire burned in the tiled stove at the near end. Curtained alcoves ran along both sides, three on each, although only one of the curtains was drawn closed. Four of the open bays contained a large mattress set directly on the stone floor, a desk, and a dresser. Pegs on the wall could hold cloaks or bags. And high in the wall, short, green-glazed windows stretched the length of each space.

Eloise and Enrich sat on a bright braided rug in front of the fire, resting against a huge, leather pillow. Enrich spoke, too quietly to hear, then Eloise giggled. And the silver-blue cushion moved.

Franisa drew in a deep breath. "That isn't a pillow, is it?"

The dragon raised its head and blinked sleepy eyes at them.

"Franisa, this is Starlight." Nevan took her arm and gently urged her across the stone floor. "Starlight, this is Franisa."

The dragon's long, sinuous neck curved away from the children, and the dragon's tongue came out to taste the air around Franisa's head. Holding her breath, she stood still, hoping this one would be as gentle as the other. Starlight pulled back a little and turned her head so one large eye stared directly at Franisa.

"Franisa."

"Mama!" Eloise leapt up from the ground. "Isn't she pretty? She's Starlight, and she flies, and she swims, and she let me sit on her back and..." The little girl grabbed her hand, bouncing with excitement as words tumbled out of her. "...Enrich is going to be an apprentice, and when I'm bigger I can be too! And Nevaaaaan!" She turned her big eyes on the giant. "Starlight says I can ride on her, 'cause you have the straps and I weigh nothing!"

"Starlight said that, did she?" Nevan chuckled as he stroked the dragon's neck.

Eloise nodded solemnly. "Soon. Tomorrow, maybe. She's ready. She promised."

"Riding the dragon? In the air?" Despite Franisa's attempt to keep her voice even, the questions came out high and harsh. "I don't think that's a good idea."

"Why not, Mama?" Eloise squeezed her fingers. "She said she can do it. She's ready."

"The dragon *spoke* to you?" Franisa raised a brow at her daughter, then turned to Nevan. "You didn't tell me they can speak."

With an apologetic glance at the girl, Nevan shook his head. "They don't."

"She does." Eloise stomped a foot and pointed at the dragon. "She talks to me."

Franisa leaned closer to Nevan and lowered her voice. "She thinks the house talks to her. And fairies."

Nevan frowned. "The pixie *does* talk to her."

"The pixie talks to everyone. Has Starlight ever spoken to you?"

Nevan's brows drew together. "Maybe?"

"She talked to me." Enrich finally rose from the floor and came to stand beside his sister.

Nevan's jaw dropped. Franisa felt her own go loose and made an effort to keep her mouth closed while her mind grappled with this new information.

"Starlight?" Nevan put his hand on the dragon's neck again. "Can you speak?"

The big head swung toward him, nuzzling against his neck. His eyes popped wide, and he pushed her head away, staring into her glittering silver-blue gaze. "You really can talk!"

CHAPTER FOURTEEN

"I thought I was imagining things." Nevan stroked Starlight's flank. "No one ever suggested dragons could speak."

Sitting on the built-in bench beside the stove in the dragon lair, Franisa stared at the two of them.

"Franisa?" With another pat to the dragon's side, he moved closer. "Are you—what's wrong?"

She looked up. "Nothing. Well, so many things. Not wrong, but new. It's too much."

He nodded in agreement. "Definitely too much."

The children, who had been dispatched to retrieve the other dragon riders, pelted back into the stables with Cala and William in their wake.

"They speak?" William limped up to the dragon with a frowning glare. "How is that possible? Ternath never spoke. Finn has never said anything. What do you have to say for yourself, Starlight?"

"She doesn't talk out loud. And I think you're scaring her." Nevan stepped between the agitated guild master and the dragon. "I don't know. Maybe it's only Starlight. Or maybe she just learned first. You know she learned to fly sooner than the others."

The dragon didn't say anything, but a wave of smug pride rolled off her.

"If she doesn't speak aloud, how do you hear her?" Cala moved closer, stroking the dragon's neck. "And you said she spoke to the children, not just to you?"

"She talked to me!" Eloise jumped excitedly beside Cala, tugging at her sleeve. "She likes me!"

"I'm sure she does." Cala put a hand on the child's head, but the little girl whirled away, full of energy. "What has she said?"

"I've only heard single words." Nevan's head tilted as he thought. "Names." He pointed at each of the children, then at Franisa. "Eloise, Enrich, Franisa."

The baker's eyes went wide. "She said my name?"

"When we came in. After I introduced you. I thought I was imagining it." Cheeks heating, Nevan turned back to the dragon. "Didn't you?"

"Franisa." The deep, velvety word seemed to ring inside his head.

The baker clutched a hand to her chest. "I heard that! This time *and* before. The first time I thought... I didn't know what I heard."

William frowned and stuck a finger in his ear. "You heard something?" He turned to his wife. "Did you hear it?"

Cala shook her head slowly, side-to-side. "Nothing."

"Maybe she only talks to people who is nice to her." Eloise appeared beside Nevan, facing off with William, her arms crossed, chin up.

"Eloise!" Franisa whispered, her tone appalled.

William gazed down at the child, eyes hooded, face set, except the tiniest twitch of his lips which betrayed amusement.

Eloise turned to Starlight. "Cala is nice."

"Nice."

"I heard that!" Cala grabbed William's arm. "She said 'nice.' Who knew dragons would prefer friendly people?" A smile played about her lips.

William gave her a sardonic look. "I'm nice. Maybe not warm and friendly, but I'm not mean." He moved a few steps closer to the dragon. "Will you speak with me?"

The dragon sized him up for a long moment, then nodded. *"Speak."*

"Incredible!" William looked as struck as Franisa had a few moments before, but he recovered faster. "Has Nari exhibited this behavior?"

"Behaver." Starlight's distaste for the mangled word was clear in her mental tone.

"Please excuse William's clinical tone, Starlight," Cala said. "He's used to working with war dragons who obviously aren't as smart as you. He thinks of them as animals, not people."

Ignoring the woman's words, and the dragon's smugness—or maybe he didn't feel it—William strode out of the stable. "Finn!"

"Finn no talk," Starlight said.

Cala, who had followed William, paused by the door. "Doesn't talk? Can't talk? Won't talk?"

The dragon lifted her wings and dropped them in an obvious shrug.

"How about Nari?" Not waiting for an answer, she headed out into the darkness. "Nari?"

"You are the smartest dragon!" Nevan wrapped his arms around his friend's neck, giving her a gentle hug. A sense of smug agreement rolled over him. "You're going to get a big head, though." Her puzzlement came through as strongly as the agreement. "It's a human saying. It means you will be..." He turned to Franisa. "How would you explain it?"

"A big head?" Franisa's gaze settled on her daughter, dancing around the dragon and singing a wordless song. "That's a tough one. I'd probably say, 'no one likes a know-it-all,' but that isn't exactly right. Maybe, 'you'll understand when you're older'? Although I hated that when I was a kid."

"Me too. But it's true." Nevan turned back to the dragon. "I can't explain it right now."

The dragon's mouth opened wide, showing off her two rows of small, sharp teeth. She let out a fishy yawn, ruffling Nevan's hair, then snapped her jaw shut.

He patted her neck. "You can go to bed. I'll be back shortly." He crossed the room and pulled the curtain aside from their little stall. The dragon padded after him, curling up on the stone floor, her head on the mattress beside his pillow. She settled her wings and heaved out a loud breath as she relaxed.

Eloise scampered up beside him, watching the dragon, bouncing on her toes. "Is she sleeping? Is that where she sleeps? When will she wake up?"

"Hush, Eloise." Franisa rose and moved toward them. "Let the dragon sleep."

"It's okay. Once she goes to bed, not much can rouse her." Nevan pulled the curtain across the space. It wasn't quite large enough. The dragon's hind quarters pushed the fabric away from the floor, and her tail curved out into the main room. He didn't normally close it, but he hoped Eloise would understand that meant bedtime.

As if in response to his thought—or maybe reacting to the dragon's even breathing—Eloise yawned. A moment later, Enrich did too. Nevan felt his own jaw trying to drop and chuckled.

"We'd best head home." Franisa looked around the room, then out the door where William and Cala huddled in a hushed but intense conversation. "I'm not sure how to get there, though."

Understanding took a moment—Nevan was tired too. "You can't walk home. It's at least an hour to the village. We should have thought of that…" He looked around the stable. "There are plenty of empty beds if you want to sleep here. Then you can go back in the morning."

"I suppose we could do that…" Franisa trailed off. "I have to start the bread early, though. Really early. Before sunrise. I'm not sure it matters if I walk home now or in six hours. Either way it will be dark."

"I'll take you on the faerie trail in the morning," Cala said with a smile as she returned to the stable. "I'll actually be on time for once."

Franisa chuckled. "Or I'll be late."

"Would it be the end of the world?"

"Not until Goodwife Terman shows up demanding a fresh loaf." Franisa lifted both hands. "But unless you're willing to escort us home tonight, what will be will be."

Cala looked out at the courtyard where William still stood with Finn. "I think we'll go in the morning. I'll protect you from the goodwife."

Decision made, Franisa settled the children in the cubicle next to the sleeping dragon. "These beds are huge."

Nevan gestured to himself. "Some of us need that much space."

Her cheeks went pink, and she looked away. "I suppose so."

"Why don't we go back into the house." Cala gestured to the door. "Unless you're ready to retire?"

Franisa cast a look at the darkness outside. "Normally I would. Dawn comes early! But I don't know if I'll be able to sleep at all tonight."

"I know what you mean." William came into the stable, followed by the two larger dragons. As he pulled the heavy wooden door closed, the dragons curled up together in the empty stall closest to the door. They both snorted out heavy sighs and relaxed in the warmth of the efficient stove. William cast a fond look at the two beasts, then limped past Nevan and Franisa to follow his wife into the house.

"After you." Nevan gestured toward the door as he'd seen William do. Over their months of association, he'd picked up some of the Verduunian's manners and patterns of speech. He hadn't really noticed until his mother commented on it at dinner this week when he'd pushed her chair in. But she seemed to appreciate the courtesy.

Franisa cast a worried smile at him but loitered on the stair, gazing at the sleeping children. "They'll be okay here?"

"There aren't any predators on the island who would take on one dragon, let alone three of them." He moved closer, trying to get her moving.

She looked up at him, then back at Nari and Finn, barely visible in the far cubicle. "It's not predators that I'm worried about."

Nevan reared back. "The dragons won't hurt them. Besides, Eloise and Enrich were here with Starlight all evening. That didn't bother you."

She flushed. "I guess I didn't really think about it until I saw all those teeth. I'm a terrible mother!"

"You aren't a terrible mother. Starlight wouldn't harm a fly. No, that's not true. I've seen her eat a fly. But she already loves Enrich and Eloise. She may not have spoken before, but I could feel that. They mainly eat fish. And honey. Not children." He chuckled. "As far as the teeth—have you seen Koni's? You aren't afraid to leave your children with him."

"Koni has sharp teeth?" She backed up until her heels hit the top step.

"No, I don't think his teeth look any different than ours. But you've obviously seen Brenet the butcher's teeth." He used his fingers to illustrate the orc's crooked tusks. "My point was you don't judge people by their teeth, so why the dragons? Starlight speaking tonight should have proven she's people too."

"I didn't really think about that…" She cast one more glance over his shoulder, then turned. "If you and Cala trust the dragons, I will too."

Nevan's heart warmed to be placed in the same category as Cala. He knew the two women had formed a strong bond. "What about William?"

She shrugged and threw a mischievous smile over her shoulder. "Only because Cala trusts him."

When they reached the kitchen, Cala had poured wine into two small crystal glasses. She handed one to Franisa. "This is a special vintage from Sonnenuhr Winery in the Borgonne. Elspeth has quite the connections in the wine trade. I save it for special occasions. I would say this qualifies."

Franisa took the glass carefully and held it to her nose. "I've tried some of her wine, but I don't really like it."

"This one is different," Cala said with a shrug. "Just try a sip, then. You might not like it. William doesn't. Nor Nevan."

William lifted his tankard of ale and clanked it against Nevan's.

Franisa sipped the wine and hummed as she considered. "I'm not sure." She tried another sip. "It's very sweet. And fruity."

Cala sat and gestured to the table. "Don't worry—if you decide you don't like it, you won't hurt my feelings. More for me." She winked and sipped from her own glass.

Nevan downed a gulp of ale. The day had evolved very differently from what he'd anticipated this morning, and the emotional turmoil had left him exhausted. Franisa might think she wouldn't sleep, but he could barely keep his eyes open.

"Nevan." Cala reached across the table to pull the empty tankard from his grasp.

His head snapped up, and he tried to remember what they'd been discussing. "What?"

"You're asleep in your chair. Go to bed. We can talk about—and to—Starlight in the morning." Cala made shooing motions at him.

His gaze darted to Franisa. "But—" It seemed like they had so much to discuss, but none of it was coming to mind at the moment. A huge yawn overtook him, and he ducked his head apologetically. "Sorry. I guess I'll see you in the morning."

BUT IN THE MORNING, THE TWO WOMEN WERE ALREADY GONE. He met William in the kitchen where the old dragon rider had heated some water and begun steeping the tea. The two men exchanged nods but didn't speak, as often happened when they broke their fast together.

Once he'd gotten some of Franisa's delicious bread into his gullet, Nevan cast a glance at William. The older man sat in his armchair beside the side table, his tea grown cold as he read from a large, leather-bound tome. The turn of the page and the creak of the house as a gust of wind hit it were the only sounds. Nevan settled in to enjoy the quiet morning.

Until Eloise whirled into the room. "Hallo, Nevan!" She bobbed a swift curtsey. "Oravai, Sir William! When will the dragons wake up? Do they eat breakfast? Will they like Mama's sea shell rolls? How many do you think Starlight will eat? When—"

William put up a hand, and the girl's incessant questions cut off at once. "It's too early for so many questions, child," he said, his gruff voice kind but firm. "Dragons eat fish. When they're hungry. The rolls are for humans. I suggest you enjoy one."

"Oops. Mama says I'm a chatter pixie." She bustled across the room, dragging a chair closer to the tall dresser.

Before she could climb up, Nevan rose to help her. "Let me get that for you." He cut one of the sweet rolls in half and put it on a plate, then added some of the sliced melon. "If you're still hungry when that's gone, you can have more."

The little girl beamed and climbed onto a chair next to Nevan's. "I can clean house, you know. Even without Aislin. Do you want me to do that after we break our fast?"

Nevan tried to suppress a smile as he glanced at William. "Maybe you can help me sweep out the dragons' den. They track a lot of sand inside."

"I can do that! Enrich and me have chores every morning." She took a bite of the roll, and blessed quiet descended… until she swallowed. "Do you have any milk?"

William rose and went to the cold box, returning with a small pitcher. He added a bit to his tea, then poured the rest into a small clay tankard and set it before the girl. "I will ask Cala to bring more if you will be staying with us."

"Thank you, Sir William!" She beamed at the older man.

His lips twitched up, as if he couldn't help responding. "You're welcome, Mistress Eloise. I will leave you to your repast." With a courtly bow, he took his tea and book and left the room.

"Where is he going?" Eloise picked up a slice of fruit but couldn't seem to stem the questions long enough to eat. "Is he going up to the tower? Is that where Finn is? He wasn't in the stable when I woke up. Why is it a stable? There are no horses—"

Nevan tapped her hand. "Stop. Eat. You can learn everything about the dragons when we're finished."

"You're already done eating," she said in a wise tone.

"True. But I haven't drunk my tea." He lifted his cup. "Where's Enrich?"

"He's a sleepyhead. He doesn't wake until Mama shakes him. Or Aislin pokes him." She stuck her finger into Nevan's arm.

"Ow!" He clasped a hand over his arm as if injured. "You have a mean poker."

She looked seriously at her index finger, then up at his face. "You're joking."

"I am."

Nodding decisively, she went back to her food. "Pixie pokes are ticklish, not pokey."

He grunted in response. She seemed to understand this meant they should enjoy the rest of their meal in quiet.

That lasted about three minutes. "Are you gonna marry my mama?"

Nevan choked on the last of his tea. Eloise stood on her chair to pound on his back. He wiped his eyes and nodded his thanks. He still hadn't gotten used to the idea of being betrothed to Franisa. Even if it wasn't real.

He cleared his throat, not wanting to lie to the clever little girl. But Franisa had made it clear she shouldn't be entrusted with the truth. "That's what betrothed means."

"I know. But when Trudi, at the pub, got betrothed, there was a party. And she was happy. You and Mama don't seem happy. More—" She broke off, considering him, her little brows drawn down in serious thought. "More worried."

Nevan's jaw dropped. This child was perceptive. He sipped his tea but found the cup empty. Still, the action gave him a moment to think. "Does Trudi at the pub have children?"

"No, silly. She's not handfasted yet!"

He pointed at her and nodded. "That's the difference. Your mama has you and Enrich. Two people pledging a life together is a big deal. Four people doing it is... even bigger."

She nodded, her brow still furrowed. Then her sunny smile reappeared. "You're gonna be a good daddy." Without waiting for a reply, she started stacking the dirty plates. "I'm gonna wash the dishes. Mama and Aislin teached me how. Can you put a chair by the sink?"

Speechless, Nevan moved the chair and helped her fill the sink with warm water from the heater built into the stove. He tied a tea towel around her middle to keep her dress dry, then put some food on a plate for Enrich. While the child washed, he added the remaining wooden plates to the pile, then pumped more water into the heater. Eloise sang to herself as she washed, a nonsense song about soap suds and bubbles.

Enrich came in, rubbing his eyes.

"Good morning," Eloise sang out. "Did the sleep faeries catch you?"

The boy muttered something under his breath, then sat at the table, eyelids drooping, his head propped up on one hand. Nevan slid the filled plate closer to him. "Do you want tea?"

Enrich shook his head. "Milk?"

Nevan peeked into the pitcher, then shook his own head. "Sorry. Wasn't enough today." The boy grunted in response.

"We're gonna learn to take care of the dragons today!" Eloise jumped down from her chair and wiped her hands vigorously on her towel.

Nevan untied the sodden cloth and turned the girl to inspect her front. Wet blotches marked her bodice and skirt. "You stand over there by the stove to dry while your brother eats."

"Okay." She skipped to the stove, keeping up a rambling narrative of what she thought they should do.

Nevan let the words wash over him. When she mentioned swimming, he bit his lip, trying not to smile. "It might be a bit chilly for swimming today."

"The dragons swim in the winter." She turned to face him.

"Yes, they do, but they dry faster than we do." He made a circular motion with his finger, and she turned back to the stove.

"Nevan!" William's voice carried faintly through the house. "Time to work!"

CHAPTER FIFTEEN

Push and fold, turn and dust. Franisa shoved the heel of her hand into the ball of dough, muttering the mantra under her breath as she stretched and folded with even, practiced movements. As she breathed in the yeasty air, she tried to let her mind clear. Most mornings, the routine comforted and calmed her. Or energized her, if that was needful. But this morning—she slapped the ball of dough onto the counter and groaned.

Cala looked up from a bowl of flour, a measuring spoon poised over it. "That sounded heavy."

Taking a metal flask from the shelf beneath the thick maple counter, Franisa poured a little oil into the bowl, then dropped the dough into it. A practiced swirl and flip oiled the ball of dough and bowl at the same time, and she dropped a cloth across the top, moving it to the proofing shelf above the stove. "Things are way more complicated than they should be. A year ago, life was so much simpler. Hard work, sure, but I knew what I was doing. Bake the bread and pastries. Send the kids to school. Clean the kitchen. Sell the baked goods. Then Gnollis had to—" She broke off and whirled across the room to pull an empty bowl from the shelf.

Early this morning, Cala had brought her to the village by the elven path. The short walk through the early morning darkness had passed quickly, the two women too sleepy for conversation. But now that they'd gotten the first batches of bread started, she needed to talk.

It was one of the things she'd missed most after Keldan's passing—another adult to share her thoughts with. And even though he'd rarely contributed anything useful to the conversation, he'd acted as a sounding board for her ideas. When she decided to start making the fancy Verduunian pastries she'd found in a bakery book in Milli's bookshop, he'd listened and even encouraged her. When Enrich was going through the terrible twos, he'd been there to nod and grunt.

Since she'd returned to Safe Haven, Cala had offered a little of that human interaction, and Franisa craved more. With the recent events, she *needed* more. "I can't let Nevan ruin his life for me."

Cala put the little spoon back into the salt cellar, turning in surprise. "He's not ruining his life. If you ask me, he's happy to be betrothed to you." Her lips quirked. "Actually happy, not just helping a friend happy, if you know what I mean."

"I do!" Franisa dumped a cup of sourdough starter into her bowl and added some warm water. "But what if he—"

Bringing the dry ingredients, Cala stepped closer and put a hand on her friend's arm. "He's not. You've given him an out. The two of you can call off the handfasting at any time. If he meets someone new…" She smirked and shook her head. "He isn't going to. He's head over heels for you."

"I know." Franisa took Cala's bowl and dumped the flour into her own, sending a cloud of white over the tabletop and her own front. She absently swiped at her apron then looked at her friend. "But I don't feel that way… and that's not fair to him."

Cala raised a brow. "Even in love matches, one person is often more emotionally invested than the other. But feelings change over time. Love can develop even within arranged partnerships. Didn't you and Keldan grow into your relationship over time?"

Hands sticky with dough, Franisa paused in her mixing to consider the idea. "I suppose. We barely knew one another when our parents arranged the pairing. My affection for him grew as we got to know each other. I won't say I was in love with him, but I cared for him. In many ways, he was more like a child than a husband."

"I don't think your experience is the norm." Cala took her empty bowl and returned to the other end of the room to measure more ingredients. "But I'm hardly an expert at marriage. I have learned a bit about love these last few months, though."

"Your situation with William is completely different!" Franisa protested. "You two were obviously made for each other."

"Right. War witches from the Borgonne frequently partner with Verduunian dragon masters."

"Maybe not, but—" Franisa threw up her hands in surrender, sticky globs of dough splatting down on the work surface. She blew out an exasperated sigh, used her sleeve to push a few loose hairs away from her damp brow, then scraped a wooden blade across the table to scoop up the dropped bits.

The two women worked in silence for a while, then Franisa put another kneaded and oiled batch above the stove. She nodded at Cala. "You're getting the hang of kneading."

"It's soothing." Cala sprinkled a bit more flour across her workspace and folded the dough. A fine dusting of white spread across the table in time with her movements.

"How are you staying so clean?" Franisa gestured at her own front, then at her friend's pristine white apron.

"I haven't been throwing dough around with emotional abandon," Cala said with a little smirk. "And Aislin helped me put a spell on this dress. I think it's protecting the apron too. And my shoes, apparently. Not so much the floor." She gazed at her feet where little drifts of flour outlined the perfectly clean circle in which she stood.

That surprised a laugh from Franisa. "As long as she doesn't blame me for the mess. That pixie is surprisingly judgmental for someone who loves cleaning as much as she does. You'd think she'd be grateful to have a slob to look after."

Cala snorted a laugh of her own. "She's just astounded at our lack of ability. She told me in very certain and very disappointed tones that I don't have Milli's affinity for cleanliness. It took a lot of pixie magic to make this." She gestured at herself, then reached for the oil. "It's a good thing I'm better at dragon riding."

~

AFTER THEY FINISHED THE MORNING BAKE, CALA RETURNED to Safe Haven while Franisa opened the shop. She sold her goods to the usual customers, trying to respond graciously to the repeated felicitations. After the first rush, she went to the back to clean up, marveling over the pristine circle left by Cala and Aislin's magic as she swept up the dusting of flour around it.

Once the dishes were washed and the last tray of pastries were out of the ovens, she banked the fires and took a moment to rest. When the church bell tolled noon, she nibbled on a leftover crust spread thick with butter fresh from the creamery. The orc dairy farmers were good customers, trading milk and butter for bread and sweets on a regular schedule. But she slathered the last of this week's delivery on her lunch, so she'd need to replenish her supply before the morning.

She took the little wooden sign from its hook on the door. Enrich had made the little thing ages ago, and now that she'd worked on reading with Cala for six months, she could puzzle out the words: "Open" on one side and "Taking a break. Be back soon" on the other. She flipped it, then closed and barred the door and went out the back. The doors didn't lock from the outside, and the bar on the front was more to prevent customers from entering unaware than to keep out marauders. Like the name said, Safe Haven was a safe place to live.

Pausing in the doorway, she spoke to the empty kitchen. "Aislin! If I'm not back when the children return—"

The little pixie popped into the room in a cloud of pink sparkles that disappeared before they hit the floor. "Aislin will listen." And in a blink, she was gone again. Probably back to the bookstore to clean.

With her shopping basket over her arm, Franisa strolled up the lane and across the square to the street leading toward Cala's bookstore. The half-timbered houses leaned inward a bit, casting deep shadows over the little lane in the winter sunlight. A cold sea breeze snuck between the buildings, flapping her skirt against her legs and chilling her. The heat of the bakery combined with the bright sun had fooled her, and she'd neglected to take a wrap.

Once she emerged into the next square, the sun provided enough warmth to counter the chilly wind. She passed by the bookstore and the mercantile, greeting the other residents busy on their own errands. Brenet waved from the door of his butcher shop, his leather apron stained with things she didn't care to question. But the orc had always been a good friend, so she overlooked his less than savory apparel.

"Good afternoon!" She paused beside his shop, casting a swift glance at the dark bookshop. It had been vacant for years before Cala returned to Safe Haven, but in the few months between her arrival and pairing with Nari, Franisa had gotten accustomed to seeing it brightly lit and often bustling with children. Now that Cala was busy at FarPoint, it was closed more often than open.

The orc noticed her glance. "It was nice having a neighbor, and Romulus certainly misses the afternoon story hour."

"Perhaps someone else can take over the shop." Franisa suppressed a sigh—her husband had dreamed of buying the store from Cala's aunt, but he had died not long before Milli. Now that Cala had revived the place as a lending library, maybe someone else would show interest. "But at least she's open a couple times a week."

"True enough. And I don't need young Romulus spending all his free time with his head in a book. He needs to learn a trade." He winced. "No offense."

Franisa pretended she didn't know he was referring to her husband and ignored the muttered excuse. "Is Romulus working with you?"

"Somewhat." Brenet wiped his hands absently on the once-white towel hanging from his belt, but they looked no less blood-stained when he finished. "Like the rest of the village, he's obsessed with pairing with a dragon." The orc shrugged. "I suppose it's possible he'll succeed in such a venture. I'm not sure it puts food on the table."

Franisa frowned. She hadn't thought about the financial implications of the dragon guild. How did William and Cala provide for themselves and Nevan? Had she inadvertently tied herself to another man who would offer little in the way of worldly support? Not that she intended to follow through on the betrothal. "I suppose the bookshop..."

Brenet shook his head. "She's not charging for the books anymore. Turned it into—what did she call it? A 'lie berry.' People can take a book, read it, and return it. For free! That's not how you keep a business afloat. I don't hand out roasts. You wouldn't give fresh bread away."

"True, but no one returns the bread after they eat it." She wrinkled her nose at the idea. "Perhaps dragon riding is a part-time venture. Once the training is complete." She stared over the roof of the mercantile as if she could see FarPoint from here.

"Time will tell. But in the meantime, I must teach my son the family business and keep his head out of the clouds."

They both looked up at the clear blue sky and chuckled a bit. Then Brenet rubbed his bald head. "I've heard your boy was working with the dwarves."

Franisa lifted her chin. She ached to expose Gnollis's perfidy, but she knew angry gossip would only poison their relationship further. "Not anymore. It makes no sense for him to train for work he'll soon be too large to do." Dwarven mines weren't tall enough to accommodate an adult human, and even with his shorter stature, Enrich was bound to grow once he reached his teen years.

"Is he going to become a baker, then?"

She sighed. "He doesn't seem to have any interest. Or affinity for the skills." She chuckled dryly. "He burns the toast."

"Hmm. You don't suppose he'd be interested in butchering? Once we get them past this dragon fixation, that is? Mayhap we can trade apprentices." Brenet pointed across the street. "My daughter is learning tea mixing from Mistress Thistlewick. Koni said something a few weeks ago that got Vlina and I thinking. Maybe Safe Haven businesses don't have to stay in the family. The butcher's son can become a baker. Or the baker's daughter can run the mercantile." He gestured at the shop at the end of the square.

She blinked at him. "I... Eloise seems to enjoy making bread, but she's only five. Who knows where her interests will lie in the future. But Enrich definitely needs to learn a skill in a few years. He's only nine."

"Agreed. We didn't start Romulus in the shop until he was ten. And he still goes to school in the mornings. But when you're ready… Koni said he'd help us set up—what did he call it?" He turned to call through the doorway of his shop. "Vlina! What did Koni call that apprentice idea of his?"

A rough but feminine voice answered, her words muffled. Snapping his fingers in agreement, Brenet turned back to Franisa. "A 'co-op.' He said it's short for 'co-operative.' A way for businesses to work together. Mistress Thistlewick and I have an informal arrangement, but Koni thought it would be better to come up with some rules. So no one gets stuck with a lazy apprentice." His eyes went wide, and he looked away. "Not that I think Enrich would—"

She touched his burly arm. "It's all right. I know Keldan was not regarded as the most productive member of society." She grimaced at the carefully worded disclaimer. While she might call him much worse things in the privacy of her own mind, she wouldn't complain about him to others. "Enrich takes after me, not his father. Although he's as dragon besotted as Romulus. Maybe more."

Brenet laughed. "Well, if dragon riding is a useful career, Enrich is fortunate to have the inside track through his new father. Congratulations to both of you—or all three if we include Enrich." He laughed again.

Cheeks burning, Franisa muttered her thanks. "I must go. Good afternoon."

"Think about the co-op." Brenet lifted a hand as he turned toward his shop. "It could be good for all of us."

"I will. Thank you. Good afternoon."

Mind abuzz, she turned down the lane beyond the butcher shop, heading for the dairy farm. Because the cows and goats required pastureland, it stood on the very edge of town, much like the stables at the other end of the village. The lane wound between a variety of single and two-story buildings housing residents of the town. Laundry hung from ropes across the narrow lane, flapping in the breeze. She breathed in the fresh scent of drying sheets. And a tang of something harsher.

She took in another experimental breath. It smelled like woodsmoke—not uncommon at this time of year. But there was an acrid undertone, as if someone were burning garbage. Her steps quickened, and as she rounded a corner, she saw the plume of smoke she'd subconsciously expected. "Fire!"

CHAPTER SIXTEEN

Dragon training while watching a five-year-old proved to be almost impossible. Enrich had been helpful the previous day, but the little girl required much more supervision. While Nevan and William put their dragons' harnesses on, Eloise decided she'd like to ride Nari. The dragon didn't mind having the little girl on her back, and she carried her around the courtyard, getting in the way of the others.

"Nari, wait for Cala!" William snapped more than once, but the dragon didn't respond. "Sure, they can talk, but they don't listen." He slapped the dragon's neck as she lumbered past, the happily squealing little girl on her back.

Nevan tried to suppress his nervous snicker. "Eloise, can you come down, please?" He put a hand on the dragon's flank. "Nari, time to dismount." He whistled one of the commands they'd drilled the dragons on.

Obediently, Nari crouched, and Nevan reached up. "Come down."

Eloise kicked her leg over the dragon's neck and slid into Nevan's arms. "Wheee!"

He caught her and swung her to the ground. "It's time to sweep, Eloise."

"But we already sweeped!" She put her fists on her hips and stared up at him. "Two times!"

He darted a glance at William's still thunderous face, then crouched to the little girl's level. "Sir William is trying to train the dragons, and we can't do that if they're playing."

Her face fell. "I'm sorry. I can sit quietly in the corner." She pointed at an old mounting block by the door, her shoulders drooping, her voice mournful.

Nevan fought the twinge of guilt her downcast expression inspired. "That's probably a good idea. For a few minutes." Ignoring William's indrawn breath—the man was certainly going to suggest a few hours—he gave Eloise a gentle push toward the corner. "You can play in a bit."

William glowered, then turned back to his dragon. "Finn, are you ready to fly?"

The dragon crouched, and William climbed aboard. He buckled his flying straps to the harness then looked back at Nevan. "Water scooping, with a drop at the designated place."

Nevan tapped a hand to his chest—the signal they'd established to mean "understood and will comply." They'd learned early on that talking while flying, even with the enchanted communication disks, was problematic.

Finn jumped to the low wall on the seaward side of the courtyard, then launched off the side of the cliff, using the thermals to rise swiftly over the ocean. He banked toward land, moving into a waiting circle overhead until Starlight and Nevan could join him.

But then the dragon banked again and descended toward the stony ground outside the courtyard. Nevan hurried to the big door, pushing the well-hung slab of wood and metal aside.

The dragon had landed a few yards from the stable entrance. Cala stood on tiptoe beside the big beast, greeting her husband with a kiss.

Nearby, Koni watched indulgently, like a benevolent uncle. When he spotted Nevan, he skirted the dragon and came to greet him. "Well met, Nevan. I am here like a big yellow bus, to take the children to school."

"A big yellow what?" Nevan clasped hands with the elf.

"Bus. It's a means of conveyance." Koni waved a negligent hand. "Not important. But I am here to relieve you of the youngsters."

"I meant to come back and get them earlier, but the bakery is a busy place in the morning." Cala came around Finn to greet them. "And I enlisted Koni's help."

"That will teach me to shop in the morning." Koni peered past Nevan. "Here are my charges now."

Nevan turned as Eloise skipped up to them, Enrich following a few steps behind. The girl grabbed Nevan's hand and faced the elf. "Did you bring the unicorn?"

Koni shook his head slowly. "One does not 'bring' a unicorn. One requests the fair one's assistance in times of great need. You can easily walk to school. Thus this is not a time of great need."

The little girl drew in a deep breath as if to argue, then let it out with a little raspberry. "I wanted to see the fair one."

"Perhaps she will deign to be admired by you in the near future." Koni held out a hand. "For now, we have a destination. And I have other duties, so let us depart. Enrich, are you ready?"

"Yes, sir." He slowly moved around Nevan as if emerging from shelter while a storm still raged. "I'm going to school, right?"

"You are indeed." The elf gestured at Nevan. "That is the will of the clan of your father-to-be, and so it will be done." When the boy continued to stare at him, Koni grinned. "The giants send their kids to school, so now that you're under the protection of Nevan's family, you follow giant rules."

Enrich smiled, and the furrow between his brows disappeared. "Then I am ready to go."

"We bid you adieu!" Koni swirled around, the force of his turn pulling Eloise from the ground. Her feet flew out, and she squealed happily then landed beside the elf, kicking up a little puff of dust. "Take your sister's hand so we don't lose you on the elven lines." When Enrich had complied, Koni pumped his free hand in the air. "Onward!"

Cala watched them walk away, a bemused expression on her face. "He is endlessly entertaining."

"That's one way to put it." William still sat astride Finn's back. "I could do with a little less drama and a little more efficiency."

"Then he wouldn't be our Koni." Cala gestured toward the courtyard where Starlight and Nari waited, dozing in the winter sun. "Shall we get to work?"

They spent the morning running fire drills: scooping water from the sea and attempting to hit targets William had previously painted on the stone of the peninsula. Each had a large red number, and they tried different elevations and directions of attack. Finn and Nari proved to be more accurate initially, but by the end of the morning, Starlight had begun to outperform her siblings. As noon approached, William called a halt.

They unstrapped the dragons' harnesses, then sent them out to fish, swim, and sun themselves. Cold, wet, and tired, the humans retired to their rooms to change clothes, then congregated in the kitchen for lunch.

William carved some meat from a joint of ham. "What did you do differently, Nevan?"

He stopped slicing the bread and looked up. "What do you mean?"

"On that last run, it looked like Starlight was targeting the upper left corner of the target. She hit it right on, three times." William slid some meat onto Cala's plate, then held up the laden fork.

Nevan nodded and held out his dish. "Oh, that. I told her where to hit."

Cala put her food on the table and pulled out a chair. "And you weren't telling her before?"

"No." Nevan put his plate down and added a slice of bread. "I was visualizing what I wanted her to do. But now that she's learning to talk, I thought I'd tell her. In words. And it works much better. That last part was just showing off. She was trying to hit the wet splotch from the previous run. And she did."

William frowned. "Indeed. Did she tell you that? In words?"

Nevan rocked his head side to side. "It's hard to explain. I told her to hit the target. And when she did that, I told her to try the top left. I had to visualize top left. When I praised her for doing it right, she said she'd do it again."

The older dragon rider rose and went to the smaller table beside the window. He lifted the heavy book he'd been reading that morning. "This book is about training. I'm not sure where Koni got it..." He raised a brow at Cala.

"Not from my store," the witch said. "And not from any bookshop in the Borgonne or Verduun. The construction is like nothing I've ever seen."

"Agreed." He looked at the cover again, then flipped it open. "It talks about learning styles. And how some people are visual learners, and others are auditory—they learn from hearing. Let me ask you this, Nevan. When I tell you to visualize the target, what do you see?"

Nevan screwed his eyes shut and tried to imagine the target. They were big red numbers painted on the stone with a rectangle around them. He knew that and knew where they were on the peninsula. But trying to *see* the target in his mind was impossible. "I see black." He opened his eyes. "I know what they look like, and where they are, but I don't *see* anything but black."

Cala sat up straighter. "I've seen this before. We had a young woman at the academy when I was there. She had power—immense power. But when she tried to visualize the spells, she couldn't see anything. They finally taught her to write her spells in words, instead of drawing them like I do. It was incredible. She immediately became the most adept student in her group." She peered at Nevan. "Do you mean to tell us you've never been able to visualize?"

Nevan spread his hands helplessly. "I—can you actually *see* things inside your mind? Like they're real? Or like a drawing?"

William and Cala both nodded.

"Like a picture?" Nevan pointed at a framed painting of the Verduunian Dragon Guild Hall on the wall by the door. "You can see *that* inside your head."

Cala closed her eyes briefly, then opened them again. "Yes. And I can change the colors, move the trees beside the river, add some snow..."

“It doesn’t snow in Verduun.” William frowned at the picture, then looked up at the ceiling. “I can visualize that scene, but I can’t change—wait, no, I can. Look at that! Snow! I never thought of trying that.” He met Nevan’s eyes and shrugged. “I’m not an artist—it never occurred to me to make my own pictures. I just remember targets and locations.”

Nevan sat down so hard the chair creaked. “Do you think that’s why Starlight hasn’t been able to learn? Because I can’t *see* what she’s supposed to do?”

“Maybe.” Cala leaned toward him, grasping his forearm. “But maybe that’s why she can speak? You can’t communicate visually, so she adapted. This is remarkable!”

“I’ve never heard of a dragon rider giving verbal commands to his mount. War dragons don’t speak.” William sat, the big book in his lap, a stunned expression on his face. “Maybe because we didn’t need them to?”

“Did you test riders and eliminate those who couldn’t visualize?” Cala asked.

William snapped his fingers. “Of course we did! The guild is prestigious. We get many more rider candidates than dragon eggs, so we have a thorough testing and elimination process.” He hummed under his breath. “I wonder how many people we disqualified who might have taught our dragons to speak?” He tapped the leather cover of the tome. “Do you think Koni knew that?”

“How would he know?” Cala gestured at the book. “That book doesn’t talk about visualizing, does it?”

“Not in so many words. But it does say people learn differently. Maybe he suspected Starlight… or Nevan? That one of them might need a different way of thinking. Or maybe we got lucky.” William slid his fingers across the gilded edges.

“Luck seems to follow Koni.” Cala picked up her fork. “More than anyone I’ve ever known.”

“He is an elf.” Nevan shrugged. “Maybe their magic is just luck.”

Something crawled on his leg. Nevan jumped in his seat,

suppressing a yell as he realized the source of the vibration wasn't a creature, but the communication medallion.

At the same moment, William jerked in surprise. He yanked his disk from his own pocket. "I wish it wouldn't do that!"

Both devices vibrated again, and Koni's voice rang out. "Fire! At the tannery!"

William leapt to his feet, staggering a little as his magic prosthetic failed to compensate for the quick movement. He recovered swiftly and ran for the door. "Come! Our first real test!"

In the stable, they scrambled into their riding belts, hung near the door for easy access. They seized the harnesses they had removed from their mounts only an hour before and hurried out into the yard. The dragons, alerted mentally by their riders, landed in the courtyard, jockeying for position. Finn stood nearest the door, with Nari crowding in beside him. Starlight perched on the garden wall, waiting her turn.

"Good plan, Starlight! We'll catch up with the others easily." Nevan muttered the words under his breath, trying to think them at his mount. A rush of excitement and smug agreement came back to him.

"Remember our training! The closest water to the tannery is the pond at the dairy farm. Perfect location." William sat atop Finn, buckling his riding straps. "Counterclockwise circle from the pond to the tannery and around, so we don't run into each other. Maintain your distances, watch for people on the ground. If there aren't flames on the roof, aim for the windows." He slapped a hand against Finn's neck and pumped his arm—the signal to launch.

Finn bunched his legs and leapt, his strong wings barely clearing the tall wall on the landward side of the courtyard. Nari waited a couple of seconds, then followed in his wake, beating her wings hard to gain altitude.

Starlight dropped into the courtyard as soon as the bigger dragons had departed. Nevan slid the harness over her front legs, then scrambled up her side, quickly buckling the leather straps. He'd barely gotten the first one attached when Starlight jumped to the lower wall overlooking the cliff.

"Hey! I'm not done!" Nevan cried as the dragon prepared to jump.

"And you're going the wrong way!" He slipped the second strap through the loop.

"Nevan safe." Starlight dropped over the cliff edge, wings still tucked in. She gained speed as they plummeted toward the sea, then her wings snapped open and they swooped upward. She raced over the water, then wheeled around to catch an updraft. They crossed high above the beach and over the land at a tremendous speed, soaring past the top of the tower. Within seconds, she'd overtaken the other two dragons, still laboring at a lower altitude.

As part of their training, William had taught the other riders what Koni called *fisicks*. It was a dry subject with terms like "lift" and "air speed" and "angle of attack." Nevan had dutifully—and painfully—learned the figuring required, but he preferred to let Starlight do the flying. He was convinced there was more magic involved than the others believed. And since Starlight was a sea dragon, it made sense to him that she'd do her best flying over the sea. Clearly, launching over the waves gave her greater height and speed.

"Yessss. Sea magic." Starlight bugled.

Far below, the others looked up. Cala pointed up at him, and William yelled something whipped away by the wind. After a moment, he extended his arm and pulled it back—the signal to come closer.

"Close formation," Nevan said, both aloud and in his head.

Starlight obediently folded her wings and dropped, slowing to swing in behind Cala.

Ahead, a plume of smoke rose over the village. The tannery was on the western side of town, closer to the rolling hills that rose to the forested slopes of Seaview Ridge. The heavy black cloud spread slowly, roiling from the heat of the fire.

The dragons beat their wings faster. As they approached, the flames became visible—the whole thatched roof was engulfed. William peeled away to circle around the pond in the dairy field. The herd of cows, already shifting nervously, scattered to the far corners of the pasture as the dragon swooped low above their heads.

Lining up on the pond's longest axis, Finn dove at a shallow angle, skimming above the glassy surface. He opened his mouth, and his lower jaw sliced into the water, scooping up the liquid. Then with strong downbeats of his wings, he slowly rose and banked toward the fire.

Cala and Nari followed. Waves splashed at the edges of the pond, and a small flock of ducks took wing, complaining loudly. Nevan patted Starlight's neck. "We're next."

"No need." Starlight cut across the pond well over Nari's flight path, headed directly to the burning building.

Nevan pushed his right leg against the dragon's neck, trying to change her course. "You need water!"

"Got water."

Below, Finn spewed his load of water at the fire, hitting the burning roof with impressive precision. Over the wind rattling in his ears, Nevan thought he heard a cheer. As they approached, he caught sight of a swiftly forming bucket brigade leading from the front of the building down the lane. Villagers hurried from the pumps in the square by the church, water sloshing from their pails.

Starlight dropped, flying perpendicular to the line Finn had taken. She spewed water across the roof, hitting the unburnt portions before expelling a gout on the flames. Then she rose swiftly and banked clockwise around the building, flying over the dairy.

"We were supposed to go the other way!" Nevan leaned close to the dragon's back, his eyes streaming with tears from their speed. Or maybe from the excess water blown back in their flight. Eye protection would be a welcome addition to their gear. He pressed his leg against Starlight's neck again. "We have to get more water!" Why wouldn't she listen to him? He gritted his teeth in frustration.

"No." Starlight swung around. Nari had just completed her pass and banked to the right to fly over the lane and around to the field behind the tannery. Beyond the burning building, Finn dropped toward the pond. Starlight came around the opposite direction and made another pass, spitting more water across the entire roof.

"How are you doing that?" Nevan hollered.

Ahead, Finn came straight at them, his wings beating furiously to gain altitude. Starlight twitched a wing and seemed to rise almost effortlessly on the hot air of the smoke plume, wheeling to the right to get out of Finn's flight path. They passed around the outer edge of the dark column, but the smoke made Nevan's eyes water and sting.

The mission became a tedious but terrifying loop. Rise over the dairy barn. Swing around to the right. Dive over the tannery, expelling a seemingly endless supply of water, the salty blowback stinging his face. Swoop upward and around the cloud of smoke, often coming face to face with Nari or Finn. Then bank around over the dairy barn and begin again.

Nevan's eyes stung, and his lungs burned. He clutched the flight straps, knowing it would do little good if they broke but unable to let go. The light started to fade, and the cloud of smoke seemed to strengthen. They flew and spewed, over and over. Until suddenly Starlight dove toward the shore of the little pond.

"Done. Off." She landed with a thump.

Startled by the sudden change, Nevan scrabbled at the buckles. "Is it out?"

"Most. Need water."

"Then go! You can scoop it up like Finn." He paused, one belt loose in his hands.

"Need more." Starlight's head swung around to look at him, her tone urgent. *"Now!"*

"Go!" He frantically tried to buckle the loose strap again, but his tired hands didn't seem to work.

With an almost human shrug, Starlight launched into the air. But instead of following Finn and Nari's flight path, she beat upward, wheeling over the village at a startling speed. As she flew low over the thatched roofs, Nevan squinted back at the tannery. Smoke still drifted from the windows, but no flames were visible. The bucket line seemed to have slowed as well. Then the building was lost beyond the others in the town.

Starlight swooped across the crescent-shaped plaza along the port. Three big ships rocked gently in the waves beside the piers. The little dragon seemed to lose altitude as she slipped past their furled sails. Then she dove.

Waves engulfed them as Starlight plunged into the bay. Nevan gasped, pulling in a lungful of sea water. He scrabbled at the buckles of his flight straps, but the wet leather wouldn't move. Panic pounded in his ears as the water pressed against him.

Then his head broke the surface. He choked out water and sucked in a deep breath of blessed air. His lungs seized in a coughing fit, but that passed.

"I thought I was going to drown." The words came out hoarse.

"Nevan safe." Starlight floated, her wings and neck extended, her body low in the water. She ducked her head under, then came back up. *"Off now."*

"I'm trying." Nevan fought with the wet leather and finally got the second strap unbuckled. He'd never managed to refasten the first one.

"You stay." With a mental sigh, Starlight dove from beneath him, sinking into the waves.

"Starlight!" Nevan cried as she disappeared into the dark water. What was happening? Was she… dying?

"Safe. All safe." The words seemed to fade from his mind as if the dragon had swum out of reach. But a surge of comfort and security wrapped around him as he floated on his back in the bay.

CHAPTER SEVENTEEN

Franisa hurried across the muddy cow pasture, heedless of her shoes or the hem of her dress. The dark plume of smoke above the tannery had lightened as the dragons and the bucket brigade extinguished the fire, but thick clouds low on the horizon still blocked much of the remaining light cast by the setting sun.

Nari and Finn had landed beside the little pond, waiting while their riders unbuckled their flight straps. As she approached, William slid down and slapped Finn's side. "Magnificent!" His voice, hoarse with smoke, still rang out across the pasture. He leaned against the dragon's side for a moment, then hurried to Nari to help Cala.

Franisa hovered a few feet away. She turned slowly, looking for Starlight, but the smallest dragon wasn't visible in the darkening sky. "Where's Nevan?"

William looked up in surprise as he helped his wife slide down her dragon's side. Once she reached the ground, he stepped away and tipped his head back, scanning the sky. "He's... I have no idea where he is." His rough voice went hard. "He didn't follow the training. None of my instructions! We had a plan!"

Cala put a hand on his arm, stilling his voice. "It probably wasn't his fault. He's told us many times Starlight isn't as compliant as Finn and Nari."

He flung up his arms. "I thought we fixed that! The whole visualization thing!" William took a surprised step back as both dragons suddenly launched into the sky. They flew low across the field before banking around to head over the town. "Where are they going?" Then he answered his own question. "The sea."

Cala and William turned and hastened across the pasture.

Franisa ran to catch up. "Why?"

Cala stumbled and both William and Franisa caught her arms. She shook them off. "I'm fine. Uneven ground. Hard to see." She lifted a hand and flicked her fingers in a gesture Franisa had seen before, but a flame didn't appear. "Squall take it! I'm too tired to light it."

William let go of her and dug into a pocket of his soaked trousers. "I have one of your glow stones." He pulled the little round rock out and displayed it on the palm of his hand. The glow illuminated their tired eyes, smoke-streaked faces, and soaked hair.

Cala plucked the stone from his hand. "Aim it down." She held it from above, so it lit the rough field beneath their feet. The three trudged across the muddy grass to the fence. William climbed over, but the two women ducked between the rails. They headed up the dirt road toward the front of the tannery.

A group of residents stood in the small square, light from the gas lamp casting long shadows across the cobblestones. They surrounded the muddy orc tanner and his disheveled wife, their faces as haggard and exhausted as Cala's and William's. Discarded buckets lay at their feet, and puddles of filthy water covered much of the square. But when someone spotted the dragon riders approaching, a cheer went up.

"You've saved our home!" Goruk Hidehand surged forward, wrapping his arms around Cala and William. "Without you, we would have only stones and ashes."

William turned to look up at the big building. "The bucket brigade must have worked fast. We didn't do that alone."

Goruk clapped a heavy hand on the dragon rider's back, nearly sending the older man to the ground. "They did. But your dragons turned the tide. Especially that little one! It was twice as fast as the other two. Was that you, Sir William?"

William and Cala exchanged a look, swift but meaningful. Franisa wasn't sure anyone else noticed.

"That was Nevan and Starlight," Franisa said. "They were—why were they so much faster?"

"I don't know." William squinted through the darkness beyond the little huddle of people. "But I aim to find out. Has anyone seen Nevan?"

Mavila, the tanner's wife, pointed across the square toward the main part of town. "At the end, they flew that way."

"The sea," Cala said softly. She met her husband's gaze again, then slowly stepped back.

He nodded but continued answering the questions of the gathered townsfolk.

"Is Nevan okay?" Franisa whispered. "Why is he—you didn't go with the dragons. Why did he?"

Cala put an arm around her shoulders and took another step back. "Let's find out." The witch kept moving backward, one slow step at a time, drawing Franisa with her, until they stood in the shadow of the pump in the center of the square. Damp from Cala's clothing soaked into Franisa's dress, but she didn't say anything. She wasn't sure if Cala was doing magic or simply letting William distract the others as they drifted away from the group.

Once behind the pump, Cala released Franisa and turned decisively, striding across the dark little square. Franisa hurried in her wake, the voices fading behind them as they moved down the lane toward the center of town.

In the darkness of early evening, Cala somehow avoided the notice of townsfolk straggling home after the excitement of the fire. They caught snippets of the conversation as they passed. Most everyone marveled over the contributions of the dragons and their riders. And none of them saw the two women making their way swiftly toward the port.

As they passed the Crab and Tankard, the door opened, and

cheerful voices rang out. A cloud of savory spices enveloped them, and Franisa's stomach growled. Or maybe it was Cala's—she couldn't tell.

The witch laughed at the sound. "I am exhausted and starving," Cala whispered. "Elspeth is sure to feed us. But let's find Nevan first."

They reached the bayside crescent, pausing at the mouth of the lane. To their right, the Silver Acorn did their usual business, the patrons seemingly unaware of the drama of the afternoon.

"There!" Cala pointed across the plaza toward the water. Out in the bay, the three dragons floated, their long necks silhouetted against the low moon. Closer, voices drew their attention.

Gas lamps glowed at the landward end of each wharf. A rowboat bobbed beside one long wooden dock in the shadow of a larger ship moored there. One figure huddled in the bow of the boat while another tossed a rope to a third person standing on the quay. They secured the boat, and the seated man rose, climbing slowly to the pier.

"Is that him?" Franisa whispered.

Cala nodded, and they hurried across the cobblestone crescent. Nevan trudged under the lamp, the light glinting on his dark, wet hair, a blanket wrapped around his shoulders. His boots squelched as he walked. Water dripped from his clothing. "Cala! Is everyone safe?"

"Yes. What happened? Why are you here?" Cala gestured at the sea.

"Starlight needed... she said water. I didn't get the flight straps off fast enough." He ran a hand over his tired face. The blanket slipped, revealing his sodden shirt. An even larger man stood at his back, his face impossible to see in the shadows. He caught Nevan's blanket before it hit the ground and draped it across the smaller man's shoulders.

Nevan looked up and nodded his thanks. "Sorry. This is Sigrun Tidemark. Captain of the *Ironwind*. They had just put into port. Saw us... fished me out of the drink."

"I've never seen anything like it." The giant's voice was surprisingly high-pitched and Franisa realized with a jolt of surprise that she was a woman. "That little dragon dove straight into the sea with Nevan here on her back. I was on the deck and figured he might need some assistance."

"Thank you for your help." Cala shook hands with Sigrun. "I'm Cala—one of the other dragon riders. And this is Franisa, Nevan's betrothed."

The giantess looked between the two of them, her brows drawn down. Then she nodded. "I know humans are bashful, but you can give your man a kiss. He deserves it if half of what he told me is true." She gave Nevan a little shove.

Staggered by the force of her playful push, he jolted into Franisa. He grasped her shoulders, and she stumbled back, throwing her weight forward to stop his fall. The move was much more effective than she'd expected. She gripped his forearms. "Are you all right?"

"Just a little loose on my pins." He gazed down at her.

"Go on! We don't mind," Sigrun said with a deep, hearty laugh. "Kiss the man!"

Franisa glanced over Nevan's shoulder at the watching giant. She wasn't going to let this go. Nevan stared helplessly at her. Moving into the shadow cast by his body, she stood on her tiptoes and reached up to pull his head down. Nevan stiffened, and she squeezed his neck gently. "Don't worry, she can't see anything." She pressed a soft kiss on his cheek.

Nevan jerked and broke away to cough rather violently. Sigrun pounded his back. After a moment, he straightened. "I'm a little waterlogged."

"I saw that plunge!" Sigrun said. "A little waterlogged is an understatement. That dragon dropped like a knife into a Honeybone pie at my family's mid-winter feast!" She laughed again, then gripped Nevan's shoulder. "Let me buy you a drink."

"I think I'll—" Nevan broke off, his gaze on Cala's face. The witch shook her head side-to-side just a fraction. "That would be quite generous of you."

"I think *we* should be buying the drinks." Cala took the giantess's arm and turned her toward the street leading to the Crab and Tankard. "You saved Nevan from a long swim."

"Ah, we giants float, you know. He'da been fine. But I won't say no to a tankard of ale."

"Bring your sailors, if you will. It would be our pleasure to buy a round for your valiant crew." Cala gestured toward the little rowboat.

"Nah, Brynj and Yrsa are on duty. But I'll pass on your appreciation." She linked arms with Cala "Where's this pub of yours?"

While Cala steered the big woman toward the dark street they'd hurried down only a few moments before, Franisa hesitated. "I need to get home. Enrich and Eloise are there."

"The pixie is with them, right?" Nevan's arm tightened around her shoulders, as if he couldn't bear to have her leave.

"She is..." In the last few months, Aislin had proven to be a reliable child-minder and would not leave the bakery until Franisa returned. "But I don't want to impose..."

His grip loosened and he sighed. "I understand."

Cala turned back. "Nonsense. Aislin loves playing with Eloise. She'll be delighted to have more time with them."

"Are you sure?" Franisa bit her lip. She didn't want to take the pixie's help for granted. But she really wanted to know how Nevan had ended up in the bay.

"I'm sure." Cala gave her a meaningful look and tipped her head toward the giant. Then she continued up the lane.

Franisa understood the message. Her betrothal to Nevan was the only thing protecting her son from the mines. And while a random sailor's opinion might not matter, running away instead of celebrating his success at the pub might raise more questions than she was willing to entertain right now. With an indecisive nod, she took Nevan's arm. Leaning close, she whispered, "What happened?"

Nevan gestured helplessly at the bay. "Starlight—she was amazing. She made run after run without a single dip in the lake. I don't know where all the water came from. She just kept circling and spewing!" He ran a hand over his face then pushed the damp curls from his forehead. "Then suddenly, she said she needed water. She landed by the pond, but I dunno. Maybe the water was too shallow or muddy from Finn and Nari sloshing through. I tried to get off, but the flying straps were wet. Then she launched and flew into the sea, like she couldn't wait any longer. And sank to the bottom."

Franisa gasped, her fear for Nevan making her feel faint, but he waved a hand to cut her off. "No, she's fine. Out there floating with Finn and Nari now. But at first... I'm a good swimmer, and as Sigrun said, we float. But with the flying straps holding me on—if she hadn't come up for air, I'd be a goner. She knew that. She saved me." He staggered a bit as he said this, his voice going thick.

"Hush." Franisa flung an arm around his waist, steadying him. "You don't need to talk. William and Cala are going to want to know. Save your strength."

"I'm fine." The words sounded uncertain, and his steps wavered.

She tightened her arm, pulling him close. His wet clothing soaked into hers, and she snorted a little laugh. At least she'd have matching damp spots on both sides now. She guided him down the street, aiming toward the warmth of the Crab and Tankard at the next intersection.

Light spilled through the little windows, casting bars of light across the lane. Cala and Sigrun went down the two steps and opened the door, a cloud of savory steam and the chatter of many conversations pouring out around them. As they entered, Cala glanced back, then nodded approvingly and went inside.

Unsure why Cala had insisted the clearly exhausted Nevan join them in the pub, she nevertheless guided him down the steps to the door and pushed it inward. Noise assaulted them again, and Franisa's stomach growled in response to another blast of beef, spices, and yeast. This time, Nevan's responded, and the giant chuckled as he leaned in to hold the door open. "After you."

She slipped out from under his arm, her body cold for an instant from the damp dress. Then the warmth of the pub wrapped around her, banishing the chill. She spotted Cala and Sigrun settling in at a table near the window. It looked as if the place had been hastily vacated. Trudi, the publican's daughter, cleared a basket and some bowls while a group of dwarves slid in beside the orcs at the next table.

Nevan took the seat by the window, leaning against the wall as if he could barely hold himself upright. Franisa slid in beside him, with Cala and Sigrun across the table, leaving the places on the end for William and whoever might accompany him.

"Bring a round—six, if you please, Trudi," Cala said to the serving girl. "And whatever Elspeth has on the stove."

"You got it." The young woman swiped a cloth across the table, holding the tray of dishes in the other hand. "That was quite the show you gave us today! Never seen anything like it!"

"I doubt anyone has," Sigrun said. "I've sailed the world and never encountered dragons doing anything but bringing fire and destruction. How'd you teach them to breathe water?"

"Those are our sea dragons," Trudi said proudly before the others could respond. "Been here all my life. But they've never doused a fire before. That I know of." She raised a brow at Nevan and Franisa who dutifully shook their heads. Swinging the tray high overhead, she turned on her heel and waded through the rapidly filling pub.

While they waited for their meal, a steady stream of people filtered into the bar. Some stopped by the table to congratulate the dragon riders while others watched from their seats, nodding and whispering. Franisa and Nevan sat quietly, letting Cala and the gregarious ship's captain do all the talking. Despite having missed the spectacle of the fire, Sigrun had no problem asserting her opinions on the topic to all who stopped by.

Trudi finally returned with ale, food, and a glass of wine for Cala. She plunked the bowls and tankards in front of each of them, dropping the basket of bread in the center of the table. "Is Sir William joining you?"

"Yes." Cala half-stood to peer toward the entrance. "Is he here?"

"Just arrived." Trudi nodded at the clump of orcs by the door, then flipped the empty tray under her arm and plowed between the tables toward the kitchen. Customers called out orders as she went, to which she nodded pleasantly but didn't slow.

William appeared at the end of the table and introduced Goruk Hidehand, the tanner, to the others. Cala explained why Sigrun had joined them, then they all dug into their food. Cala muttered something about the bread as she ripped a piece off her roll and dunked it into her bowl. Franisa wasn't sure what she said but nodded in agreement as she ate. Even Sigrun stopped talking while they inhaled the savory and filling meal.

When they finished, Goruk rose. "I cannot stay but wanted to at least buy you a meal in gratitude. We have a lot of rebuilding to do, but it would have been so much worse without you and your dragons."

"Do you have a place to sleep tonight?" Franisa wasn't sure where she'd put the tanner and his family of eight, but she wouldn't leave them out in the cold.

Goruk waved a hand. "We're fine. Marnel Skorra has offered us space in his hay barn. Mavila is already getting the kids settled. They think it's a fine adventure. I'll pick up some food for the family and be on my way."

"If you need anything..." Franisa let the offer trail off. She suspected Elspeth would already be arranging for the family's needs—the publican was a dynamo.

Almost as if summoned by the thought, the plump little woman arrived at the end of their table. "Hidehand! I hope you weren't leaving without this." She hefted a big basket filled with crockery. "There's stew for the family, and bread too." She nodded at Franisa. "And more for the morning."

"I'll send Enrich over with some rolls at daybreak," Franisa said. "And we have clothing—I've been meaning to go through the things that are too small for the children."

"My thanks, Elspeth, Franisa, but there is no need." The orc twisted his hat in his hands. "We can—"

"This town takes care of those in need." Elspeth shoved the basket into his arms. "You've contributed to others in the past. Let us do the same for you."

"But I want to pay for the dragon riders' meals." Goruk pointed at the table. "And Franisa and the captain, of course."

"No need!" The captain clapped one hand on Cala's shoulder. "We're square here."

"You won't pay for anything tonight, Hidehand," Elspeth said. "Now get home and feed your family." She pushed the basket at him again, urging the orc toward the door.

With a rueful shrug, he bowed low to each of them, then clutched the basket to his chest and left.

"That was a nice thing." Sigrun nodded then downed the remains of her ale. "I've always liked this town. Might just retire here myself." She nudged Cala with an elbow. "In a decade or five. Too much adventure to be had right now. Thank you for your hospitality, my friends. I must go. We sail on the dawn tide."

William grasped her arm. "I'd appreciate it if word of this didn't get out. Verduun is a might touchy about dragons."

Nodding in agreement, she rose. "I'll do my best, Sir William, but my ship isn't the only one in port. Word will spread." Scanning the room, she let out a wordless shout, cutting through the clamor of conversation. Silence fell as everyone looked toward them, and a few of the giants rose, dusting off their clothing and finishing their drinks. "*Ironwind*! Prepare for departure!" With another nod, she slapped William on the back and made her way out of the room, her sailors falling in behind.

After the giants left, William rose. "We need to check on the dragons. And find out what happened out there, and why." His steely gaze settled on Nevan, and the younger man ducked his head.

As they slowly got to their feet, Elspeth returned, bearing another basket. She pressed it into Cala's hands, whispering something to her friend. Cala embraced her with one arm, then laughed. "Sorry, I forgot I'm still wet."

"No matter. I'll dry soon enough in here." Elspeth escorted them to the door, cutting through the patrons waiting for a seat. "Get away with ye!" she hollered when someone tried to intercept William. "The dragon riders are tired. You can walk out to FarPoint and talk to them on the morrow."

"That'll stop most of them," Cala said in a low voice.

"As intended." Elspeth pulled the door open, letting the four of them pass by. "But not me! I'll be out to hear the tale!"

When they reached the street, the dragon riders turned toward the port. Franisa touched Cala's sleeve. "I don't expect to see you in the morning."

The older woman chuckled dryly. "That's good, because I doubt I'll be awake before sunrise." She glanced at her husband and Nevan. The two men trudged slowly down the street, shoulders stooped, feet shuffling. "That was exhausting."

Franisa nodded, watching Nevan. A little spurt of disappointment cut through her—he hadn't said goodbye. Or anything, really, since they reached the pub. She knew he was tired, but—she dragged her gaze away, reminding herself their relationship wasn't real, and if his infatuation with her was finally abating, that was best for both of them. "I hope you can take the elven trail home."

"Either that or fly." Cala's eyes drifted upward, as if listening. "The dragons may have recovered enough to carry us."

"Can you hear them?" Franisa whispered.

"No. I can't. But I can tell they're still in the bay. Waiting." She shrugged. "We'll find out soon enough."

The pub door opened, and a whiff of sour pipe smoke curled the hairs inside Franisa's nose. Rolph strolled into the street and bowed to the two women, his sharp gaze taking in the dragon riders at the far end of the lane. "Ah, Franisa. May I escort you home?"

Drawing in a deep breath—an action she immediately regretted when she got a throat full of Rolph's odd burnt scent—Franisa turned to nod at Rolph. "Thank you, no. I don't require an escort." She gave Cala a brief hug, then strode down the side lane that led toward the bakery.

With a muttered comment to Cala, Rolph hurried after her, poking his elbow out when he reached her side. "You don't need an escort, but I would be honored to offer one."

Franisa glanced up at the man. He was easily twice her age, and now she understood Eloise's comments about his smell. He reeked of a burnt scent, not pleasant like a wood fire, but sharp, like the tannery fire today. Perhaps from his odd tobacco. How could anyone enjoy a pipe that tasted like that? She continued up the street, keeping her hands tucked inside her wrap.

Fortunately, the bakery wasn't far. They crossed another intersection, where a gas lamp illuminated the fronts of the shops and houses, then passed into the darkness of the lane. A little farther on, they reached the square in front of the bakery. Light flickered in the upper windows, welcoming her. Franisa paused at the mouth of the narrow alley leading to her backyard. "Thank you for the escort, Rolph. Unnecessary though it was. Good night."

"Franisa, wait!" The skinny man followed her down the side lane. "I wish to speak with you."

"We could have spoken on the walk. I must get back to my children. They've been in another's care for long enough." She reached for the gate.

Rolph's hand closed over hers. "I've heard a rumor you're betrothed to the giant. Surely that is not true? You and I have been developing a… relationship—"

"His name is Nevan, not 'the giant.' And I'm sorry if you thought something has been growing between us." She pulled her hand from his grasp and stepped through the gate, closing it between them. "That was not my intention. I'm not looking for a relationship. With you," she added belatedly. "I have one."

"With a giant," he sneered. "You deserve more than that, my dear. After your disastrous first marriage, you should belong to a man with intelligence and fortune."

Anger flared in her chest. "I won't *belong* to any man! Handfasting isn't bondage, and I don't care about your fortune. Nevan is intelligent and kind." She poked a finger at his chest. "And don't you dare speak about Keldan in that tone of voice again! Goodbye, Rolph." She whirled through the kitchen door, slamming it shut.

CHAPTER EIGHTEEN

Nevan trudged along behind Cala and William as they took the elven trail home. William had sent the dragons back to FarPoint, not wanting to burden the exhausted creatures. He held the glowing stone, lighting the path at his feet while Cala did whatever magic was required to make the journey. She didn't seem to do anything, but the darkness closed around them, then the moonlight glinted on the tower in the distance.

The dirt track underfoot transitioned to the stone of the promontory, and they climbed the last few yards to the front of the house. Apparently holding hands on the journey wasn't required—he'd been able to follow the other two without touching them.

William bypassed the front of the house, going around to the courtyard at the right. Once he'd ascertained the dragons were safely asleep in their favored place, he turned to Nevan. "We'll speak in the morning. I want to know why you deviated from the plan."

Nevan opened his mouth, but William lifted a hand, his tone harsh. "In the morning. We aren't as young and resilient as you." He limped across the stable and up the steps to the interior door.

Cala put a kind hand on his arm. "Don't worry about him. He's always grumpy when his leg is hurting. I'm sure it will be better on the morrow." She patted him gently. "Good night."

Nevan closed the big doors, leaving the latch undone so the dragons could get out if they wished. Then he peeled off his still wet shirt and poked up the fire. His giant blood burned warmer than humans', but his dunking had definitely chilled him. The food had helped, but he needed some warmth before he sought his bed. That was the disadvantage of sleeping with a dragon. Unlike a dog or cat, dragons didn't provide any warmth.

Once he'd dried off and warmed up the room, he climbed over Starlight and snuggled under his blankets. He thought he'd stay awake for hours stewing over his coming conversation with William, but the warmth from the fire and the bed lulled him to sleep.

HE WOKE LATER THAN USUAL, AS THE SUN PEEKED ABOVE THE horizon. The big door stood ajar—the dragons could push it open but frequently didn't bother closing it, though they knew how. Nevan got the impression they didn't understand the need. And since three-quarters of the year the mild weather made an open door preferable, he hadn't worried about reinforcing that skill.

After dressing, he went out into the courtyard. Climbing over the low wall, he made his way along the narrow path between it and the sheer cliff. His first time walking out there had been terrifying, but he'd overcome that fear since Starlight loved to perch on the higher wall at the end. Normally, he'd go through the house and into the garden, but after Starlight's performance the previous night, he'd decided to avoid William as long as possible this morning. He didn't know if the older dragon rider was awake, but he wasn't going to chance running into him.

At the end of the point, he put his back to the stone wall surrounding the garden. The cliff dropped away on two sides here, leaving a little triangle of space. Starlight would land atop the wall by his head when she came back, but he didn't expect her until later in the morning. The dragons liked to fish early, then play in the sea with their wild siblings. He shaded his eyes, trying to pick out their three among the flock in the sea below.

Flock? Thunder? Pack? They still hadn't settled on words to define their endeavor. In Verduun, the guild was broken into fighting wings, which in turn were made up of squadrons. But with only three of them, the terms seemed pretentious. Maybe when they grew their numbers.

He let the crash of the surf far below his feet, the squawks of the gulls, and the whistle of the winter breeze calm his soul. Before he paired with Starlight, he'd never realized how soothing the sea could be.

The creak and thud of a door opening and closing brought him out of his reverie. "Nevan?" Cala called softly. "Are you out there?"

He thought about not answering, but they'd find him soon enough. Time to face the guild master. "Yes, ma'am. Coming."

Taking the slightly wider path on the left side of his perch, he came around the wall and ducked through the doorway into the garden. The wooden door shut behind him with a final-sounding thud.

Cala stood by the door into the kitchen, a sprig of herbs in her hand. "Come inside. William is making omelets."

Nevan froze, gaze darting to the windows. William only cooked if he was in a particularly good mood. "He is?"

Cala smiled and nodded. The tension drained out of Nevan, and he followed her into the room.

William stood at the stove with a towel tied around his waist. He held a cast iron pan in one hand and a flat metal utensil in the other. "Sprinkle them in."

Cala pulled the leaves from the sprigs and dropped them into the pan, tearing the larger ones into scraps. The fresh scent of the herbs mixed with the cooking eggs, sizzling butter, and rich tea steeping on the table. Nevan took the dishes Cala indicated and set them at three places.

He raised an extra plate. "Is someone joining us?"

"Koni will be here soon." William folded the omelet and slid it onto a platter, then sprinkled some crumbled cheese on top. "Grab the toast, will you?"

Nevan flipped the bread browning on the stove top onto a plate and set it beside the eggs. As Cala poured the tea, the front door opened.

"Hallo!" Koni breezed in, a cheerful smile on his face. "How are my favorite fire fighters? You are the talk of the town!"

"How would you know?" Cala indicated the empty chair with a tip of her head and took the largest tankard from the shelf. "The town is barely awake." She poured a generous portion of ale and handed it to the elf.

"It's late, my dear dragon rider!" Koni waved at the clock. "You forget sunrise is later this time of year. Most of the town is awake and discussing the tremendous feat you accomplished yesterday." He sat and picked up his napkin, dropping it into his lap with a flourish. "Especially Starlight's exceeding skill and speed."

William's iron gaze settled on Nevan as he took his seat. "Yes, that was... unexpected." He picked up his fork and snagged a piece of toast from the plate.

"Honey?" Koni produced a little brown crock and lifted the lid. "This one is from the vineyard." The elf kept bees in a wooden box, a trick he claimed to have learned in "another reality." Each box was placed in a different environment around the island—his vineyard, the village garden, the wildflower field, the berry bramble. The location seemed to imbue the honey with its own flavors through a mechanism Koni would explain at length given the opportunity.

Nevan had never managed to stay awake long enough to hear the whole thing, but the result was delicious. Avoiding William's gaze, he dunked his spoon into the crock and slathered some of the golden honey on his toasted bread.

They ate, the silence broken by the clink of cutlery against plates and the occasional muttered compliment or request. At the foot of the table, Koni drank deeply but ate little, a pleased smile playing across his face as he watched his friends.

William finished his meal. Leaning back in his chair, he picked up his tea and turned to Nevan.

The older dragon rider's gaze felt like a weight on Nevan's shoulders. The toast seemed to curdle in his stomach, and he pushed the remains of his meal away. With a deep breath, he straightened his spine and turned to meet William's eyes.

"Perhaps you'd care to explain what happened yesterday," William said, his gruff voice surprisingly gentle.

Nevan gulped. He'd expected anger and disappointment, not eggs and understanding. "I—I don't know." He didn't want to blame his dragon, but the truth was she hadn't followed his instructions. At all.

William sipped his tea. "I was too busy to watch, although I certainly noticed you coming straight at me on more than one occasion." He demonstrated, bringing his hand toward his face.

Koni unrolled a scroll he must have brought with him. "If I may." He pushed the dishes away from his end of the table, using some of them to hold the curled edges down, and Nevan recognized it as a type of map. Koni tapped one of the rectangles drawn in charcoal in the center of the scroll. "This is the tannery. That's the dairy barn. The pasture and the lake. This line is the flight path Nari and Finn followed." He tapped a large oblong drawn in a broken line, then shifted to a smaller, more circular one that overlapped. "This is Starlight's. Smaller, more passes, more efficient." He paused. "Never once dropping to the pond for water."

"How did you—" William put both hands on the arms of the chair and heaved himself to his feet, grunting with the movement. Shoving the chair away, he slowly circled the table to the far end, his eyes on the drawing. "Who made this?"

"I did." Koni grinned. "I answered the call for the bucket brigade, of course." He held up a hand, displaying the already healing blisters on his palm. "Once the dragons arrived, I decided my observations might be more useful than my continued bucket slinging. I sketched it out on the spot." He patted his chest, then spread his hands over the map with a flourish. "And enlarged and refined the results."

"Is this another of your 'alternate reality' schemes?" Nevan eyed the papers with suspicion.

"Not at all. Basic training techniques. I'm sure William is familiar with the practice." Koni raised a brow.

William nodded. "We had analysts who observed our training—and on occasion actual missions—who did something similar. They worked with sidelined riders—those whose mounts were injured—to refine training plans." He shifted the paper a little, dragging the honey pot across the table.

"We often had observers as well." Cala leaned her elbows on the table and peered at the drawing. "Improving tactics requires understanding successes *and* failures." She tapped Starlight's line. "This flight path offers a longer line of attack on the fire. But how could she —" Her hand shifted to the pond, smudging the charcoal a little.

"Exactly!" Koni flung out both hands. "How could she continue to spew water when she never refilled? Where did it come from? Is this something the other dragons could learn?"

"How do we find out?" William dropped into his chair again.

Koni's eyes sparkled as he turned his gaze on Nevan. "We ask her."

Nevan closed his eyes, trying to "hear" Starlight. "She's swimming right now. Not answering."

"Tell her to come back!" William's voice took on a commanding edge.

Cala put a hand on his arm. "It has become pretty obvious Starlight doesn't respond well to that kind of demand."

"She's a child. Literally." Koni chuckled and flung out both arms. "We've been so invested in the outcome, we haven't taken the time to appreciate how much we—and they—have accomplished in a very short period of time. How long does it take to train a war dragon, William?"

The older man rubbed his eyes. "Years. We don't start riding until six months after hatching. Then pairs spend months learning drills. Formation flying. Attack techniques. Trainees won't go to the front until they've been flying at least a year—and then only if they pass the trials and prove their abilities."

"A year and a half before operational deployment." Koni's lips twitched at their reactions to the unfamiliar words, but he went on.

"And yet our dragons are barely eight months old. Obviously, sea dragons differ from the war dragons, but they're literally just fledglings."

"They learned so much faster!" William took a turn around the room, his limp more pronounced than usual. "They were ready. I'd swear they were."

"Undoubtedly." Cala met him by the windows, putting a gentle hand on his arm. "We didn't push them too hard. Finn will confirm."

"Will he?" The question burst out before Nevan could stop it. He'd stayed quiet, hoping to avoid any blame. He and Starlight had started flying weeks before the others, but in secret. He hadn't encouraged the others to start. He hadn't even told them they'd been experimenting with flight. Starlight had been ready. He could feel it. How could William not realize that? And if he couldn't, how would Finn confirm it?

William's head came up. "Yes. And you're right. Finn was ready to carry me. He made that very clear." He stomped back to the table and dropped into his seat. "And I can't explain the 'how,' Nevan. I can feel it." He clenched his fist and tapped it against his heart.

Nevan smiled. "That's how I know too."

"Tower." Starlight's voice intruded on his mind.

Pushing his chair away from the table, Nevan rose slowly, his muscles complaining. "Starlight is on the tower. Let's go ask her."

The others followed even more slowly. Only Koni seemed to have his usual vigor, but he hadn't spent the previous day riding a sea dragon. The elf bounded ahead, reaching the top of the tower well before the rest of the group.

Nevan rounded the last curve, the small room at the top coming into view. Koni sat on the lowest rung of the ladder, peering at something in his hand. He slipped whatever it was into a pocket before Nevan got a good look and rose. "I'm never one hundred percent sure I should go up without one of you." He pointed at the trapdoor in the ceiling.

"You aren't afraid of the dragons," Nevan said with certainty as he climbed the ladder.

"No, of course not. But I'm not one of you. And the bond between a dragon and their rider is magic. I don't like to interfere with magic I don't understand."

As Nevan shoved the door open, he glanced down at the elf in confusion. "As long as you don't cast random spells up here—" The wood banged against the stone roof like a gong.

Koni waved a hand and started up the ladder behind him. "Of course not. But elves *are* magic. Well, all beings are magic. We each exude a little just by existing. But elves emit more."

Nevan climbed out onto the roof, startled to see all three dragons perched on the rail, facing inward, their tails hanging over the side. Their bodies blocked much of the stiff breeze. "That's new." He stepped closer to Starlight, sliding a hand up her neck. "Hello, friend."

She nuzzled his neck and head, ruffling his hair, but didn't say anything. Nevan thought speech was still difficult for her, and unnecessary most of the time. Unlike many humans—and orcs, dwarves, giants, and especially elves—she didn't seem to feel the need to fill silence with chatter. He appreciated that about his dragon. He hoped it lasted once she became fluent.

Koni popped out of the open hatch as if launched, landing lightly beside Nevan. He turned back to help Cala up the ladder.

"—not sure I want to think about exuding anything," the witch said as she ducked past Nevan to stand by her dragon. "It sounds so... unsanitary."

Koni laughed. "We can use a different word. Expel, discharge, excrete. Eject, spew, disgorge—"

"Enough!" Cala flung up a hand. "The academy taught us everything vibrates at a unique rate. And the vibrations are stronger in those with magic. It's one of the excuses the instructors used to explain why we couldn't learn other races' magic. Elven vibrations interfere with human vibrations. We've already proven that belief wrong." She shrugged and looked up at Nari. "And I don't think your elven vibrations will interfere with the dragons."

"I appreciate the sign of respect, however." William finally joined them on the roof, his bad leg making the climb slower and more painful, despite his magic prosthetic. "Something we encouraged at the guild. Non-riders wouldn't dream of approaching a dragon without explicit permission from the rider."

"That explains why you didn't like Franisa's children chatting with the dragons." Cala laughed sympathetically and touched her husband's arm.

He glowered, perhaps a little more theatrically than he really felt, then turned to face Nevan. "Now that you've convened this meeting, let's get on with it."

"Me? I—" Nevan gulped. He looked away from the man's intense stare. "I didn't—"

William raised a brow then tipped his head at Starlight.

"Right." With the hatch open in the center of the tower and the dragons perched along the outside, the space felt almost claustrophobic. He looked up at the open sky, drew in a breath of salty sea air, and turned to face his dragon. "How did you do it?"

"Magic." Starlight lifted and dropped her furled wings in a draconic shrug.

Stiffening his spine, he turned to face William. "She says it's magic."

William growled, then blew out a breath. "Magic. She just... magicked up a continuous stream of water. Out of nowhere."

"It wasn't continuous—"

Starlight puffed out a cloud of vapor right into William's face. The man gasped, mist glistening on his cheeks and in his short beard.

Nevan cringed. "Starlight!"

"Magic." The dragon turned her long neck and spewed a stream of water away from the tower.

"That proves nothing." William angrily blotted his face with his sleeve. "Nevan said you were just swimming."

She turned back to look at the guild master, blowing a little spurt of water at him this time. It hit his nose, dripping down to the roof. *"Magic."*

William growled louder, wiping the water from his face.

Starlight tipped her head back, spitting upward. They all watched, transfixed, as a little plug of water sparkled in the sunlight, reached its zenith, then curved back toward the ground. William lurched to the side as the water splashed onto the stone roof right where he'd been standing, wetting his boots and pantlegs.

As the man drew breath to speak, Starlight blew another stream over them, waving her head back and forth to create a mesmerizing arc of water. William's jaw snapped shut, as he stared, transfixed by the display. The dragon continued spitting water for much longer than should have been possible.

Starlight stopped, the water falling around the tower. Her head swung to make eye contact with her siblings. Then the other two dragons joined in, streams rising and falling around them.

Koni turned slowly, arms outstretched, laughing as the dragon mist dampened his clothing. "Incredible! An endless supply of water." He rubbed his fingers together, then sniffed them and tasted. "Sea water."

William swung around to face the elf, stabbing a finger at him. "Do you think that's—we were using water from the pond. *Drinking* water for the herd."

Cala put a hand to her forehead. "Sea dragons. Sea water! Why didn't we realize—"

"They drink fresh water," Nevan put in. "It wasn't a crazy idea." He stared proudly up at his partner. All three dragons had extended their necks to full length as they continued to spray water into the air.

Then, as one, they wheeled away and dropped off the side of the tower. The dragon riders and elf all gasped, rushing to the low rail. The three dragons curved around the tower, arrowing towards the sea below. Starlight dove in, followed by Nari and Finn. They disappeared under the gentle swells for a long moment, then surfaced far from shore.

"That's what Starlight did yesterday. She dove in. Like she had to get completely immersed. She was insistent." Nevan put a hand to his waist. "I couldn't get the belt off fast enough."

Koni stroked his chin. "Maybe their magic allows them to pull water from the sea, but they need to reconnect after? How long did they stay in the water yesterday?"

"A few hours?" Nevan shrugged. "Long enough for us to go to the pub and eat dinner. But they could have been fishing."

"That's not fishing." William pointed at the three dragons who had spread out, their wings lying flat on the surface, like a child floating on the surf. "I think Koni is right. They're connecting."

"Or soaking up more sea water?" Cala shaded her eyes. "Like a sponge, after it's been wrung out?"

Koni snapped his fingers and pointed at Cala. "Exactly." He turned to look at each of the dragon riders. "We need to find out how much water they can shoot and how long they need to recover."

CHAPTER NINETEEN

The morning after the fire, Franisa woke late. She pulled on her dress, calling to the children, then hurried down the stairs. Thanks to the blaze, she hadn't gotten the butter and milk she needed for today's sweet rolls. She'd have to focus on plain bread today and hope none of her regulars were disappointed enough to make the trek to Valebra.

When she reached the kitchen, she found the firewood cubby completely filled, the stove burning hot and bright, and Eloise perched on a chair, her arms elbow deep in very sticky dough. Aislin fluttered around her, shooting little blasts of pixie dust at the girl's arms and the table beneath, attempting to keep up with the mess.

"Mama! We's helping!" Eloise pulled sticky fingers from the bowl and plunged them in again, managing a credible imitation of her mother's mixing technique.

"*We're* helping. I think you might have a bit too much liquid in there." Franisa hurriedly tied on her apron and reached for the flour, considering, not for the first time, the impact the pixie had on Eloise's grammar. "What did you put in?"

Eloise tapped her dough-covered finger against her chin, leaving a sticky blob on her face. "Starter, flour, sugar, butter, milk..."

"Where did you get butter and milk?" Franisa turned to take in the kitchen. Two heavy crocks sat on the floor beside the chair. She bent down to lift the smaller one. A big knob of butter filled the little jar. A ladle protruded from the top of the larger one—milk with a thick layer of cream on top. "How?"

Enrich pulled aside the curtain leading to the shop. "Goodwife Skorra came early this morning." He showed her a scrap of brown paper with heavy black lettering.

She took it and smoothed the wrinkles, her finger tracing along the lines of words. "Grat... Milk. Eggs." With an exasperated sigh, she snapped the paper at Enrich. "Read it. I can't—I don't know all the words."

"It says, 'In gratitude to the family of the dragon riders. You saved our home. We pledge milk, eggs, and butter for a year.' They're giving us free stuff!" Enrich laughed, brandishing the paper.

"That's for Nevan, not for us!" Her face burned at the thought of being part of his family. "It should go to the smithy."

"He's going to be our daddy." Eloise nodded decisively as she continued mixing her sticky dough. "He can take some for the dragon den too. Do dragons eat milk an' butter?"

"I don't know, Pumpkin. I suspect we'll find out."

~

AFTER PREPARING MORE DOUGH—ELOISE'S ATTEMPT KNEADED into a surprisingly nice batch—she got the children off to school. With her late start, she was a bit behind her normal schedule but managed to get the first loaves out of the oven as the church bells tolled nine. A few villagers clustered outside the door when she opened it.

"I'm sorry I'm late." She held the door wide, then flipped the little sign to "open." Yrsadra Skorra, Mavila Hidehand, and Goodwife Wrenright marched into the building with cheerful greetings. Franisa let the door swing shut and hurried around them to the counter.

Mavila, the tanner's wife, waved a hand. "We're all a bit off schedule this morning. I came to pledge support for the dragon riders."

Franisa frowned at the woman then looked at the dairy farmer behind her. "Yrsadra already brought milk and—"

"That was nothing," the little goblin woman said. "The least we could do. There will be more."

"But I didn't do anything—"

"Your man saved the tannery." Mavila gestured to her companion. "And the dairy barn. Without the dragons, our homes would be completely gone. We want to make sure they continue this valuable work, so we're pledging support."

"But that support should go to the dragon riders." Franisa wrung her hands. "I can pass the goods on to them, of course."

"We discussed it." Mavila tipped her head at the others. "The tannery—when we're back in business—will provide all the dragons need for harnesses, belts, boots even. Anything leather, it's theirs."

"That's very generous of you. On behalf of the dragon riders, I thank you. But you need to speak with Sir William—"

"Goruk walked out to FarPoint this morning." Mavila dusted her hands together. "Now that's done. I'd like some rye bread, if you please."

Franisa opened her mouth, then caught a whiff from the oven. "In a minute. The bread is done!" She pushed aside the curtain and hurried into the back. Using her big wooden peel, she slid the hot, golden loaves out of the oven and onto the cooling rack. The one in the back was a bit overdone—she'd save that for the family. Slipping the next batch in took a moment, then she selected the prettiest of the new loaves, put it into the basket, and took it to the front.

"This is still hot." She set the basket on the counter. "If you'd like, I can have Enrich run it over after school. Or you can come back a little later. I'm so sorry. I was late getting started—"

Mavila lifted the loaf and set it into her own basket, then held up her hand, rough palm up. "Calluses. Heat doesn't bother me. It'll cool fast enough on the walk home." She turned to the other women. "Are you getting bread?"

Franisa got another hot loaf for Yrsadra. "I'll have sweet rolls in a bit."

With a smile, the plump dairy farmer patted her stomach. "Maybe tomorrow. How much do I owe you?"

Frowning in confusion, Franisa shook her head. "Nothing. You gave me the butter and—"

"That's not how this works," Mavila said firmly. "Our goods are for the dragon guild. Not in trade for your bread. We'll pay for this." She pulled some coins out of her pocket and slapped them on the counter. "Two different transactions."

Yrsadra nodded in agreement and put her own coins down.

"But you just lost your home—"

"No, your man just *saved* our home. We have some rebuilding to do, but most of our belongings are undamaged." Mavila shrugged. "Or a little damp. And we have a tidy sum saved up over the years. We can give coin to the dragon guild, if that's preferable. But we will support them. And we'll pay for our bread." Mavila swung around and swept out of the bakery with Yrsadra in her wake.

Left standing alone in front of the counter, Goodwife Wrenright lifted a hand. "I'd like a sweet roll."

The morning passed quickly, with her usual brisk business. By noon, most of the fresh bread and a good number of the late sea shell rolls had been sold. Franisa layered a slice of cheese on a chunk of the over-browned loaf for lunch, then tidied up. Time for another trip out to FarPoint. She wasn't going to run her bakery on the charity of others, even if her supposed betrothed had saved the town.

She packed a few of the remaining rolls into her basket, wrapped her shawl around her shoulders, and headed out. The walk took much longer without Koni's escort. If this phony betrothal meant regular trips to the tower, she'd have to figure out a better means of getting there. A brief vision of flying with Nevan on Starlight appeared in her mind, a flush of excitement taking her breath away. Then she shook her head. Dragon riding was for the young.

With a little snort, she recognized the ridiculousness of that idea. Both Cala and William had several decades on her, so clearly youth wasn't the defining characteristic. Maybe it was better to say dragon riding was for the brave. Her one visit to the hatching cavern had solidified in her mind that she'd never be among their number. The big creatures with their leathery hides, translucent wings, and many teeth made her tremble with a fear that must harken back to her ancestors.

An hour later, she emerged from the forest. As the trees thinned, the path continued up the rise and across the rocky promontory toward FarPoint tower. The sea crashed unseen on the sandy beach below the point, and sea birds wheeled through the pale blue sky. One of the dragons sat atop the tall tower, watching the sea. The two-story cottage came into view as she continued to climb, its whitewashed walls bright between dark beams. The scent of the sea mixed with wood smoke from the home's chimneys.

The dragon on the tower bugled, and a moment later the front door opened. Cala stepped out onto the shaded stoop, looking around. She spotted Franisa and waved. The witch disappeared into the building, then returned a moment later, bundling a wrap around her shoulders as she hurried toward her guest.

"I'm sorry I wasn't at the bakery this morning—" Cala paused at the top of the crest, waiting for her friend to meet her.

"Don't be silly. You said you weren't coming." Franisa handed the basket to Cala. "I will let you carry that, though. The walk out here is longer than I remembered."

Peeking under the cloth covering the basket, Cala smiled as she turned back toward the house. "The boys will be grateful!"

"The boys?" Franisa quickened her steps to keep up with the taller woman. "You don't usually call William that, do you?"

Cala laughed. "No. I'm referring to Koni and Nevan, of course. If I'd known you were coming, I would have asked Koni to bring you on the elven route."

"The exercise is good for me." Franisa put a hand to her chest. "Even if my body doesn't agree right now. That hill is steep." She paused and turned to look back toward the town. From the top of the rise, she couldn't see even the point of the church steeple.

"It is. Why do you think I waited up here for you?" Cala chuckled again as they walked to the house. She led the way up the steps and opened the door. "Come in. The draconic council is in session."

Franisa froze, her shawl in her hands. She hadn't heard about a council. "I don't want to interrupt—"

"Nonsense." Cala took the wrap and hung it on a peg next to her own beside the door. Then she beckoned her friend into the kitchen. "It's just William and the boys."

With a scraping of chair legs, William and Koni rose, Nevan lurching up a moment later, his cheeks going pink. He met her gaze, then ducked his head and looked at the table.

Koni made one of his elegant bows. "Who are you calling 'the boys,' Cala? I'm at least a decade older than you."

"But you behave more like Nevan." Cala set the basket on the table and whisked the towel away. "And I suspect you're still a child in elven accounting."

Koni drew himself up in faux indignation. "I assure you I am a fully grown elf. And Nevan here is a fully grown giant. We are men, not boys." His eyes twinkled. "That doesn't mean we always have to act like adults."

Nevan glanced up again, his cheeks even redder. "My ma often says I'm half-grown."

"She's referring to your size, not your maturity." William dropped back into his seat with a little grunt. He rubbed his leg absently, looking up at his much larger friend. "And you're plenty grown from my perspective."

Somehow, Koni had managed to get one of the sweet rolls out of the basket and onto a plate without anyone noticing. He pulled a section of the rolled bread away, releasing the cinnamon and cardamom like a sweet breeze.

Cala looked at the stack of plates in her hand, then at Koni's place. Shaking her head, she set the remaining dishes in front of her friends and took her seat. Koni smiled gently.

"Franisa, sit. Have some tea." Cala poured a cup and handed it to Nevan, who set it in front of the seat next to him.

"I—I don't want to intrude." Franisa gripped the top rung of the ladder-back chair she stood behind and waited for their denials to die. "But I need to—the Skorras brought me eggs and milk. For you." She pointed at Nevan. Realizing her finger looked accusing, she waved it limply at the others then shoved it behind her back.

William sipped his tea. "What seems to be the problem?"

"It's for the dragon riders. You saved the tannery and the dairy. But they think it's helping Nevan to give it to me." Her cheeks went hot, and she focused on William, so she could ignore Nevan across the table from him.

"Yes, well, we probably need to discuss an accounting system." William gestured to the seat beside Nevan. "Please, sit down. This could take some time to negotiate."

Nevan pulled the chair away from the table. With a sigh, Franisa let go of the one she'd been clutching and went to sit next to him. His hesitant smile sent a sweet little arrow of something through her chest. Ignoring it, she turned to William, grateful for a topic to focus on.

"Yes, an accounting system. I understand they want to support you, and they think they're doing so by giving things to me. Since you probably don't use as much butter and eggs as I do, it makes sense for them to provide that to me rather than you. I can pass that on in the form of finished bakery goods. But you don't eat that much." She gestured at the empty basket. "Except maybe Lord Koni."

Her cheeks went hot again. Somehow, the statement had popped out of her mouth without thought. She had always viewed the mayor as a being of exalted stature, and the idea of poking fun at him terrified her. But he behaved so much like Enrich sometimes, the inhibition seemed to have worn off. She clasped a hand over her mouth.

The elf laughed as if her sass delighted him. "So true."

William frowned at the elf and turned his attention back to Franisa. "When we started this venture, we didn't really think about sustainability. You, as a businesswoman, probably have a better grasp on how this needs to work than any of us. Our esteemed mayor being the possible exception." His thick brows came down, and he cast a dark glance at Koni again.

"I am a terrible businessman." Koni spread both hands cheerfully. "Just ask my wife. It's why I went into politics."

Shaking his head with mock disgust, William tapped a sheet of paper Franisa hadn't noticed before. "We were just trying to work out how we could run this fire brigade in a fair way yet still provide for ourselves. When I came to Safe Haven, I had saved enough coin to live out the rest of my life in comfort. Or so I thought. That was before I knew how much repair the place required. And before I started this." He waved at the people sitting around the table.

"In Verduun, the crown pays for the operation of the dragon guild, of course. And they tax the citizens to provide that and other necessary services." His glower became real. "And several unnecessary ones."

"It's the same in the Borgonne." Cala put a hand on her husband's arm and he visibly relaxed. "Not for dragons, of course, but to fund the academy. And the army, which paid and fed us."

"I guess we need a tax." Koni sighed. "And for that we'll need to hold a vote."

Cala and William both frowned at the elf. "A vote?"

"The people of Safe Haven elect their leaders." Koni gestured to himself. "And they decide what the government will provide. Through a vote."

The two older humans exchanged an amazed look. Koni's lips twisted and Nevan smirked.

"You let the people decide?" Cala asked the question as if tasting each word. "Normal, everyday people?"

"That we do." Koni slapped the table with both hands. "It wasn't always this way, but when they asked me to organize things around here..." He swirled his fingers in a circle, then he shrugged. "I've seen how it's done in other places, and I wanted people—normal, everyday people—to have control. It's messy, but it works. And people are happier."

"Well, then." Franisa pushed her chair back a little. "If we vote on a tax, everyone can support the dragon guild that way, and I don't have to worry about accepting donations on your behalf." While a tax might strain her coffers a bit, she knew the guild deserved to be supported by the entire town.

"It will take a bit of time to set up." Koni pulled at his lower lip. "And a bit of explaining to get enough people on board. They'll need to understand the importance of the guild—is that what we're calling it? The dragon guild? Because there are a few folks who might object to that name." He raised a brow at Nevan.

"Because we call it that in Verduun?" William folded his arms. "It's an honorable name."

Cala smirked. "The Verduun dragon guild isn't as highly regarded everywhere as you seem to think." She pointed at herself.

William waved this off. "You're the only person from the Borgonne. Everyone else loves the—"

Nevan cleared his throat.

The former guild master looked at his young friend in surprise. "Really?"

"My family is from Verduun." Nevan lifted a defensive shoulder. "The dragon guild isn't—my family weren't fans. And now that Pierr is there..."

"That's right. Your brother joined the Verduunian army. Definitely not a career move I would have encouraged had I been here before he left." William drummed his fingers on his chair arm. "I suppose giants probably don't like anything associated with the Verduunian government. And I can't say I disagree since Astorov came to the throne."

Koni slapped the table again and jumped to his feet. "It's decided, then. We need a new name. And then we'll hold a vote on the tax."

"But what about the butter and eggs?" Franisa tried to keep her tone even. She'd walked all the way out here to decide this issue, and she wasn't going to let the mayor and the guild master overrule her. "I can't keep taking those gifts if they're meant for you."

"This betrothal is really muddying the waters." Koni sat back down. "Maybe we should make it official."

CHAPTER TWENTY

Nevan's vision went dark, like a cave closing in around him. He drew in a deep breath, trying to ground himself. Koni wanted him and Franisa to formalize their betrothal with a handfasting. The idea both thrilled and terrified him. He'd gladly marry Franisa, if that's what she wanted. But what if she preferred to be alone? Or worse, she wanted someone else. Like that carpenter.

Koni burst out laughing. "You two should see your faces!" He slapped the table again then flung himself back in his chair, overwhelmed with mirth.

Nevan stole a look at Franisa. Her cheeks were red, and her eyes were closed. Was the idea of marrying him so repugnant to her? He drew in another deep breath and looked away.

"Koni, stop." Cala smacked a hand into the elf's arm, then poked a finger at him. "This kind of disregard for the feelings of normal people is what gives elves their bad reputation."

Koni sobered at once. "I deeply and humbly apologize for my joke. Please don't lump me in with other elves. I thought we were friends. Human friends tease each other."

"*We* are friends." Cala swung her finger at herself then back to him and dropped her hand. "But Franisa and Nevan aren't as comfortable with you as William and I are. It takes most humans a while to adjust to your lofty stature and view you as 'one of us.' They'll get there."

Koni caught Nevan's eye, then looked at Franisa. "I'm sorry. There's no reason for you to get married if you don't want to. As I said before, the betrothal should be enough. Gnollis has stopped taking Enrich from school, has he not?"

Franisa nodded. "Yes. As soon as Nevan—" Her cheeks reddened as she said his name. "As soon as I told him about the betrothal, he washed his hands of us."

Koni raised a brow. "Forgive me, but was he providing other support? Does this arrangement place you in need?"

"What? No. He's done nothing for us since Keldan died. Until he demanded Enrich learn the trade." She lifted both hands. "If I had been able to come up with a way to leave the clan, I would have."

"Well, you have now." Koni tapped the paper by William's place. "And if you won't simply accept the tithe from the dairy, we'd best work out an equitable accounting system until we can get the taxes in place."

Nevan pushed back his chair. "Do you mind if I skip all of this? Numbers were never my thing, and I trust all of you to work out the details." Besides, it would undoubtedly be easier for Franisa to discuss all of this without him present, but he didn't like to say that aloud.

When the others agreed, he went through the stable to get his jacket and headed outside. Starlight came in response to his whistle, landing on the low wall in the courtyard.

"Name," Starlight said.

Nevan couldn't tell if she was actually saying the words or simply putting the ideas in his mind which then translated them to words. In the long run, it didn't matter as long as they could communicate. "I should use your name instead of the whistle?"

"My name." Starlight jumped down into the courtyard and crouched low so Nevan could put her harness on.

"But if you're out playing in the sea, will you hear me?" He buckled the straps onto the rings, then put the whole thing around her body.

"Always hear Nevan." She wiggled with anticipation. He could feel

her desire to fly with her best friend, and her love and excitement soothed his soul. Maybe Franisa didn't want to marry him, but he'd always have Starlight.

THAT EVENING, NEVAN FLEW INTO TOWN TO SEE HIS FAMILY. At least that's what he told himself. The trip had nothing to do with checking on Franisa. But when Starlight landed in the field beyond the stables, he took the long way around, coming up the lane to the square to enter the smithy through the front instead of the back.

He paused in the square to look at the bakery. The windows of the lower floor were dark, but faint light shone in the uppers. It looked as if an open door allowed light from another room to shine through. He watched for a few minutes, but no one came into view. With a sigh, he turned to the smithy, opening the smaller, yet still giant-sized, entry cut into the huge front doors.

Banked coals burned in the forge, not casting enough light to pick his way around the equipment. He pulled out the magic stone Cala had empowered for him, the little pebble shining bright in the darkness, and made his way through the big building. Beside the back door, a stairway led to the upper floor. He opened the door quietly and climbed, stepping over the creaky second-from-the-top step out of habit. Another door at the top led to the living quarters.

He knocked gently against the wood as he opened it. "Oravai!"

"Nevan!" His mother jumped and turned away from the aromatic pot she had been stirring on the stove. "What are you doing here? Did you come for supper?" She hurried across the living space to embrace him.

Lilabeth Smith was a full giant. She stood well over eight feet tall, and when she embraced Nevan, it took him back to his childhood. He didn't remember his birth mother—Lilabeth had always been the safe haven in his life, even before they'd moved to the island of the same name.

She pulled back to look at him and shook his shoulders before she released him. "What's this I hear of a betrothal?"

Heat flooded Nevan's face. When he'd agreed to continue the charade, he hadn't considered how his parents might take the news. Somehow, the idea that they'd learn of it hadn't crossed his mind. He tried to think of something—anything—to say.

"Aye. I heard the story as well." Nevan's father, Derwin, walked into the room, the dishes rattling on the dresser in response to his heavy footsteps. Although giants generally weighed much less than humans seemed to expect, his father managed to shake the floor every time he entered a room.

"It's... complicated." Nevan stepped away from his mother and turned to clasp forearms with his father.

"What's complicated about it? You see someone you want, you marry them. That's what I did with yer ma." Derwin slid closer to Lilabeth and squeezed her rear end.

"Get on with ya!" Lilabeth smacked Derwin's hand with her wooden spoon and went back to her stove. "Bring your lady to supper. We have plenty."

"She has... obligations." Nevan bit his lip.

"Do you think we don't know who she is?" Derwin pulled a chair from the table and dropped into it. The wood creaked. "She lives across the square. Why you thought you'd be able to keep it from us—"

"Why did you want to?" Lilabeth sprinkled something into the pot and stirred again. "You should be proud to be handfasted to that one. She's a strong woman. Very strong for a human." Chuckling a bit, she lifted the spoon out of the pot, blew on it, then tasted. "More pepper."

She placed a big, red-skinned pepper on the wooden block beside the stove and cut off the end with her wicked-looking knife. As she chopped, she looked over her shoulder at Nevan. "You're young to be the father of a boy as old as Enrich, but you're a good example for a young man. Strong, capable, stable. And that little Eloise—she's a charmer! You'll have more children, of course. Franisa isn't past bearing yet."

"Ma, watch your knife." Cheeks burning, Nevan pointed at her hands. It made him nervous when she didn't look at her work, but that wasn't the only reason he tried to distract her.

Lilabeth laughed. "Haven't cut myself yet, boy. Your father made this knife. It isn't going to hurt me."

"It's not magic."

"It's about knowing where your hands are." She laughed again and turned back to her chopping. "Make yourself useful. There's some bread in the box. Now that you're marrying the baker, can we expect fresh bread every day?"

"I can't promise that, Ma. The bakery is her livelihood." He took a half loaf of hearty bread from the box on the dresser and handed it to his mother.

"Once you're married, you'll help provide for her." Lilabeth scraped the chopped pepper into the pot, then put the bread in its place on the maple block. She set the chopping knife aside and took a longer, slender one from the slot in the back.

"How do you plan to do that, boy?" Derwin squinted across the table at him. "Is that dragon rider paying you?"

Nevan squirmed under his father's glare. "Not yet. We're still in training. Once the fire brigade is up and running, the town will provide for us."

Derwin eyed him, one brow raised. "You going to live at the dragon farm or the bakery?"

"I—we haven't discussed that yet, Da. And it's a dragon den, not a farm." He frowned at the ceiling. "Although I don't quite like 'den.' It sounds too… land-based."

Downstairs a door slammed, then heavy footsteps pounded up the steps. Gebhard burst into the room, an envelope clutched in his hand. "Ma, Da! We got a letter!"

Lilabeth dropped her spoon into the pot, splashing gravy that hissed on the hot stove, and hurried across the room. "From Pierr?"

"You know anyone else who sends us letters from Verduun?" Gebhard brandished the letter, holding it above his head, the thick paper brushing the ceiling. "Hey, look! My little brother is here!"

Lilabeth smacked a hand into Gebhard's stomach, hard enough to make him double over. “Give me that.” She snatched the letter from his hand and dropped into a chair by the table. “And show your *eldest* brother some respect.”

Nevan smothered a laugh. Some things never changed.

“Nevan, bring the lamp.” Lilabeth pried the wax seal up with her fingernail and opened the rough envelope.

Nevan took the lamp from its stand beside the stove and carried it to the table. He stood behind his mother, so the light fell on Pierr’s messy handwriting. He followed along over her shoulder as she read aloud.

Dear Family,

Greetings from Perthan. The weather here is much like the rest of Verduun—hot and sticky. The sun shines every day, and the locals complain of the drought, but it don’t feel dry to me. Rumor says the Borgonne war witches are pulling the clouds away to drop floods on the deserts to the east, but I haven’t been there yet.

I haven’t seen any dragons in weeks. They must be deployed elsewhere. Without them harrying the B army, we’ve been busy collecting rocks for the catapults and digging trenches as we advance. No one tells us what’s going on, of course, but I hear stories from the injured. They don’t allow giants in the medical tents, but I’ve made friends with a healer. She tells me bits and pieces when I help her move the injured and dead.

Giants can’t learn to read here, so I don’t have access to the post. I’m hoping my friend will send it for me. And if you write back, you can send it to her.

Healer Hawthorne

Black Lantern Brigade

Verduun

I miss you all. The adventure continues!

Pierr

Lilabeth sniffed and blotted a tear with the back of her hand. “That stupid boy. Does he think we can’t read between the lines? We were there!”

As Nevan returned the lamp to its stand, Derwin rose and came around the table to grip his wife's shoulder. "The young have to learn their own lessons. At least he's found a friend."

"You think that's all she is? Or is this a repeat of you and—" She broke off, glancing over her shoulder at Nevan.

"A repeat?" Nevan moved closer. His parents rarely spoke of their lives in Verduun. "Was my mother a healer?"

Derwin dropped into the empty seat beside Lilabeth but didn't answer.

"Da. Was she?"

"You should tell him, Derwin." Lilabeth smoothed the paper in her lap. "If Pierr is following the same path..."

Derwin heaved a sigh. "I tried to tell him not to go. Verduun treats giants so poorly. But he insisted. Never would listen to reason, that boy." He glared into the distance for a long moment. Finally, he heaved another sigh. "Serve the meal, and I'll tell the tale."

Nevan carried the steaming pot to the table while Gebhard placed the bowls and Lilabeth brought the bread. Gebhard poured ale for the four of them, and their father said the blessing. They dug into the stew, muttering compliments to Lilabeth as they ate.

After a while, Derwin pushed his empty bowl away and crossed his arms, his head down. "Orlaith—your mother—was the daughter of a Verduunian officer. He wanted her to marry a noble or merchant, but she wasn't interested. She convinced him to let her study healing. When she'd finished her studies, she took an assignment with the army. I never understood how that came about. Someone with higher rank must have taken a liking to her and overruled her father. He was not pleased.

"She was assigned to the headquarters—near the dragon guild. There's no way her father would let her anywhere near the front lines. She treated those who had been badly hurt but not killed. Men who survived but would be leaving the army. People like Sir William, who had lost a limb. She worked with the magical healers, but she had no magic herself. In Verduun, the only place to learn magic is the healer's college."

When Nevan nodded, Derwin lifted his tankard and finished off his ale. Lilabeth rose quietly and poured some more, then began clearing the table. Nevan sat across from his father, transfixed. He'd never known more than that Orlaith was human.

"There was a ceasefire. They happened often enough in those days. A few days and someone would break it, and we'd be back to war. But this one actually took. The army used the peace to rearrange things. Move units around. I was with the Skyforge Wing. When I wasn't working with the smith, I hauled things for the dragon riders. When they went back to the guild house, some of us were detailed to move their belongings. That's how I ended up in the capital city."

He sighed and stared at nothing for a while. "I helped an injured dragon rider... what was his name? Haveren? Haver-something. Doesn't matter. He was done flying. His dragon was hurt, bad enough he couldn't carry a rider no more. And he lost his arm from here down." He pointed at his elbow. "I brought his gear to his room in the healer college, and there she was."

Derwin picked up his tankard again but didn't drink. "She was beautiful, your mother was. Long, dark hair. Bright green eyes. Like yours. A big, strong girl, for a human. Came up to here." He gestured at his own sternum, then drank.

"We became friends. More than friends, very quickly. When the ceasefire ended, we found a priest and were handfasted. Like I said, you see someone you want, you marry them. Before they change their mind. Or their father objects. She came to the front with me. Her father hated me, of course. Refused to acknowledge our union. Wasn't much he could do once you came along. So he disowned her." He laughed bitterly.

"We didn't care. We were in love, and we had a baby on the way. Learent, the smith, taught me the trade, and I was able to earn extra coin doing work for villagers along the march. Fix a wagon trace here, shoe a horse there. As far as the army was concerned, I was still part of the giants' pack, of course. Hauling heavy stuff. That's what we did."

"You were a few months old when Orlaith was killed. She was treating a soldier too close to the front, and—" He broke off, gritting his teeth and breathing deeply. "Gone, in an instant. And I was left with a baby." Derwin looked over his shoulder at Lilabeth, quietly washing the dishes. "Your ma saved us. She took care of you, got you adopted into the giant clan, despite your human ma. And when I gathered the funds to move us to Safe Haven, she came with us."

"You never told me." Nevan sat across from his father, staring. How had he never heard this story before?

"Never asked."

"I thought you didn't want to talk about it. About her." Nevan darted a nervous look at his stepmother's back as she placed the last plate in the draining rack above the sink. "I have a mother. I didn't think asking about the first one was right."

Drying her hands, Lilabeth came to stand behind Derwin. She gripped his shoulder and squeezed gently. "I never met her, but Orlaith must have been an extraordinary human. My clan said she treated all soldiers, regardless of race, with equality and dignity. She healed humans, giants, dwarves. It didn't matter to her. When she was killed, we—the giant community—knew her son would need protection. I didn't have a family, so I volunteered to take him. You. I found the family I needed." She smiled down at Derwin and squeezed his shoulder again. Quick as a snake, her hand snapped out, and she slapped Gebhard's arm with a teasing laugh. "And the family I didn't need showed up on their own."

"You must be talking about Pierr. I'm a blessing. Everyone says so." Gebhard puffed out his chest. "And a much better apprentice than that little runt." He thrust his chin at his half-brother.

Nevan chuckled, hearing the affection in his brother's voice. He responded in kind. "You are correct. My petite frame is better suited to riding a dragon than dragging buckets of water around."

CHAPTER TWENTY-ONE

Once the children had gone to bed, Franisa had a few hours to herself. Not that she didn't get plenty of time alone—except when Cala came to help, she did most of the baking on her own. But that time was active, her mind focused on her work. In the evenings, she had time to think. And that wasn't always pleasant.

She sat by the stove, darning one of Eloise's socks. The oil lamp flickered. Along with yesterday's aborted visit to the dairy, the fire had distracted her from her regular shopping. She'd meant to get more oil at the mercantile. With a sigh, she put the sock aside, lit a candle, then blew out the guttering lamp.

With the wavering flame casting weird shadows across the wall, she crept down to the bakery. She'd double-check her supplies and prepare a shopping list for the next afternoon so she wouldn't forget anything else. The strange events of the past few days had distracted her from the routine of the bakery, and she craved a return to normalcy.

At least the discussions at FarPoint had gone well. She would continue to provide bread and sweet rolls to the dragon riders, along with a portion of the eggs, milk, and butter from the dairy. And she'd pay a small amount to William to keep the balance even. It still came out to her benefit, she feared, but once they had another class of dragon riders, the balance would shift, and it would even out in the long term.

She inventoried her supplies, marking her needs on the little slate Keldan had made for her so many years ago. She touched the paintings of a bag of flour, a canister of sugar, a jug of milk with a gentle finger. He'd been useless in the business end of the bakery, but he'd put his artistic skills to good use from time to time. She drew a mark next to the oil jar then moved to her spice cabinet.

A loud noise in the square startled her. She set the slate aside and ghosted through the curtain to the shop. Light from the gas lamp over the fountain cast a greenish glow through the thick window glass, lighting the shop enough to cross the room without stumbling. She peered through the clear pane in the door, grateful Keldan had convinced her to spend the extra coin for the more expensive glass.

Two hulking forms passed in front of the lamp, casting a heavy shadow across the door—giants. A deep voice rumbled, and Franisa pressed her ear to the window, trying to make out the words.

"—what Da said. You see someone you want, you marry her." The loud voice wasn't Nevan's, but similar—his younger brother.

She opened the door and stepped out into the cool night. "Gebhard. Is that you?" she hissed as she moved closer. "Keep your voice down, will you? The children are sleeping." She pointed up at the windows over the bakery.

"Look, there she is!" Gebhard's whisper could have woken the dead. "Go get her!"

"Gebby!" Nevan's low voice was slightly less slurred. The brothers had obviously imbibed a fair amount of ale. "Shut your trap. She's right there."

"Tha's what I said! Hallo, Franisa!" Gebhard waved and hollered.

"Gebhard Goodhammer, lower your voice at once!" Franisa marched up to the two men and shook a finger at them. "You're waking everyone in the square."

"'Snot *that* late. Where's the clock?" Gebhard swung around, peering upward, and lost his balance. He tilted precariously, and Nevan jammed his shoulder against his brother's chest, stopping his fall.

"The clock is in the church steeple, where it's always been." Franisa put a hand on the giant's arm and pushed. "You're drunk. Go sleep it off."

"I tried to tell him," Nevan said. "He insisted on walking me out." He turned to look up at his brother. "I'm out now. Go to bed."

Gebhard's big head turned from side to side, but in the darkness, she couldn't see his face. He laughed and pointed a finger at Nevan. "Ah ha! You want to be alone with her!" He slapped a hand on Nevan's back, sending him staggering into Franisa.

Instinctively, she stepped back and tripped over an uneven cobblestone. Nevan grabbed at her arms, trying to hold her up, but they both went down. She landed on her backside, with Nevan on top of her.

"Marry her, little brother!" Laughing like a maniac, Gebhard ambled away.

With Gebhard's head no longer blocking the light, Franisa looked up at Nevan. His body lay across hers, warm but surprisingly light. His hands slid along her arms, gentle as he gazed into her eyes.

In the past, she'd always viewed Nevan as a child. When they were growing up, he was the little boy who lived across the square. Later, after she'd married and taken on the bakery, he was the apprentice carrying water to his father's smithy. More recently, the young dragon rider who still had a crush on her.

But when she saw him flying with Starlight, heroically saving the tannery, something had shifted. He was a man protecting his town. And now, her betrothed, protecting her family. Protecting her. Their relationship had changed into something deeper, and she wasn't sure she was ready for it.

Their eyes held for a long moment, and her breath caught in her chest. Then he pushed to his feet with surprising agility. He reached a hand down, pulling her up, then released her and turned away, disappearing across the square in his brother's wake.

THE LITTLE BELL OVER THE BAKERY DOOR RANG. "JUST A minute!" The morning had been surprisingly busy, and Franisa had barely had a moment to breathe. Hands wrapped in her apron, she pulled a pan of sweet rolls from the big oven. She set the tray on the cooling rack, slid the last one into the oven, and closed the door.

Pushing aside the curtain, she stepped into the shop, stopping when she saw Nevan standing near the front door. He wore a long waxed-cotton coat and a brimmed hat similar to the one William usually sported. A fine mist beaded on the fabric.

He stared across the little shop for a long moment, his green eyes seeming to connect with something inside her chest. Then he looked away, pulling off his hat.

"Oravai, Nevan." Her voice came out a little raspy, and she cleared her throat. "Are you here for the tithe?"

"I, uh, I guess so? Cala told me to pick up something." He looked around the little room as if it might be hiding under a bench or shelf. "She didn't say what."

Franisa raised a finger. "Let me get it." She darted into the kitchen and returned with a basket covered by a cloth. "We decided I would send a loaf of bread, a selection of whatever sweets I baked, and some of the butter and eggs each day. I'm sorry you have to play delivery service." She set the heavy basket on the counter. She wasn't really sorry—his arrival had sent her heart into a happy quickstep.

"We don't mind." Nevan crossed the room, the brim of his hat crushed in his hand. "Starlight and I like flying. And it's good practice for us." He grinned. "We strafed a few buildings this morning."

"Strafed?"

"That's what William calls it. Flying over and spitting water—like we did at the tannery." He used his free hand to mime flying. "That's why I'm wet."

"You sprayed a building that wasn't burning?" She fiddled with the towel, tucking it securely around the bread.

"Sure. It's just water. We're trying to gauge how much Starlight can spit without needing to—" He raised his hand and pushed it down fast.

"That makes sense."

"I'd better go." He reached for the basket.

Strangely reluctant to let him leave, she hurriedly asked another question. "Did you fix the buckles? You need something that will release quickly. Like untying a bow." She turned and pulled the end of her apron string, watching him over her shoulder.

Nevan's gaze dropped to her lower back, and he drew in a deep breath, his face going red. Then he jerked his eyes away.

Franisa's cheeks burned, and she swung around. She hadn't intended to draw his attention to her backside. "I mean, obviously, you can't use a string."

"Right." His voice sounded rough. "My da can probably come up with something. Thanks for the reminder." He gripped the basket and turned away. At the door, he paused, not looking at her. "Sorry about last night. Gebby was drunk." He slunk out the door.

She stared after him. Did he regret their little moment last night? How much did he remember? Why did she care if he didn't? She crossed to the door, peering out the little window. Nevan crossed the square, disappearing into the smithy with his basket in hand.

Enough. She'd decided yesterday—before the incident in the square—that life needed to get back on schedule. Time to make that happen. She hung the little lunchtime sign in the window, barred the door, and went back to the kitchen. Wrapping her shawl about her shoulders, she took her shopping list and basket and headed out.

The mercantile sat at the end of the same square that held Cala's bookstore. Franisa took a deep breath—dealing with Goodwife Terman always set her on edge. But today was a new day and a new normal. She was a businesswoman like Terman—no reason she shouldn't expect the same respect she showed the older woman. With a decisive nod of her head, she opened the door and strode into the shop.

She took a metal tin of lamp oil from one of the lower shelves and put it into her basket. A card with some sewing needles went in next to it, and a bar of soap. Then she approached the counter at the back and rang the little bell.

Goodwife Terman stomped in from the back room. "You've interrupted my luncheon."

Franisa's heart quailed, but she raised her chin. "You should close for lunch if you don't want to be disturbed. I can have Enrich make you a sign like mine."

Terman gaped at her for a second, apparently unprepared for anyone to talk back to her. "I've never liked that practice. A shopkeeper should be available for their customers."

"Then I guess I didn't interrupt you after all." Franisa put her basket on the counter. "I'm a customer."

"Well, of all the nerve!" Terman looked around for an audience, but there was no one else in the shop.

Anger kindled in Franisa's chest. She was tired of this woman's insinuations and insults. Tired of being viewed as "less" because of her age or race or sex or whatever stupid excuse people made. She narrowed her eyes and took the items from her basket, dropping them on the counter. "If you prefer I take my custom elsewhere, I can. Valebra isn't so far if one has a dragon at their disposal." The words seemed to come from nowhere. How could she dare to speak so to the most formidable matron in the town? And to use her supposed relationship with Nevan in such a way?

Terman took a half step back, her gaze darting to the items on the counter. Her mouth opened and closed several times, then she pursed her lips and picked up the first item to check the price. "No need for that, Mistress Hearthwell. I'm happy to assist the wife of a dragon rider." She put the items back into the basket one by one and told Franisa the total.

Franisa set the coins in the finicky little tray Terman insisted everyone use and picked up her basket. "Thank you and good afternoon." With a little zing of smug pride in herself, she sailed out the door.

A gaggle of children swarmed into the square from the lane leading to the schoolhouse. Eloise skipped with a couple of other girls, singing as they headed for the bookstore. Enrich sauntered along with Koni's son Int and Romulus the butcher's son. The boys paused by the butcher shop, jostling each other and laughing.

Franisa stood in the shaded corner of the square, watching. In the last two days, Enrich had gone from sullen and quiet back to his former cheerful self. She had Nevan to thank for that. She'd never forget his willingness to stand by her.

Cala opened the front door of the bookshop and came out. After a quick conversation with the girls gathered on the step, she went back in and shut the door. The girls wandered over to the boys and held a huddled conversation.

Curious, Franisa crossed the square. "No story time today?"

"Mama!" Eloise called out cheerfully, hurrying to her side to take her hand.

Enrich glanced at her, his shoulders tense. Then he relaxed. "Mistress Cala said she can't today. Right, girls?"

Sala, Koni's daughter, dropped a graceful curtsey. "She said there's dragon business at the port." The girl's keen blue eyes seemed to challenge her. "My papa is already there."

"Ah." Franisa wasn't sure how to respond to the statement. "I'm sure we'll hear more about it from Nevan."

Romulus elbowed Enrich and said something in a low tone to the younger boy. Enrich darted a glance at his mother, then back at his friend. He shook his head. Sala's twin brother Int—or Intereph the Intrepid as he preferred to be called—smirked and swaggered forward, bowing to Franisa. "Oravai, Mistress Hearthwell. Romulus, Enrich, and I are going to join the other dragon riders at the port."

Franisa's eyes bulged, and she clamped her lips tight to hide a smile. Int sounded so much like his father, but the boy was only ten. "The *other* dragon riders?"

Int's confidence faltered. "Enrich is an apprentice dragon rider. He should be there." He pushed Enrich forward.

She raised her brows skeptically. Surely if Koni wanted her son there, he would have asked her. And she would have said no. Nine-year-olds weren't necessary for "dragon business." Not in her family. "Really? And you and Romulus are going because...?"

"For support," Romulus said shrilly.

"We're potential apprentice dragon riders?" Int's voice swung up on the end, turning his brave declaration into a question.

Eloise grabbed the orc girl's hand. "We're potencha princesses too!"

The older girl shook free with a gentle smile. "I have to work. But maybe Sala can go with you."

The half-elven girl shook her head and her chin lifted. "Papa didn't ask us to come." She crossed her arms and glared at her brother. "If he wanted you, he'd have said, Int."

"How do you know he didn't?" Int stuck his tongue out at his sister.

Sala started to retort, but the front door of the bookshop opened again. They all turned as Cala came out. "Franisa! Well met. Your presence is requested." She brandished her magical communication disk, then dropped it into her pocket.

Franisa looked at the children still clustered around them. "I assume it was only *my* presence?"

Cala smirked a little and reached for Franisa's basket. "Enrich, take this home for your mother. The rest of you had best head home as well. Or to work." She took in the children's crestfallen expressions. "Apprentices follow instructions. Sala, will you escort Eloise home and stay with her until Aislin arrives?"

Koni's daughter dropped a quick curtsey and took Eloise's hand. Wenda, the orc girl, bobbed a sloppy imitation of her friend's graceful dip and scurried across the square toward the tea shop. The older boys shuffled their feet, then disappeared into the butcher shop.

With a scowl, Enrich took the basket. He glared after the girls as they skipped across the cobblestones. "I don't need a babysitter."

"She's watching Eloise, not you." Cala tipped her head to the side.

The boy lifted his chin. "I want to come to the port."

Cala's expression hardened, instantly transforming her from bookshop owner to war witch. Or dragon rider. "Apprentices do what they're told."

Enrich gulped and gripped the basket handle so tight his knuckles whitened. "Yes, Mistress Cala." He turned and darted after his sister.

Franisa watched for a moment, then turned to her friend. "I need to learn that look. He's starting to ignore my motherly glares."

Cala snorted a little laugh. "I think that's natural at this age, isn't it?

And his grandfather's example doesn't help." Her expression darkened again.

"What do you mean?" Franisa asked as they headed down the lane toward the port.

"Children learn from their elders. If Gnollis treats your decisions as optional, it's not surprising if Enrich starts to follow suit." Cala squeezed her arm gently. "You said you want a solution that doesn't involved Nevan. A way to keep Enrich safe without the betrothal."

Franisa nodded slowly. Although she was starting to think being handfasted to Nevan wasn't a terrible idea.

"Take a page from your mother-in-law's book. Why does Gnollis let her make the decisions? He's the head of the clan. Yet he let her raise Keldan how she saw fit. From what I've heard, your husband never set foot in the mine."

"That's why Gnollis was so insistent Enrich had to take his turn." Franisa pushed the hair back from her forehead. "He said Philomena ruined Keldan. And that he wasn't going to let me spoil Enrich."

"That's what I mean. I'm not saying I agree with him—from what I've heard, Keldan had an academic's heart, and there's nobility in study. But as head of the clan, Gnollis had every right to insist Keldan work in the mines. He bowed to Philomena's rule. Why?"

Franisa stopped in the street, frowning at the older woman. "He's besotted with her. Everyone knows that."

Cala laughed and pulled her forward. "He's terrified of her. I've seen them together. It might have started as infatuation, but he's scared to death of his wife. And do you know why?"

"He's afraid she'll poison him?"

Cala barked a laugh, then pondered for a moment. "I suppose she could. But she's a smart woman. She knows Koni wouldn't turn a blind eye to that. And he has the ability to sniff out wrongdoing. And probably poison." She shook her head. "No. Philomena *knows* she's right. Always—even when she isn't. People defer to that kind of confidence. And they come to expect that deference, which reinforces their confidence. But when you stand up to them, they deflate very quickly. I'm sure you've seen that."

Franisa thought of her interaction with Goodwife Terman that very afternoon. The mistress of the mercantile had always terrified her. And yet, when she called the woman's bluff, the goodwife had folded. "But I told the schoolmaster Gnollis couldn't take Enrich—"

"You told the schoolmaster. You need to tell Gnollis." Cala shook her arm a little. "You are a successful business owner. You told me you don't need Gnollis's financial support—that you've provided for your family since the beginning. Just because he's the head of your clan doesn't mean he calls all the shots."

"That's not what Koni said..." Franisa bit her lip.

Cala rolled her eyes. "You don't have to argue with Koni. You just have to convince Gnollis."

CHAPTER TWENTY-TWO

"Why are we here?" Nevan followed William down the long wooden pier to a fishing boat tied up at the end. The dilapidated vessel had seen better days—better centuries even. Mottled grayish paint peeled from the wooden sides and deck, the cleats were corroded and rusted in places, and the door to the little house that protected the helm hung at an angle. But the hull looked solid, and the tall mast sported a new coat of paint.

"All will become clear in a moment." William reached out and knocked his knuckles against the deck. "Ahoy! Ship!"

A trapdoor flipped open, slamming against the deck. Nevan winced, sure the ship would shake apart from the impact, but it held. A head popped out, a worn tricorn casting a shadow on the face. Teeth flashed, and the man levered himself out of the hold. "William!"

The unfortunately familiar voice grated. Nevan grabbed William's arm. "That—tell me that isn't your..." He stopped, unable to think of a polite phrase to describe his feelings for Tyge de Xerrist, the arrogant Verduunian dragon rider.

"Yes. Tyge. Remember what Koni said." William shook off Nevan's hand and raised his own in a wave. "Good to see you, Tyge."

As Tyge carefully navigated the gently swaying deck, Nevan ground his teeth. "What did Koni say?"

"Right. You weren't with us. Tyge wouldn't be here if he was a danger to us. Koni's magic prevented him from returning to Safe Haven unless he'd had a change of heart." William reached up to clasp Tyge's forearm, then tipped his head at Nevan. "I'm sure you remember Nevan?"

Tyge gave Nevan a considering look, then nodded. "Well met, Nevan."

"Sir Tyge. What brings you to Safe Haven?"

Beneath the brim of the tricorn, it was hard to read Tyge's expression, but his shoulders tensed as he cast a look back at the hatch in the deck. "A grave matter of utmost secrecy."

Nevan tried not to roll his eyes. "We're hundreds of miles from Verduun. And far from the Borgonne as well. What matter of utmost secrecy could bring you to Safe Haven?"

William took a step back, then leapt up to the deck of the boat. The boat bobbed, and he wobbled on his bad leg. Tyge caught him, then the older man pulled free, turning back to Nevan. "Come and see."

"Are you sure?" Both Tyge and Nevan asked together. The two men glared at each other for a long moment before Tyge swung away, heading for the hatch.

Nevan didn't trust Tyge, but he had complete confidence in William. Putting a foot onto the ship's deck as it dropped in the gentle swells, he easily stepped up onto the storm-worn planks. The faint bobbing of the ship as it sat tied to the pier made his stomach gurgle uneasily. It was nothing like sitting on a dragon floating in the sea.

A waft of sulfur and brimstone overwhelmed the familiar salty, fishy tang of the bay. Perhaps years of associating with fire dragons had imbued Tyge with their signature stench? Then something rumbled under his feet, like a massive, restive dog shifting in its sleep. "What did you bring with you, Sir Tyge?"

William glanced down into the hold, then turned back to Nevan, his expression a strange mix of excitement, regret, and worry. "Sundri."

Nevan stopped cold. "Sundri? His war dragon?" His gaze darted to Tyge who crouched beside the opening. "Inside the boat?"

"Come. He won't hurt you." William knelt beside his friend, peering into the darkness. "What happened?"

Tyge glanced at Nevan again. "You're sure..."

William sat back on his heels, arms crossed. "I trust Nevan with my life. And that of my dragon. If that isn't good enough for you—"

"No, of course. I forget myself. I just—" The Verduunian's voice cracked, and he looked away. "When I came last year..."

"To kidnap my sister to Verduun." William's hard tone made it clear he might have forgiven Tyge for attempting to abduct his sister, but he wouldn't forget.

Tyge shook his head. "To retrieve a prisoner of war. I thought the prisoner was willing—happy to go home! And I didn't know it was Sarai. How could I? We thought she was dead."

William lifted a hand and shook his head. "I know. My anger is directed at your liege lord, not you."

With a loud swallow, Tyge nodded. "Not my liege lord anymore. I have foresworn my vows."

William's jaw dropped, but he recovered quickly. "I should have expected that. Koni said you couldn't return if Astorov still held your loyalty. What happened?"

Tyge gave him a frowning look but went on. "Sundri was injured. His right wing was mending, but he still couldn't fly, so I was detailed to retrieve Sarai. When I returned without her, King Astorov held me responsible even though the ship's captain corroborated my story. He brought in a truth reader from Pyrantien."

"What's a truth reader?" Nevan asked. "And where's Pyrantien?"

"Far to the east. They have a different magic—Cala would have to explain." William lifted both hands, his gaze locked on Tyge. "They can read thoughts. Uncover deceptions. What did he discover?"

"Nothing," Tyge said in surprise, looking past Nevan toward the town. "I don't know what your Lord Elf did, but the truth reader confirmed my story. The agent sent to the Borgonne failed in his quest to find Sarai. No prisoner had been delivered to Safe Haven for me to bring home."

"Koni is a powerful mage. And you believed it to be the truth, so why wouldn't the reader?" William looked into the hold again. "But..."

"Sundri healed. Mostly. He was almost to full strength when..." Tyge drew in a ragged breath. "Even with the truth teller backing me, I don't think the king believed my story. Maybe the agent who put her on the ship told him something different."

"Sarai's abductor went to Verduun?" William's voice was sharp with alarm.

"I don't know. I don't know who it was, so I have no way of knowing if he came to court. But I've felt a target on my back since my return."

"That's probably my fault." William rubbed the back of his neck, as if he felt a weapon sighted on his own back. "You were my chosen successor, and the king hates me. Why else would he import a truth teller, then refuse to believe his word?"

"Anyway, we were sent out on another mission before Sundri was ready." Tyge shook his head. "I knew he shouldn't—and I tried to get Petron to back me up. But he thought Sundri looked fine. The man has so little experience. And Sundri hid his injury well. Dragons don't know their own weaknesses! That's why they need us to protect them."

William gripped Tyge's arm. "That's why Astorov promoted Petron to guild master. He's young, headstrong, and inexperienced. Someone Astorov can manipulate and control. Sundri was injured again." It wasn't a question.

"Yes." Tyge choked a little. "Badly. Astorov—William, he told me to —" The man seemed to crumple in on himself.

William waited, his hand firm on Tyge's shoulder. After a long moment, Tyge took a deep breath and wiped his eyes. "He told me to *put him down.* Like a wounded duck shot by a badly placed arrow. He said our service to the crown was over, and *useless* dragons couldn't be allowed to—to *waste* resources needed by the thunder."

The former guild master went still, his hand dropping to his lap. "Has he—what happened to Byrion? And Wasali?"

Tyge waved a hand. "No. They're still alive. Jener and Yolando—they bought a property far from the capital. Moved their dragons. Their families helped."

William glanced up at Nevan. "Jener and Yolando were both riders. Their mounts were injured, oh, years ago. Separate incidents. They survived. It doesn't happen often, but the guild has always cared for our veterans—both human and dragon. Until Astorov." He turned back to Tyge. "Why didn't you go to them?"

"I was going to." Tyge peered into the hold again, the hat falling from his head and disappearing into the darkness. "Then I remembered. It was like—like opening a door in my mind. One that I didn't know was there, but suddenly—" He sat back and met William's gaze. "I remembered everything. Sarai. Lord Koni. The war witch." His cheeks went red. On his previous visit, Tyge had made no secret of his distrust of Cala, despite William's obvious feelings for her.

"Dragon rider." William's hard tone brooked no argument. "And my wife. She's a war witch no longer, and if you want to stay here, you'll remember that."

"Of course." Tyge ducked his head. "Anything. Just tell me you can help Sundri."

"I don't know if we can, but we'll try." William pushed up to his knees, and Nevan hurriedly offered a hand to help him rise. "How do we get him out of there?"

"Where will we put him?" Nevan asked.

"FarPoint, of course." William released Nevan's hand and looked toward the mouth of the bay. "Do you think your ship's captain would sail around to the tower?"

"For enough gold, he'll sail *up* the tower." Tyge grimaced. "But this voyage took all I had."

"And gold is one thing we don't have much of here."

Nevan coughed. "Even if we can sail around to the point, how will we get an injured dragon up to the nest? If he can't fly, he can't—" He lifted both hands. "It's a hundred feet."

"That's why we need Cala." William looked past Nevan, then smiled and moved toward the side of the boat. "And Koni."

Nevan turned to see where the older man was looking and spotted Cala and Franisa coming down the dock.

"Who is that?" Tyge rose, his tone suspicious. "Another war witch?" He asked the question softly enough that it wouldn't carry to William's ears.

Anger burned in Nevan's chest at the question. "No. And what if she were?"

"Nothing. I meant nothing by it. I will abide by William's rules—" Tyge shoved both hands through his hair. "But more people—a secret shared is no longer a secret."

"Franisa won't tell anyone," Nevan said firmly.

"How can you be sure?"

Taking a page from William's book, Nevan lifted his chin and met the dragon rider's skeptical gaze. "She's my betrothed."

"Oh. Of course. Is she a healer? Even a human healer could be helpful…" Tyge looked down into the boat again.

"No." Nevan turned away before the Verduunian could complain. His insistence on secrecy was laughable. Did he think no one would notice a war dragon at FarPoint? Leaving the dragon rider, he jumped to the dock, landing beside William. He lowered his voice. "Why is Franisa here?"

"She's got a sharp mind. Cala and Koni thought she could be helpful." William shrugged and stepped forward to kiss his wife. "Ladies, you remember Tyge?"

Cala nodded cooly at the man aboard the boat. Franisa moved a little closer, gazing up at him. "I don't think we met last time."

"Franisa, this is Sir Tyge de Xerrist, a dragon rider from Verduun." William swept an arm toward his friend, still perched on the edge of the boat. "Tyge, this is Mistress Hearthwell, the town baker and Nevan's betrothed."

"Enchanted." Tyge's curt tone and abrupt bow belied the word. He turned back to William. "How can we get Sundri to FarPoint without anyone seeing him?"

"We won't." Koni appeared beside Nevan seemingly by magic.

"Lord Elf!" Tyge jumped to the dock and bowed low. "Thank you for allowing us safe haven here in... Safe Haven."

"I'm surprised to see you." Koni glanced at Cala with a raised brow. "I tied your memory of our isle to the death of your dragon, yet William tells me he lives?"

Tyge did a double take at Koni's words, as if he couldn't believe the elf could be fallible. Then he lunged at the ship, stumbling as it surged upward just as he jumped. He caught himself and dove at the hatch. "Sundri?" After a long moment, he rolled away and sat up. "Yes, he lives!"

"I didn't mean to suggest he might have died just now." Koni leapt gracefully to the boat's deck. "But you weren't supposed to remember unless you blamed Astorov for his death."

"Oh, but I do!" Tyge stopped short, turning to face the elf. "The injury nearly killed him. And then he ordered me to—" Tyge looked away, blinking rapidly. "The man is a monster who ordered the death of my beloved dragon."

"That makes sense to me," Cala said. "Koni's magic is mysterious, but it follows logical rules. Well, maybe not logical. Emotional rules? I can't explain it—" She waved both hands to ward off the question Nevan opened his mouth to ask. "But it makes sense."

"How are we going to get Sundri to FarPoint?" Nevan asked softly. "How are we going to get him out of that boat? How'd they get him *into* the boat?"

"The deck comes up." Franisa gripped the rail that ran around the edge of the boat, letting her hands rise and fall with the gentle swells. She released one hand to point. "See those latches? That whole section comes up. It's for cargo that's too big for the hatch."

"How do you know about boats?" Nevan frowned at the deck, noting the location of the latches.

"Keldan had one similar to this." She glanced up at the sun. "We'll lose light in a couple of hours. If we want to move the dragon, we should do it soon. How big is he?"

"Good question." Cala held out a hand to Nevan. "Help me up on deck, will you? This would be easier at low tide."

With a shrug, Nevan gripped Cala's waist and lifted. She squeaked in surprise, then laughed as he deposited her on the deck. He turned to Franisa.

"I'll get myself up there." She pulled her skirts up to her knees and waited until the boat dropped, then jumped.

Nevan dragged his gaze away from her legs as she released her skirt, then followed the women aboard.

"He's larger than Finn." William stroked his chin as he gazed down through the open hatch. A little puff of smoke—like that from a pipe—wafted up.

Nevan chuckled under his breath as he wondered what Eloise would make of this dragon's scent. Was it too similar to Rolph's? The thought made him smile.

"What?" Franisa whispered.

He shook his head—he'd tell her later. "Can we lift him?"

"They used a crane at Verduun." Tyge crossed to the latch Franisa had pointed out earlier and tapped it with a foot. "They took the deck off and used a sling to lower him in."

"Where did you embark?" William grabbed Tyge's arm. "Does Astorov know you were coming here?"

Tyge gave William a disgusted look. "How dumb do you think I am? I faked his death. After Astorov demanded I do it, I got a farmer to help me take Sundri out to the Joordenal Marsh. Then Varient—the guy who owns this boat—came out with a raft on the slough lines. Darius helped me wrap Sundri in an old sail, and we kind of rolled him onto the raft. Varient took us to Mardeel, near Port Hounsmath. It's a little fishing village, far enough from the city to attract little attention. They have a crane for lifting large fish, and they used it to—" He mimed lowering something toward the deck.

"Darius helped?" William released Tyge's arm. "And you weren't followed? Remember that spy at the Drunken Dragon—"

"We were careful. Yardeni was still on the no-fly rolls. Everyone else was out on a mission. Astorov didn't care about a send-off for Sundri." Tyge gritted his teeth and his lip curled. "None of the old traditions are important to him."

"Well, we don't have a crane." Nevan frowned down into the darkness of the hold. Was there a little red glow or was that his imagination? "Could we rig up a sling and lift him with the dragons?"

"That's how we got him back to the camp after the injury," Tyge said.

"Normally, if a dragon is injured, his flight mates will make sure he gets back to camp." William put his hands on his hips and stared into the distance, as if he could see it happening. "We can build similar equipment. Leather straps, canvas. Klausi, the leather master, can help with that. We'll lift him out of the boat, but they won't be able to carry him far. Maybe we can get a big cart and carry him over the elven trails."

"What about sailing around to FarPoint?" Franisa suggested. "Then lift him—could the three of them take him up that high?"

William wagged a hand back and forth. "Hard to say. It won't be easy, but we've tested how much the dragons can lift. Back in Verduun, we use a team of four war dragons—it was considered an honor. Under battlefield conditions it could be done with two. The sea dragons are smaller, but they've proven to be more capable in many ways..." He hummed as he continued to stare into the dark hold.

"We still have the problem of getting the ship to FarPoint." Tyge heaved a sigh. "Varient made it very clear he wanted three hundred more for that trip."

"Three hundred? That's highway robbery!" Cala exclaimed.

"Or high seas piracy." Koni chuckled a bit. "I'm afraid we don't have that much in the town treasury. And I'd need to convene the council to authorize it anyway."

Tyge frowned at Koni. "You have a council? But you're an elf."

"I'm not royalty. I'm the mayor. Elected to do a job, not rule over the island in unquestioned authority. I follow the rule of law." Koni muttered something under his breath. Nevan thought he said, "Unlike some people."

Franisa raised a hand slowly. "It's not exactly following the rule of law, but I have an idea."

"Let's hear it." Cala gestured at the elf. "Koni, maybe you shouldn't listen."

Koni laughed, then turned away, sticking his fingers in his ears and singing loudly, “La, la, la, la, la.”

Cala motioned for Franisa to go on.

The baker darted a glance at Tyge. “How about we steal it?”

CHAPTER TWENTY-THREE

Franisa gestured to the little ship's deck with both hands. "We won't really steal it, of course. I meant, we can borrow it. Sail it around to FarPoint, offload the... cargo, then sail it back. If we get someone to buy—what was his name? Varient? Someone can buy him a couple rounds at the pub, and he'll never know we moved it."

"It will take more than a drink or two," Tyge said. "The man drinks like a fish. But as long as someone is buying, he'll be drinking. And he's probably gotten a head start—he headed that direction as soon as we tied up. Claimed it was because he didn't want to know what I was transporting, but he knew."

"Plausible deniability." Koni lounged against the railing at the back of the boat.

"I thought you weren't listening." Tyge frowned at the elf.

Koni lifted a negligent hand. "It's easy to lie if people think you can't."

Tyge spluttered, then threw up his hands and turned away.

Cala chuckled and leaned close to Franisa. "On his first visit to Safe Haven, Tyge had this crazy idea elves couldn't lie. He learned the error of his ways fairly quickly."

"I *can* lie, but I don't, unless absolutely necessary." Koni rose. "And I prefer not to. Since I trust you implicitly, I shall take myself off to the pub where I will no longer be party to this plot. And if I happen to meet up with a ship's captain, I shall, of course, extend hospitality to him and ply him with libations and questions about his travels. You're welcome." With a casual wave, he leaped over the rail, landing lightly on the dock, then sauntered toward town.

Everyone watched him go, then William turned to Franisa. "Now what?"

She gulped. "Why am I in charge?"

"I assume, since you suggested it, that you know how to work a boat like this." William pointed at the deck. "Or you know someone who does."

Nevan shaded his eyes with one hand and peered across the bay at the other ships in port. "It's a shame the *Ironwind* sailed. They could have helped. I don't know any of the other captains."

Remembering Cala's advice earlier in the afternoon, Franisa straightened her spine. She knew how to do this, even if it had been a few years since she'd been on Keldan's boat. And if she could convince them she knew, they'd follow her instructions. She licked a finger and checked the wind.

There was none. One of the hardest parts of sailing was getting into and out of port, and she was working with no wind. Perfect. "We need to get out of the harbor. We might have to wait for a good breeze—they usually come up around four."

"That's another half-hour." William lifted his hand, arm extended, and closed one eye to look at the horizon. "That will give us two or maybe three hours of useable light. Probably less." He nodded at the dark clouds massing in the west.

"The dragons could help," Nevan said. When everyone turned to him, he shrugged his massive shoulders. "I mean, if they're going to be able to lift this... cargo, they should be able to pull the boat out of harbor."

"We don't want to weary them." William propped his fists on his hips, then stumbled as a swell rocked the boat. "Lifting a war dragon won't be easy."

"Starlight says they can do it." Nevan cocked his head as if listening. "And she's getting help."

"Help?" Cala glanced up as one dragon, then a second, glided over the rooftops toward them. "That's Finn and Nari. Is that what you mean?" The two wheeled together and banked around the large bay.

Nevan spread his hands wide. "She didn't explain."

"Explain?" Tyge looked up from where he sat on the deck beside the hatch, his lip curled in scorn. "You talk about your dragon as if she can speak."

"She does." Nevan lifted his chin. "But she's just learning, so she doesn't know a lot of words yet."

Tyge snorted a derisive laugh. "Right. Dragons that talk. I knew giants weren't very brigh—"

Franisa drew in a breath to blast the Verduunian, but William beat her to it. He kicked Tyge's hip, hard enough to make the younger man grunt. "Giants are every bit as intelligent as you. Smarter, even. Smart enough to know better than to antagonize the people trying to help them. If you want to live here, you need to overcome those prejudices."

"But—"

"No buts. I figured it out, and I had twenty more years of indoctrination than you." William turned back to Nevan. "I apologize for Tyge's abysmal behavior. He'll do better." The last phrase came out as a command, clearly aimed at the man seated on the deck.

Tyge rose slowly, then bowed to Nevan. "I apologize for my rude comment and will endeavor to mend my ways." After another glare from William, he went on. "And overcome my... indoctrination."

Nevan looked him over for a long moment, then put out a hand. "Apology accepted." After they shook, he turned to face the deeper water. "Here comes Starlight."

A flight of silver blue dragons soared low over the bay, some of their number diving into the glassy sea then zipping back up into the sky. Droplets of water spun off the dragons, sparkling in the afternoon sunlight. "Look, a rainbow!" Franisa pointed, then it was gone.

"I—I thought you only had three dragons!" Tyge spluttered.

"We have three *paired* dragons. Starlight recruited the wild herd. Swarm? School?" Nevan scratched his head. "We really need to settle on a lexicon." He darted a sly look at Tyge as he said the last word. Franisa stifled a laugh.

Tyge did a double take but didn't reply.

"Tyge! Nevan!" Franisa pointed at the dock as the dragons dove into the water nearby. "Untie the boat!" Ropes hung slack from the bow and stern, their ends secured to large metal cleats at the edge of the dock.

The two men responded instantly to her command, leaping off the boat to wrestle with the heavy ropes. Nevan got his loose and tossed it up to the deck, then raced to help the smaller man at the stern. Four of the wild dragons pushed their heads against the bow of the ship and began swimming. The boat backed away from the dock, pulling the remaining rope straight then tight. Nevan loosed the last loop as the boat pulled away, the rope running quickly through his hands. He dropped it with a yelp, and it splashed into the water.

"Get aboard!" Franisa gripped the tiller, her tone shrill.

Nevan grabbed Tyge by the waist and threw him across the rapidly widening space between the dock and the boat. The toe of the Verduunian's boot caught on the rail, and he landed face-first on the deck. William offered him a hand and pulled him upright.

"Nevan!" Franisa called as the boat increased its backward speed.

The giant put his fingers in his mouth and blew a piercing whistle. One of the dragons circling overhead dove toward the dock. Her wings snapped out just before she hit, and she flipped back to land on her feet beside Nevan.

"We need to tell the dragons to turn us around!" Franisa cranked the wheel hard to starboard, but the boat kept moving in a straight line as the dragons countered her steering. She leaned over the side. "Turn!"

Predictably, the dragons ignored her. She straightened, looking back at the rapidly dwindling dock. Nevan had mounted Starlight and was buckling his flying straps. He really needed a quick latch and release system.

She ran toward the others, still gathered beside the open hatch at the stern. "I need to turn the boat. Can you talk to the dragons?"

Startled, Cala and William looked at each other, then up at their mounts. "Tell us what you want them to do," Cala said. "We can try to get Nari and Finn to show them..."

"We need to rotate the boat. So it's facing the open sea. And so we don't run into anyone else." Franisa flipped her hand at a Dorfmundish ship moored in the middle of the bay. It was far enough away that a gentle turn should do the trick. But the dragons seemed to have decided pushing the boat was a fun game and more had joined the four at the bow.

Gaze focused on her dragon circling overhead, Cala reached into her pocket and withdrew the magic communication disk. "Talk to Nevan." She held the device out to Franisa.

"I don't—" With another glance at the cargo ship behind them, she grabbed the disk. "How do I—"

"Press the center," Cala said. "Then talk."

Franisa squeezed the disk, hard enough that the carving in the middle seemed to cut into the pad of her thumb. She held it to her lips. "Nevan?"

"Here."

She couldn't tell if his voice came from the medallion or was inside her head. "I need the dragons to turn the boat."

"On it." Starlight launched from the dock, flying low over the sea, then plunged into the waves with Nevan still on her back.

A squeal of alarm burst out of Franisa before she could contain it. That dragon would drown Nevan! But Starlight emerged almost immediately, her wings tucked tight to her back, her rider drenched. She swam between the wild dragons, using her nose to push them to the side of the ship, then diving beneath them and resurfacing with the others. Like a herd dog, she chivvied the dragons into place, reorienting the boat in a masterful way. Some of the dragons dropped away, as if bored with the exercise, but others eagerly took their places.

Franisa gripped the wheel, muttering instructions into the wooden disk, astonished at the precision of their wild assistants. Nevan kept up a running commentary, except when he was underwater, but most of the comments seemed to be aimed at the dragons, not her. She kept an eye on the ship moored behind them until they got the boat turned, her heart in her throat every time Nevan disappeared into the bay.

Once the ship was pointed the right direction, Starlight leapt from the sea, water flying off her wings and splashing the boat. Franisa gasped as the cold water drenched her dress and hair. A ghost of amusement seemed to float through the air—was Starlight laughing at her?

A breeze blew wet hair across her face, and she shivered. "Get the sails up!" She hurried to the main mast and showed the others how to unwrap and hoist the sail. As they worked, the boat slowed, the dragons abandoning their new game. Most of them flew ahead of the boat toward open water, but a few tried pushing other boats. Starlight circled the bay, Nevan's hollered demands to the wild dragons echoing weirdly from the disk in Franisa's pocket.

Eventually, they got the sail raised, and the wind quickened, driving the little boat out of the bay. Franisa stood beside the ship's wheel, calling commands to the others as they picked up speed. The little housing around the helm cut the wind, but her teeth rattled as the cold bit into her wet clothing.

Once they were under way, William took the communication disk from Franisa and retreated to the stern of the boat to mutter instructions to Nevan. The sun sank lower, glinting on the frothy whitecaps as they sailed. Franisa shivered again.

Cala brought a blanket and wrapped it around Franisa's shoulders. The witch muttered something under her breath, and a wave of warmth flowed from her hand into the fabric, countering the chill that wracked Franisa's body. Franisa relaxed a little, settling against the rail by the wheel. "That's a handy spell."

"I've been saving it." Cala smiled tiredly. "If I hoard my magic, I can usually summon enough to do a little. You'd think with all the heat my own body builds up I should be able to share it, but no. My hair catches fire—spectacular but useless."

"I thought you managed to light a flame from your hair." Franisa adjusted their course to run parallel to the coast.

"I can. But I have no control over when it happens, so—" She yanked her hand away from Franisa's blanket and lifted her braid. "See? *Now* it's working." Smoke seeped from the end of her heavy hair, then it burst into flames. Cala closed her hand over the burning braid, and put her other one on Franisa's shoulder again, transferring the heat through her body.

"I'll take it." Franisa's shoulders relaxed as warmth flowed into them.

"At least it's a little more predictable than it used to be." Cala grimaced at the hair clutched in her fist. "Later in the day, or at night. Nothing in the morning."

"I'm grateful we didn't sail at daybreak." Franisa squinted at the horizon as they rounded the last curve of the island, headed toward the tower at the end of the peninsula. The sun sat atop the bank of dark clouds, like a strawberry on a pile of meringue. "Where should I stop?"

"Anywhere along here will work." William pointed up at the tower which cast a dark finger of shadow across the beach and sea. "Sail close to land. The sea is quite deep here. If the dragons can lift Sundri, we want to make their trip as short as possible."

She let the wind push them close to the cliffs, then directed the others to furl the sails and tie them. The ship's forward motion slowed, and she had Tyge throw the sea anchor overboard. The water was indeed deep—the rope played almost to its full length before going slack.

Franisa dusted her hands together. "That's my part done. Now what?"

"I sent Nevan to get equipment from the stable." William handed the communication medallion back to her and pointed up at the tower. "We'd been working out a way to carry water to a fire—before we realized we didn't need to. But the canvas bucket will be perfect for this. How do we get the deck open?"

Franisa pointed out the latches, leaving the others to do the work. Although the blanket and Cala's magic had kept the cold at bay, her fingers were chilled to the bone. She pulled the blanket tight around her shoulders and backed into the little cabin as the others opened the deck between it and the stern of the boat.

The dragon was big, its bulk filling most of the hull. Something agitated it—whether it was the late afternoon sunlight after so long below deck, or the presence of unknown people, she didn't know. But smoke puffed from its scaly red nostrils, and its dark eyes seemed to dance with flames.

William and Tyge spoke to the dragon in low, gentle tones using a mixture of nonsense and baby talk, much as she would soothe a child. The big dragon's body was wrapped in a ragged sheet of canvas, from which its head and tail protruded, both wiggling with distress. Like Starlight's laughter, pain and fear seemed to roll off the beast. Franisa suddenly realized that had been the source of the unease she'd been feeling since she boarded the boat. She tried to project calm and safety but stayed well away from the dangerous-looking tail.

The disk in Franisa's pocket shook, and Nevan's voice sounded in her head. "Are they ready?"

"I think so?" Now that she was no longer in charge of the mission, Franisa allowed her uncertainty to show.

"Coming." His presence disappeared.

She hadn't realized she'd felt it until it was gone. It was as if he'd been standing behind her, his comforting bulk like a port in a storm. She pulled the disk from her pocket, sliding her fingers across the smooth edge. The idea of having that comforting presence available at the squeeze of the disk made her wish she'd never have to return it.

"Nevan is coming!" She called across the dragon to her friends. The men stood in the hull with the beast, Tyge by its head and William near the tail. Cala sat on the bench at the back, her feet drawn up under her rather than dangling over the dragon's body.

"Excellent." William lifted a corner of the canvas enshrouding the dragon. "Do you think this will hold? Or do we need to get him into the bucket?"

Tyge muttered something, but Franisa went around the cabin to watch the tower. A dragon took off, then another, and then the third. Each had a long strap hanging from their harnesses as they flew down toward the sea. Franisa could make out Nevan astride the smallest of the creatures, leading the little group. A swell of pride took her by surprise—she had no real reason to be proud of the giant. He was simply helping a friend. But seeing him directing the group gave her a little thrill.

The dragons swooped over the boat, then Starlight hovered, her wings beating the air and flattening her blanket against Franisa's body. The dragon dropped something she'd been clutching in her front claws into the bow of the ship. Then Nevan jumped.

CHAPTER TWENTY-FOUR

Nevan landed on the roof of the boat's cabin with an echoing thud. Rolling with the fall, he went over the side of the little structure, hitting the triangle of space between it and the bow of the ship. He landed hard on his shoulder and let out an "oof" of surprise more than pain.

"Nevan!" Franisa rushed up to him as he rose to his feet.

He grabbed her shoulders and leaned forward to keep her from bowling him over. "Careful!"

"Are you hurt?" Her hands gripped his arms, sliding up them to his shoulders and down his chest.

He put a hand over hers. Not that he wasn't enjoying the sensation, but he had a job to accomplish. "I'm fine. But we need to—"

She spun away, disappearing around the little house again. Grabbing the bundle of cloth and leather Starlight had dropped, he followed, unwrapping the canvas as he went. When he reached the back of the boat, he saw Sundri for the first time.

According to William, the war dragon was bigger than Finn. But shrouded in the tattered canvas, he looked small and scared. Nevan tried to reach out to him, but unlike Finn or Nari, the dragon's mind felt like a blank wall. Earlier, even the wild sea dragons seemed to connect with him, although they didn't really understand his thoughts. But he couldn't hear this one at all, and that made him sad.

"Here's the bucket." He shook out the canvas he'd carried, letting the end fall down into the hold. The straps on the other side slapped gently against the dragon, and the beast wiggled, struggling to get out of the wrap containing him. "Easy, boy!"

Tyge crouched beside his mount's head, stroking the fearsome spines and scaly skin. Nevan couldn't hear what he said, but it probably didn't matter, since Tyge insisted his dragon didn't speak.

William took the long leather strap hanging from the canvas, folded the big metal circle into the leather, and fed it under the dragon's tail. Then he climbed around the injured beast and worked the leather beneath it. Once he'd gotten that strap under the bulk of its lower end, he moved to the head.

"Help me get this under his shoulders." William lifted the other strap and waved it at Tyge. "Keep him calm."

"I'm trying. He's not receiving very well."

"You've done this before." William threaded the strap under the dragon's neck. "Grab that ring."

"We weren't in a rocking boat with a bunch of civilians!" Tyge's voice ratcheted up, and the dragon's tail lashed harder, thudding against the interior of the hull.

William poked a finger at Tyge to get his attention, then breathed in deeply. He spoke in a soft, even tone. "Calm. We're here to help. You need to make sure Sundri feels that. And there are no 'civilians' here. We have four dragon riders and the ship's captain. Essential personnel. Here to help."

William's placid, almost sing-song tone seemed to soothe both dragon and rider. Nevan felt the dragon's terror lessen, just a bit. Tyge took the leather strap and pulled it under Sundri's shoulders, working it downward until it was beneath his upper body.

"Perfect. Now give that to Cala." William pointed.

Tyge handed the ring on the end of the strap to Cala, still perched on the box-like bench at the back of the boat. Nevan let more canvas fall gently into the hull, holding the big rings riveted to the ends of his straps. "Pull that up, if you can, Cala."

She grasped the ring and pulled, drawing it tight. The strap slid beneath the fabric-wrapped dragon, but the bunched canvas caught on the beast's side. "It's stuck. I can't pull any more." She spotted a metal cleat and hooked the ring over it. "You'll have to roll him to get the canvas underneath."

Still in the hold with Sundri, William handed the second strap to Cala. She hooked that ring over the same cleat at the stern of the boat. She wiggled the metal, but it seemed solid. "I hope that holds."

William climbed over Sundri's tail and crouched beside the creature's hind quarters. "Tyge, we're going to have to roll him and get the fabric underneath. Can you do that?"

"Yes, of course." Tyge moved around his partner's head, gently patting and whispering as he went.

"Cala!" Nevan kept his shout to a whisper, hoping he wouldn't agitate the beast. "Come hold these rings so I can help move the dragon."

Nodding, Cala crossed the narrow strip of deck between the rail and the open hold as if it were a wide dance floor. The wind had started to come up, and the boat bobbed more, but the witch's steps were sure, like a tightrope walker. She took the straps from Nevan and tilted her head at the dragon.

Nevan dropped into the hold by the dragon's back. At least he thought it was his back—the canvas-wrapped body had ridges on this side. He crouched beside the widest part, putting gentle hands on the animal. Beneath the fabric, the dragon felt like skin and bones. His hands traced over what had to be wingtips and found a smooth curve that might be ribs. "Ready."

"On three." William counted. "One. Two. Three."

Nevan lifted and pushed in time with William's grunt of effort. The dragon stiffened and growled, but they got him up far enough to shove the loose canvas beneath his body, then gently lowered him to the hull.

William groaned as he rose, using the edge of the deck to pull himself upright. "Other side."

They repeated the process from the other side, although rolling the dragon onto its back was harder. Still, they managed to get a good portion of the unfolded bucket fabric beneath the beast. Breathing hard, Nevan rose, then climbed out of the hold. "Starlight!"

Although the dragons had returned to the tower far above them, Starlight heard his call and dove toward the sea. Finn and Nari followed a second later, each one trailing a long leather strap. They hovered over the bobbing boat, the beating of their wings seeming to push it deeper into the water.

"We only have three dragons, and four rings!" Franisa shouted over the wind and noise.

"We'll put the two at the head on one strap." Nevan pointed toward Tyge near the dragon's head. "Finn is the biggest—he should take that end. Starlight, land on the little house." The dragon folded her wings and settled onto the roof of the cabin. The ship tilted with her weight, then shifted again as Nari landed on the bench at the rear.

William stared hard at Finn, and the dragon finally came to rest on the rail running along the side of the ship. The boat listed, and Nari sidestepped to the far side of the stern, righting the vessel.

Nevan snagged the strap hanging from Starlight's harness. He passed it to William down in the hold. Nari gripped her own strap in her teeth. Cala ran along the narrow gunwale again and took the strap from her dragon. They fed the three straps through the loops on Sundri's makeshift litter, threading Finn's through both rings at the war dragon's head. Once through the rings, the straps had to be hooked over a reinforced rivet embedded in the leather to form a loop.

"Ready?" Nevan hollered.

"Lift!" William pumped his fist at the sky.

The three dragons launched upward, their strong wings beating down at the boat. They reached the end of their straps, and their upward motion halted for a heart-stopping moment. Then they rose again, slowly lifting the injured one from the bobbing boat.

The humans watched in silence as the majestic dragons slowly climbed into the sky, their massive cargo swaying beneath them. Nevan whispered encouragement and instructions to Starlight, counting on their mental connection to reach her. The dragons flew as a single unit, the hours of careful practice paying off.

"Can they lift him that far?" Franisa whispered, staring up at the tower high overhead.

"They don't have to go all the way up." Nevan moved closer and pointed. "See that ridge, about two-thirds up? There's a cave. I was making it into a den for Starlight, but it will be a good place for Sundri to heal."

She jerked. "You were leaving the stable?"

"We always planned on the stable being for training." Nevan shrugged, his gaze still focused on the dragons. "Fully trained dragons and riders would live elsewhere. The caves were an obvious choice."

"If you don't like light and fresh air." Franisa shuddered, her shoulder jostling his arm.

Nevan chuckled. "It's not like the hatching cavern. It's barely a cave at all—just a big hollow in the side of the cliff. With windows. And a woodstove. They're almost there! Good work, Starlight!"

From this distance, it was impossible to see, but Nevan could feel how hard the three dragons were working. Every downbeat, every upswing of Starlight's wings seemed to echo through his own body. He leaned forward, as if he could send power to her.

Tyge seemed to jerk out of a trance. "We need to get up there! They'll need our help to land."

Cala put a hand on his arm. "William spoke with Koni. He's there. With Enrich."

"I thought the elf was distracting Varient?" Tyge looked wildly from the dragon riders to Franisa and back. "How—"

"How did you expect to get Sundri off this boat?" William asked. "Varient left you alone so you could do it 'without his knowledge.' He knew you'd have to move the boat if you didn't want a huge audience. And he certainly didn't want that. Koni went to the pub to make sure Varient gave us sufficient time. He arranged a meal and a bed for the man, then collected Franisa's son and headed for the cave. Relax, Tyge."

Franisa chuckled. "I'm not really the boat-stealing type."

"You made a good job of it, though." Nevan put a hand on her shoulder, gripping it firmly, and winked. "If the whole bakery thing doesn't work out, you've got a fallback career."

"Bakery… you're a baker?" Tyge stared at her in horror. "You aren't a… a sailor?"

William had introduced her as the baker. Obviously, Tyge hadn't been listening, which didn't really surprise Nevan.

But Franisa spread her wet skirt and bobbed a curtsey at him. "Bakery owner and part-time boat thief, at your service."

Irritated, Nevan ignored Tyge's spluttering. "I have complete faith in Koni, but maybe we should go up? Is there a way to get to shore?" He looked over the side of the boat, not sure what he was expecting to see.

"There's a skiff." Franisa pointed to the back. "Hanging back there."

They got the little boat lowered into the water. Nevan helped Cala and William down into it, letting Tyge fend for himself. Then he turned to Franisa. "I'll send Koni down to sail back with you."

Franisa frowned at the sun quickly disappearing behind the dark clouds still massed on the horizon. "I'm not sure we'll get back before dark."

"You can do it." Emboldened by the success of their venture, Nevan leaned forward and pressed a kiss to Franisa's cheek. "I'll check on you later." Without waiting to see how she responded, he climbed down into the skiff and pushed it away from the fishing boat. As he rowed toward the beach, he caught sight of Franisa pressing a hand to her cheek and his heart soared.

They beached the little boat and started the climb to the caves. Cala took them along the elven path that shortened the climb to a few easy steps. The sensation was unnerving because it was completely unnoticeable. They started up the stone steps carved in the side of the cliff, turned a corner, and arrived at the landing some sixty feet above the sea.

"This way." Nevan pointed out the path. It led along the face of the cliff, opposite the one that went to the hatching grounds. A few hardy plants clung to the rocky face. They ducked under a twisted little tree where the path was only a foot wide. With the cliff on one side and the sheer drop on the other, it could be treacherous, but after many traversals, it didn't bother Nevan anymore. Tyge's indrawn breath behind him made him smile smugly. The Verduunian would have to get used to it until Sundri was able to fly again.

Around a little outcropping, the path came to Nevan's cave. Starlight perched on the edge of the long shelf, poking her curious nose at the still-wrapped dragon occupying her future home. Koni and Enrich stood at the far end of the space, tucked into the corner between the partially constructed wall and the stone.

"We got the straps unhooked," Koni said, relief evident in his tone as Tyge hurried to Sundri's head. "Starlight helped us push him into the cave. But he wasn't too pleased with any of it." As he spoke, Sundri's tail lashed out, banging into the vertical beams Nevan had placed along the opening, and narrowly missing the elf and boy.

"Sundri! I'm here." Tyge stroked the dragon's head and neck, then called to the others without losing eye contact with his dragon. "You'd all probably best go. I'll get him unwrapped, then he'll be more comfortable. Do you have a healer?"

William snorted a little. "There are no dragon healers outside of Verduun. Cala knows some human healers." He turned to his wife, but she had vanished. "Where'd she go?"

"Probably hiding from the agitated war dragon." Watching the big creature, Koni carefully shepherded Enrich around the dragon and out onto the wide ledge.

"I think she's trying to do something about the weather." Nevan pointed at the clouds along the western horizon. "Franisa seemed a bit worried about getting the boat back. I told her you'd help her get it to the bay."

The elf looked startled but nodded. "I'm not particularly enamored of the sea, but I can help get a boat into port. Come, Enrich, let us assist your mother."

With a glance back at the war dragon, Enrich followed Koni around the corner and out of sight.

"Nevan, will you go to Cala? She'll need help if she's expending magic." William's urgent tone conveyed his conflict—stay with his friend or help his wife. He moved closer. "I want to see how badly injured Sundri is. There may be little we can do aside from sit watch—"

He broke off, but Nevan understood what he didn't say. If the dragon was dying, Tyge shouldn't be left alone. He clapped a gentle hand on William's shoulder. "I'll check on Cala. And make sure she doesn't do anything crazy."

William blew out a sigh of relief. With a quick nod, he returned to his old friends.

Nevan crossed the landing to Starlight and pointed upward. "Go home."

"*We fly.*" Starlight's silvery eyes glinted. She obviously meant to carry him.

"Aren't you tired from lifting Sundri?" Nevan stroked his partner's neck.

"*We fly. Together. Always.*" Starlight used her head to push Nevan toward her flank as she shifted sideways to allow him to mount. "*Always.*"

He gazed at the dragon, trying to listen to her thoughts, but he heard only certainty that she could carry him. With a shrug, he climbed on, not bothering with the flying straps. At worst, he'd hit the sea again, and he was already wet.

Starlight flung herself off the cliff edge, dropping rapidly toward the water. For a breathtaking moment, Nevan was certain they'd hit the sea and sink directly to the bottom. Then her wings snapped out and she caught an updraft, arcing upward almost as quickly as they'd fallen. They wheeled out over the water, and he spotted the fishing boat far below with Franisa on the deck, looking up at the cliff. Her hand rose, and he waved back. On the beach, Koni and Enrich pushed the little skiff into the water. Then Starlight soared over the courtyard wall and dropped to the stony ground, landing with a graceless thud that betrayed how tired she really was.

Nevan slid off, patting Starlight's shoulder. "Thanks for not dunking me again."

"Already wet." She pushed the top of her head against his side, then jumped to the wall again. *"Fishing."* And she dove over the side.

Nevan looked around the empty courtyard and peeked into the stable. The other two dragons must be fishing as well. A little wind whipped around his head, reminding him why he'd come up alone. He squelched damply across the courtyard and out the big doors to the front of the property.

Cala crouched on the ground in front of the building. She'd drawn a chalk circle filling the largest, uncracked section of stone. As he got closer, he could see she'd drawn some images inside the circle of a place he didn't recognize. Tall buildings seemed to loom over wide streets filled with people.

"That's incredible. Is it a real place?" He stopped outside the circle of chalk, not wanting to smear the drawing.

"It's the capital of Verduun. Apparently recently renamed Astorov City." Pressing her lips together in distaste, Cala sat back on her heels to survey her drawing. "I've heard they've been getting a drought lately."

"That's what my brother Pierr said." Nevan leaned closer, hands behind his back. "You're an amazing artist."

"Thank you. It's part of my magic. A part that fortunately hasn't deserted me." She rose and tucked the chalk into a pocket, dusting her hands against her skirts. "I think I can send that storm to Verduun. Or at least that direction. Stand back."

As Nevan took a couple of big strides backward, Cala raised her hands and began to turn. He cut off his wordless protest as her feet smeared the drawing—she undoubtedly knew what she was doing, but the destruction seemed so wrong.

Wind blew Cala's damp hair away from her face, then swirled around her in a miniature storm. She chanted or sang something, but he couldn't understand any of the words, and the tune wouldn't stick in his mind. Faster and faster she turned, the drawing smearing under her feet, the wind gathering, the roar increasing. He fell back a couple more steps as wisps of vapor gathered around the witch.

Within moments, she was hidden by a thick cylinder of glowing, swirling storm. Nevan squinted, the brilliance making his eyes water. With a loud, wordless shout, Cala's hands appeared above the whirling clouds as she flung them up. An instant later, the storm launched upward, flying into the sky in a gigantic arc headed east. Like dogs chasing a rabbit, the dark clouds massed on the horizon shot after Cala's little storm, covering the setting sun then leaving it behind in a clear sky.

Cala collapsed. Nevan lunged forward, managing to catch her head before it impacted the stony ground.

CHAPTER TWENTY-FIVE

The wind increased as Franisa watched Starlight and Nevan disappear over the top of the cliff. She gripped the blanket around her shoulders more firmly and crouched to check that the last of the deck panels were locked into place. The dragon riders had replaced them before they departed, but Keldan had always insisted they ensure their boat was seaworthy before sailing, and old habits died hard.

"Ahoy, Madam Pirate!" Koni called.

Chuckling, she rose and peered over the side. Koni and Enrich had rowed the little skiff out to the fishing boat as Nevan had said they would. She helped her son aboard, but Koni hopped over the gunwale as if he was out for a morning stroll. She secured the little boat to the back of the larger one, the rising waves bouncing them as she worked. "That storm system is coming in."

"Not for long." Koni stood in the center of the deck with his head back and his eyes closed. He took a deep breath through his nose and let it out slowly, turning to face the spectacular colors splashed across the western sky. The bright red sun sat half-hidden behind thick dark clouds that covered the horizon. The light cast a rosy glow on the usually pale elf. "Cala is manipulating the weather."

Franisa took a half-step back, her breath caught in her chest. "She can't do that! Putting out that fire in the butcher shop almost killed her last year!"

"She's more resilient than you think." Koni opened his eyes, shading them with one hand to look at the horizon, then swung to face the cliff above them. "The magic is harder for her than when she was young, but she's been working on reconnecting to the strands. The effort might exhaust her, but there will be no long-term damage. There! Look!" He thrust his hand at the top of the cliff.

Light glowed beyond, outlining the tower and house sitting at the point in an eerie halo. A spear of brilliant blue-white launched over the house, arcing high above their heads and streaking southeast across the sky then disappearing like a falling star. A trail of vapor left a white line, ruler-straight, pointing back at the tower.

Then the sky darkened. The clouds on the horizon seemed to boil, lifting to cover the sun. The long mass drew together from the sides and stretched upward, rising like a phoenix. They coalesced into a long dark column, flowing across the sky in the wake of the smaller, faster spear of light. The storm picked up speed, streaking overhead to the east, disappearing with a faint boom, like a distant thunderclap.

The wild wind slowed to a steady stream following the storm. Franisa turned to look west and saw only a clear horizon with the sun still a few degrees above. She gaped at it for a long moment, astonished.

"That was amazing!" Enrich shouted, pumping a fist into the air.

Franisa's heart sank. Cala's last weather magic had left the witch dangerously weakened. She tugged at Koni's sleeve. "Do you think Cala is okay?"

Koni closed his eyes and breathed deeply again. "She's unconscious, but strong. Nevan is with her."

"You can tell that from here?"

The elf nodded. "I can feel their presence. Cala is quiet—asleep. She and Nevan are moving toward the house, so I think he's carrying her. William and Tyge are in the cave with the dragon. Sundri has calmed somewhat. The other dragons are—" He turned to face the open sea, squinting across the bright water. "Out there, I think. Starlight for sure. The others are harder to distinguish from the wild dragons." He shrugged and looked at her, then Enrich. "We should probably return our borrowed vessel."

"Right." Suddenly exhausted, physically and emotionally, Franisa nevertheless pointed at the sail. "Enrich, pull that rope to release the sails. Koni, use that one to raise them. Let's get home."

The return trip took less time than Franisa expected due to the wind trailing Cala's storm-sending. They reached the bay as the sun dropped beneath the horizon, leaving the ship in a shadowy twilight. "I'm not sure I can get this thing to the pier without the dragons to help." Franisa squinted at the long wooden jetties that looked so tiny from here.

Koni waved a hand at the sea anchor. "Let's leave it here. We'll take the skiff to the dock. I'll make sure Varient knows where to find it."

Grateful to leave the details to the mayor, Franisa nodded. "Let me get a little closer to that other ship. I don't want to block the main lane." She maneuvered the boat a few more yards into the bay, stopping it a good distance from the Dorfmundish schooner. "Toss the anchor over. It should hit bottom with about sixty feet of rope. Then we can go." While Koni and Enrich threw the sea anchor over and counted the stripes on the rope, she made a quick tour of the boat to make sure it was all shipshape—another habit Keldan had drilled into her.

They climbed into the skiff, and Franisa dropped onto the hard seat in the bow, leaving the rowing to Koni and Enrich. The rhythmic splash and whoosh of the oars lulled her into a stupor, her eyes drooping lower as darkness closed in over the bay.

She roused when they reached the pier and let Koni help her up to the wooden boardwalk. Then she took her equally tired son—he'd barely said a word on the sail back from FarPoint—and trudged home.

~

THE NEXT MORNING, SHE WOKE BEFORE DAWN AS USUAL AND

got the bread dough started. By the time Aislin and the children arrived downstairs, she had formed the first loaves.

"Where's Cala?" Eloise asked.

"She did some big magic yesterday." Franisa rolled dough into a large rectangle. "That makes her tired, so she has to rest." She measured the dough with her hand, then spread a generous layer of butter across it.

"I'll sprinkle the sugar!" Eloise dragged her stool closer to the worktable and climbed up. Franisa handed her the little bowl of sugar and spices and moved on to roll the next piece. "Oops!"

"Careful!" She glanced over to see a little spill of the cardamom and cinnamon-laced sugar on the table beyond the edge of the buttered dough. "That's not too bad. Scrape it up."

Eloise took the wooden scraper and cleaned up the spill. The normalcy of the morning made the previous afternoon's wild escapade feel almost like a dream. Franisa set the first batch of rolls to proof and made breakfast, then sent the children off to school.

The morning passed uneventfully, but by lunch Franisa was dying to know what had happened with Sundri and whether Cala was recovering. She still had the communication disk in her pocket, but the act of using it without a clear need felt invasive. She wasn't a dragon rider, even if she was officially betrothed to one. Her part in the rescue had been important but peripheral.

Or maybe she was just bashful about talking to Nevan after he kissed her cheek last night. Which was stupid. She was a grown woman with two children. A little kiss on the cheek was nothing.

Taking a moment to turn the sign on the door, she drew in a deep breath and pulled the disk out of her pocket. Moving to the kitchen, out of sight of anyone peering through the window, she tipped the disk toward the light. The image carved in the center was intricate, but she couldn't make out what it depicted. It wasn't worn or badly executed, but it seemed to evade her eyes.

Shrugging at this example of elven magic, she pressed her thumb against it. "Nevan?"

Nothing.

She tried again. "Nevan? Are you there?"

A faint sound—was it inside her head or coming from the disk? She still couldn't tell. But the noise sounded like soft, heavy breathing. Someone sleeping?

Feeling like a voyeur, she pressed the image again and dropped the medallion back into her pocket. Maybe Nevan was exhausted after yesterday's adventure. Or maybe that was the dragon she'd heard.

Flinging up her hands in frustration, she stomped to the door, wrapped her shawl around her shoulders, and headed out.

~

THE BUILDING KONI CALLED "CITY HALL" WAS MAINLY A gathering space. It had a big, empty room that would easily hold half the town's adult residents and a few smaller rooms on the side where the town clerk kept her records. Occasionally Koni could be found there, meeting with various people. But today his office was empty, and the clerk had stepped out.

Franisa turned toward the port, gazing across the calm water. Both the Dorfmundish schooner and Varient's boat were gone; they probably sailed on the morning tide. A couple of other ships swarmed with activity, but she didn't see anyone she recognized. With no physical evidence, her adventure felt more like a dream than before. She wrapped the shawl more tightly against the cold wind and headed back toward the bakery.

As she passed the Crab and Tankard, she caught a few words in a familiar voice. The front door opened, and Koni hopped up the two steps to the cobblestones beside her. "Well met, Pirate Captain!" He dusted his hands together, then offered his elbow.

She took his arm. "Well met? Do you have another boat for me to steal?"

"Borrow." He chuckled and turned her toward the bakery. "We definitely borrowed that boat. But no, not today. However, I shall keep your skill set in mind should the need arise. No, I am making Nevan's daily delivery run."

Disappointment washed through her like a splash of cold water. "He's not coming?"

A little smirk twitched the corner of Koni's mouth at her tone. "No, he has other duties. They're assessing the war dragon's injuries and developing a care plan. Nevan had to fly out to Valebra to request the healer."

"That wouldn't take all day—" She snapped her mouth closed. Nevan undoubtedly had more important things to do than deliver bread and eggs to the tower. And he might have had to walk back with the healer. "Does Wedreth know about dragons?"

"Not specifically, no. The sea dragons fend for themselves, as you know." Koni stopped in front of the bakery. "But she's skilled at mending other animals as well as humans, orcs, even dwarves. They're hopeful she'll have some ability to help Sundri as well."

"What about Sarai?" She tugged his arm, taking him around to the alley that ran along the side of her shop. "Can she heal dragons?"

"Possibly. She obviously hasn't had any practice since leaving Verduun, but her magic might give her an edge over Wedreth. I've sent a message to a friend in the Borgonne. He'll get it to her when he can."

She opened the door and went into the kitchen, pausing to hang her wrap on the peg beside it. "Let me get the delivery together. I'll include some extra for Sir Tyge." She put a loaf of bread into a basket and nodded at the still-open door. "Will you get the cream and butter?"

While she worked, Koni went out to retrieve the items from the little metal box in the stream that crossed her yard. Yrsadra, the dairy farmer, left the items there each day now, and with the increase in supply, the cold storage inside the bakery had filled up.

Koni arrived with two small crocks and one larger one. "How much of this—"

"Take it all. I have plenty here." She handed him another basket. "Yrsadra will want the crocks back, though. And I'll need my baskets, eventually."

Koni placed the butter and cream into his basket. "I'll make sure Nevan returns them."

Franisa ignored the little spurt of pleasure at the thought and tossed him a towel. "Wrap that around so they don't chip."

He tucked the cloth between the heavy crocks. "If we're going to keep this up, I should have Derwin make a carrier like Yrsadra has. Have you seen them?"

Franisa nodded with a smile. "I've been buying from the Skorras for a long time. Just not at this scale." She handed Koni the basket of baked goods. "That should be enough for today."

Koni reached for the handle, then snapped his fingers. "Almost forgot. Nevan said to tell you he gave the other half of your communication disk to Cala. So you can check in with her. And he'll come by tonight to take you to the smithy for supper." Koni scooped up the basket and flitted out the door.

"Wait, supper?" she called after him, but he was gone.

CHAPTER TWENTY-SIX

"You did what?" Crouched beside the cooler in the kitchen at FarPoint, Nevan stared up at Koni, his jaw slack with shock.

Koni handed a crock of butter to the giant. "She's your betrothed. I'm sure your mother has been expecting you to bring her home."

"Well, yes, but—"

"Show your mother some respect. And your betrothed." Koni wagged a teasing finger at Nevan. "They should get to know each other."

"They've lived across the square for as long as I can remember. They know each other. And this is fake." Nevan put the butter into the cooler and rose.

"Is it?" Koni crossed his arms and stared the younger man down. How he was able to do that while staring *up* at him, Nevan didn't know. "It doesn't have to be. You've been in love with her for ages, so what are you waiting for? You're a respected dragon rider, and she admires you. It was so obvious yesterday. If you ask her to make it real, she won't say no."

Nevan gulped, his cheeks burning. "How do you know? Is that elfish magic?"

"The term is 'elven.' And no, it's just the opinion of a scholar of human nature." Koni spread his hands in a shrug. "It's not a guarantee. But you're a catch, and she has made it clear she likes you. So take the leap."

"That's what my brother said, but he's only sixteen. I'm not taking life advice from a child."

"I'm much older than sixteen." Koni put a hand on his shoulder. "But if you don't believe me, ask Cala." He tipped his head toward the doorway.

Cala stood there, her head cocked, brow raised. She looked tired, and she wore a loose dress, a woolen shawl over her shoulders, and thick, fluffy socks rather than her usual wide pants. "What are you two plotting?"

"Nothing," Nevan snapped, his cheeks heating. He wasn't sure how long she'd been lurking and how much she'd heard.

"How to woo Franisa," Koni said with a cheerful smile at the giant. "You know you want to!"

What Nevan wanted was for the floor to open up and swallow him. He ducked his head and stared at the stone, but no amount of concentration caused even the tiniest crack. Which was good for his friendship with William but did not get him out of this embarrassing conversation.

"Fine." He threw up both hands. "You're right. What should I do?"

~

LATE THAT AFTERNOON, NEVAN KNOCKED ON THE KITCHEN door of the bakery, a basket clutched in each hand. Koni had suggested flowers, but even on Safe Haven, few flowers bloomed in the winter. But Cala had agreed returning the baker's baskets would be a good start and had added a jar of Koni's honey. It felt mundane to Nevan, and he bounced from foot to foot on the doorstep, nervously waiting for her to answer.

The door swung open, revealing Eloise, the ever-present Aislin hovering at her shoulder. "Hallo, Nevan!" She leaned close and drew in a deep breath then smiled approvingly. "You smell like dragon tonight." The pixie flew a quick circuit of his head and returned to Eloise, nodding in agreement, her huge purple eyes sparkling.

"Uh, thank you." He bowed a little, then followed the two into the room. Setting the baskets on the clean worktable, he eyed the child, shifting nervously. "Are you coming to dinner?"

"Mama said we was all invited, but Aislin doesn't eat people food, so she's going home to the bookshop." Eloise glanced at her friend.

The little creature sparkled and grinned, showing off a mouthful of very sharp teeth. Nevan wasn't sure he wanted to know what she ate.

"And Enrich?"

"He's coming too. He's upstairs, getting his nice clothes on." Eloise spun in the middle of the kitchen, showing off her pink dress. "Mine's prettier."

"You look very nice." He crouched to get on eye level with her. "Girl clothes *are* prettier."

She spread her skirt and curtsied. "I think so too. Watch me spin!" She turned again, the skirt flaring out.

"Mine does not do that."

Eloise giggled, longer and louder than Nevan expected. "Boys don't got spinny dresses!"

He rose and tugged on the bottom of his linen shirt, then turned twice. "No such luck."

Feet clattered on the steps, and the door at the back of the kitchen burst open. Enrich came through, wearing a dress shirt many sizes too large and his usual britches and worn boots. Franisa hurried down the steps behind him. "Wait! You're not done!"

"It's good enough! It's just the Goodhammers. They see me all the time!" Enrich spotted Nevan and put his hands on his hips. "Tell Ma I don't need to wear fancy clothes for dinner with your family."

Franisa stopped at the bottom, framed by the doorway. She wore a flower-sprigged gown with a gathered waist and full skirt—much more elegant than her usual work dress. Her thick hair was tucked up on her head with a matching ribbon threaded through the braids.

She took his breath away.

"Oh, Nevan, you're here!" She sounded as breathless as he felt, and her gaze darted away to her son. "Enrich, at least tuck in your shirt."

"Nevan's isn't." The boy pointed at him.

"Thanks for throwing me under the wagon." Nevan tugged at the shirt protruding from beneath his vest. "Cala said this is stylish."

Franisa's eyes darted to him and away again. "You look very nice, Nevan. But Enrich doesn't have a vest. It's not the same."

"Why is your shirt so big?" Eloise tugged her brother's hand. "You might be able to spin! Show him, Nevan!"

"I think I'll pass." Nevan shoved a hand through his hair, belatedly remembering how hard Cala had worked to smooth the curls. Well, too late now.

"It's one of Pa's shirts," Enrich told Eloise. "Ma said mine aren't nice enough for company."

"Yours are worn and too small. I've been meaning to remake a couple of these for you." Franisa fussed with the shoulder seams. "Maybe you should switch back—"

"Yes!" Enrich pulled away from his mother's fussy hands and bolted for the stairs. "I'll be right back!"

"Don't rip the shirt!" Franisa called after him, peering up the steps. "Maybe I should—"

Oddly calmed by Franisa's obvious nervousness, Nevan put a hand on her shoulder. "He'll be fine. It's just dinner with my family. You've broken bread with them before."

"We've eaten together at festivals. Or at the pub. I've never been invited into their home for a meal as their son's betrothed. That's big." She didn't meet his eyes.

He gulped, the nervousness returning. "Yeah."

She darted a glance in the vicinity of his shoulder. "We're being too dramatic. It's not a big deal. It's not—" She looked at Eloise, spinning with the pixie on the other side of the worktable, and lowered her voice. "It's not real."

"It could be." The words tumbled out of Nevan's mouth before he could stop them. His heart seized for a moment, then carried on at breakneck speed. Had he really said that? "I mean, if you want—"

Finally, she looked up, her brown eyes wide. Their gazes met with an almost physical snap, and his heart stopped again.

"What's not real, Mama?" Eloise appeared at Nevan's side, her eyes jiggling. She giggled and swayed. "I'm so dizzy!"

Franisa turned away, grabbing a loaf of bread from a rack. With quick movements, she wrapped it in a clean cloth and tucked it into a perfectly sized basket. "We'll take this to Derwin and Lilabeth. And some butter. We have plenty now!" She hurried toward the door. "I think there's a small crock out in the cooler."

Enrich reappeared at the foot of the stairs wearing his worn wool shirt with a large paisley vest overtop, the shirt hanging out the bottom like Nevan's. "How's this?"

Franisa stopped by the door, one hand on the wrap hanging from a peg beside it. She gave her son a quick but thorough scrutiny. "Where did you find that vest?"

"It was in the trunk you got that shirt from. One of Pa's, I guess." The boy smoothed a hand over the purple fabric. "I like the color."

"Your father wore that the day we were handfasted." Franisa touched his shoulder with a gentle finger, then drew in a deep breath. Her tone sounded matter-of-fact rather than nostalgic or romantic. "It's a good color for you. Still too big, but we can take it in—" She glanced at Nevan, then back at the boy. "Later. Let's go."

Franisa handed Enrich the basket while she shrugged into her wrap. "Get your cloaks, children."

"It's just across the square, Ma! And I got this vest to keep me warm!" Enrich pulled the door open and darted out, still clutching the bread.

Franisa wrapped another shawl around Eloise and nudged her toward the door. As she left, the pixie popped out of existence, dropping a cloud of glitter over the little girl. Eloise giggled. "I'm fancy now!"

"Where does she go?" Nevan stepped out into the alley and waited while Franisa latched the door behind them. The moon provided enough light to see.

Franisa crouched to pull a small crock from the metal box in the little stream that ran behind the buildings. "Aislin? Back to the bookstore. She's tied to it in some way. She can spend time here—as much as she wants—but the bookstore is her home. And I think she feels loyalty to Milli, or maybe one of Milli's ancient ancestors. With Cala spending so much time at FarPoint, Aislin watches over the shop. And cleans, of course. That pixie loves cleaning." She shook the water from the crock and followed the children out of the yard and up the lane.

They walked across the square, the lamp over the pump casting their shadows large against the front of the smithy. "We'll go around the side." Nevan gestured toward the lane leading by the pasture behind the smithy. They stopped at the back of the building, and Nevan opened the gate for the others, then latched it behind them. The pasture belonged to the stables next door, but another large door at the back of the smithy led directly into the fenced yard so Derwin could shoe horses.

"Stay on the path," Franisa called. "The pasture is still muddy."

"Will we see the horses?" Eloise danced along the stone path that led from the gate to the back door.

"Probably not. They go into their shed at night." He pointed at the long, low building behind the stable. A faint whickering confirmed this.

"That's too bad," Eloise said. "What about Starlight?"

"She's probably back at FarPoint." Nevan helped Enrich open the big door. "I sent her home. I'll sleep here tonight, and she'll come get me in the morning."

"Do dragons fly at night?" Eloise paused in the huge doorway, peering into the dark building.

Nevan slipped one of Cala's magic stones from his pocket and held it aloft. It cast a soft glow into the building, illuminating the shadowy entry but not much else. He nodded at a door on the right. "That goes up to the house."

This door was only wide and tall enough for a giant, not horses, of course, and it swung easily when Enrich pulled it open. A lamp hung from the wall at the top of the steps, welcoming them.

"Dragons *can* fly at night, but Starlight prefers to sleep when it's dark." Nevan gestured for the family to precede him up the steps. "Go right in. They're expecting us."

The children ran up, laughing about how much higher and wider the giant-sized treads were. Nevan had never paid much attention to the larger than normal build of the place until he'd spent time at FarPoint. The seventy-two steps up the tower were human-sized—tiny in comparison. "They're big. Be careful."

Franisa lifted her skirts to climb. The stairway was steep but narrow, so he let her go first, following close behind, one hand hovering in case she caught a toe on the tall risers. During their coaching session that afternoon, Cala had suggested he actually put a hand on her back, but that felt presumptuous.

They made it to the top without incident. The children stood together by the door, waiting.

"You can go on in," Nevan said.

"Enrich couldn't reach the latch." Eloise pointed at the lever over her head. The boy blushed.

"Nothing wrong with that," Nevan said cheerfully. "I couldn't reach it when I was young, either. My da had to tie a string on it for me. Giants are *big*." He couldn't remember ever being as tiny as these two, but then they were a quarter dwarf, so maybe he never was. He reached over Enrich's head and pressed the latch.

"Nevan! We've been waiting forever!" Gebhard yanked the door open, and Eloise tumbled through. "And you brought your family!"

Nevan's cheeks warmed at the idea that Franisa and the children were *his* family.

"We were expecting them, Gebby. Don't you ever listen?" Lilabeth came from the kitchen, drying her hands on her apron. She smacked the back of Gebhard's head, then pushed past him. "Come in!"

"They can't come in when you're blocking the door, Ma," Gebhard jeered.

Lilabeth turned, raising her hand again, and Gebhard ducked away. She scowled in mock anger, then turned back to the newcomers. "Come in. Franisa, Enrich, Eloise, welcome to our home." She backed away, beaming, to allow them inside.

"Thank you. Enrich has some bread for you." Franisa stepped into the warm room. "And here's some butter for it. The dairy has been so generous since Nevan fought the fire there."

Derwin came up behind his wife and took the basket from Enrich. "We're proud of our boy." He beamed at Nevan, then took the bread and butter away.

"That we are." Lilabeth waited for them to come inside, taking Franisa's shawl and hanging it on a peg behind the door. "Eloise, may I take your wrap?"

The little girl curtsied. "Thank you, ma'am."

In the giantess's hand, the shawl looked more like a handkerchief. She carefully hung it across Franisa's slightly larger knit wrap, then gestured to the table. "Dinner is ready if you'd like to sit."

The table and chairs were giant-sized, of course. The children climbed the spindles much as he had as a kid and scrambled onto the wooden seats. Franisa paused doubtfully beside the chest-high chair.

"May I?" Nevan held out both hands. At her nod, he gripped her waist. The feel of her soft body sent a fizz of sparks through his brain, like the pixie dropping sparkles on Eloise's head. Suddenly his mind refused to remember what he'd intended to do. He stood there, staring down at Franisa, marveling at her beauty, breathless and brainless.

A deep cough snapped him out of the daze, and he sheepishly lifted her onto the chair, heat flooding into his face. He lifted her too high, and she landed with a little thud. Everyone laughed. Nevan ducked his head and slipped onto the chair beside her, his cheeks hot.

Once everyone was seated, Derwin spoke the blessing, and they passed the dishes. Lilabeth served a delicious meal—roasted pork, potato wedges baked in the drippings, and stewed cabbage rolls stuffed with mushrooms and spices. Nevan couldn't remember the last time she'd gone to the trouble of making all his favorites. Of course, since pairing with Starlight, he'd rarely made the trek home for a meal.

"This smells good!" Eloise leaned close to the heavy crock holding the cabbage rolls, drawing in a deep breath.

Franisa blushed. "Eloise, don't sound so surprised. You've eaten Lilabeth's food before. You know she's a good cook."

"But this is diff'rent." The little girl waited while Lilabeth scooped one of the rolls onto her plate, then poked it with her fork. "It's smoky. In a nice way. Not like Rolph."

Franisa put her hands to her face. "I'm so sorry."

Gebhard wrinkled his nose and leaned closer to Eloise. "That carpenter guy? He smells like burnt hair."

Eloise shot a triumphant look at her mother, then swung around to face Gebhard, the little piece of cabbage roll flying off her fork. It landed on Gebhard's plate. Franisa groaned, but the giant simply picked it up and popped it into his mouth.

"Hey, that was mine!" Eloise shook the fork at him.

"You fling food at me, I eat it." Gebhard lifted his own fork and poked it at Eloise's plate. "Or if you leave it lying around too long."

"This one's mine! Eat your own, giant boy!"

"Eloise!" Franisa hunched her shoulders, her face burning bright.

Lilabeth laughed. "I'm glad Gebby has finally found someone his own age to play with."

"I'm sixteen!" Gebhard protested.

"Sixteen going on six," Lilabeth retorted. Derwin grinned, nodding in agreement.

Nevan turned to Franisa, ignoring his family's mock argument. "Sorry about them."

She looked up, her face still pink. "For what? Unlike my family, they aren't throwing food or smelling people."

"Gebby just said he smelled the carpenter. And just because the food throwing hasn't started yet doesn't mean it won't happen." He bit his lip, watching her face. He still wasn't sure Cala and Koni were right about Franisa's feelings for him, but he knew any long-term arrangement between them would be better if she liked his family. Sure, they'd been neighbors forever, but getting along with the neighbors was different if they were also your in-laws.

Or so he assumed. He'd never had in-laws, but he'd heard all the usual stories. And seen how much trouble Franisa was having with her current ones. Which was why they were in this situation in the first place. Not that he regretted it one bit. Their false betrothal had given him the chance to try to make it real.

But something in her expression gave him confidence. Like she was just waiting for him to say the right thing. He had always admired her courage and independence. Until the situation with Gnollis, he'd never thought she needed anyone else. And he didn't want her to just need his protection. He wanted her to want him. Maybe Cala and Koni were right. Maybe it was time to lay his heart at her feet. At least then he'd know and could move on.

The ridiculous bickering faded to a pleasant hum as he searched her face, trying to remember the lines his friends had coached him on. Instead, as usual, he said the first thing that popped into his head. "They can be your family too."

CHAPTER TWENTY-SEVEN

Franisa gazed up at Nevan. Around them, his family and hers continued to argue cheerfully, but she didn't hear any of it. Somehow, she and Nevan seemed to be cocooned in a bubble of white noise, alone at this table full of loud children and louder giants.

She met his gaze for a long moment before speaking. "You said something… in the bakery. That this could be—" She dropped her voice to a whisper. "Real."

Nevan drew in a deep breath, his feelings for her seeming to burn in his eyes. "Say the word."

When she'd first conscripted Nevan into her daft scheme, she'd only been thinking about Enrich. How to keep him safe from his grandfather. And even now, that was still a concern. If she turned down Nevan —if she told him she didn't want their relationship to be real—would he refuse to play along? That wasn't a risk she was willing to take.

She also wasn't willing to lie to Nevan. She wouldn't *pretend* she wanted to marry him. Koni had said there were other options. And Cala had suggested she simply stand up to Gnollis and say no. If her friends were willing to back her, maybe she didn't need this pretend betrothal to keep her son safe.

But staring up at him, those arguments didn't seem to matter. Because something inside her wanted to make it real. This man cared about her. He cared about her children. And he'd offered her his heart. The idea of refusing that offer left a cold, sad little hollow in her stomach. In the few weeks they'd been playing this game, she'd gotten used to the idea. She'd become accustomed to having him at her side—that invisible presence she'd felt when speaking with him via the magic disk. The knowledge that he could be with her in moments, flying to the rescue on his dragon.

And the idea of anyone else taking that place left her cold. She'd married Keldan because her father arranged the match. And although he frustrated her and hadn't provided the security that arrangement had been written to provide, she'd come to care for him.

But since then, she'd seen the love that drove William and Cala together. She'd witnessed the happiness of Trudi-from-the-pub with her bard. And now, in the warmth of this family, she was reminded of the very real love between Nevan's parents.

She wanted that. As much as she wanted safety for her children. She wasn't sure what she felt for Nevan was the same, but it was already so much more than she'd had with Keldan.

"Yes," she whispered.

Nevan's eyes blazed. "You mean it? For real?"

"For real." She nodded. Would he kiss her? Right here in front of his family?

A chunk of bread bounced off the side of Nevan's face.

Nevan choked, whipping around to glare at his brother. Face flaming, Franisa looked at her hands in her lap.

"Nevan! Wake up!" Gebhard tossed another piece of bread.

Nevan's hand snapped up, and he caught the bread, hurling it back in one smooth move. "See?" he said to Franisa, not taking his eyes off his brother. "I told you there'd be food throwing."

After dinner, and a lively game of bones, they said their farewells. Nevan lifted a sleepy Eloise, and she snuggled into his shoulder as if she belonged there. Franisa draped the girl's shawl across her back, thanked their hosts, and nudged Enrich toward the stairs, almost sad to leave the cozy home. Derwin and Lilabeth walked them down the steps. At the bottom, Derwin pulled the big door open and shepherded Nevan and Enrich out into the pasture.

Lilabeth put a hand on Franisa's arm. "I want you to know I approve."

Franisa glanced up at the giantess, but her big form blocked the light from the stairwell lamp. "Of me and Nevan? You say that like you didn't before."

The shadowy figure shrugged. "I wasn't sure. I know the boy has been besotted with you for years. But I didn't like the idea that you might not feel the same. Now, well, you're clearly as smitten as he is. It's a good match."

Franisa stared up at her, wishing she could see the other woman's face but at the same time grateful she couldn't. "You think I'm smitten?"

Lilabeth chuckled. "Definitely. I have no worries. At all. You two are perfect for each other."

HER MORNING BAKING AND SALES FINISHED, FRANISA PACKED up a basket for the dragon riders. She tucked bread, sea shell rolls, butter, and eggs beneath a clean towel and set it on the counter. Last night, Nevan had carried Eloise up to bed, then promised to return after lunch to pick up the delivery and talk.

Talk. How could one word carry so much weight?

She flipped the sign on the front door and bolted it, then returned to the kitchen to find Gnollis standing in the open back door.

The wizened dwarf glared at her. "Where's the boy?"

"He's at school." She stiffened her back. "And he's no longer your concern."

"We need him at the mine."

"He's not going in the mine. Ever again." She moved closer, crowding him out the door. Why had she never realized her height gave her a physical advantage over the little man? His dwarven build made him stronger than her, but thanks to Philomena, he'd been conditioned to treat human women with deference.

He stepped backward off the low stoop, almost tumbling into the yard. "He'll never learn a trade if he doesn't start. He'll turn out like his father."

She crossed her arms, scowling. "He's a child. He has plenty of time to learn a trade. Here at the bakery. Or with Brenet. That's right, the butcher suggested a trade. Or maybe he'll become a dragon rider. No matter what he chooses, it will be a trade he'll be able to continue in for the rest of his life, not just until he's too tall to fit." She stalked forward, forcing him out of the yard and toward the square.

Gnollis blinked up at her, as if that had never occurred to him before. It was hard to see his expression behind that bushy beard and peaked hat pulled low over his brows, but somehow she could tell she'd taken him by surprise.

"Huh." He scratched his chin, the carved trinkets woven into his beard clinking dully. "I guess that makes sense. He is gonna get too big. Why didn't you say that before?" Without waiting for a reply, he turned and stomped up the lane.

Franisa stared after him, dumbfounded. "I did say so!" she hollered as the top of his hat disappeared behind the fountain.

Nevan appeared at her shoulder, grinning. "That was easy."

Franisa turned with a surprised shriek. "Where did you come from?" She clutched at her chest as if she needed to keep her suddenly pounding heart inside by force.

He chuckled and jutted a thumb over his shoulder. "Starlight landed in the back. It's a tight fit, but she made it. She's very interested in Eloise's pixie village."

Franisa followed him back down the lane. Her little back garden seemed to be full of silvery-blue dragon. Starlight's powerful tail curled around the little table and chairs sitting beside the windows, while her long neck curved down near the thick plants at the back. A sparkle of pixie glitter floated around her head as she sniffed at something on the ground.

"Aislin is here?"

He shrugged. "She popped in as soon as Starlight poked her nose down there. They appear to be having a silent but friendly conversation."

Franisa drew in a deep breath, trying to bring her unruly heart under control. His appearance had startled her, but his nearness kept her on edge. Last night he'd promised they'd talk, but what did he want to say? Had he changed his mind?

Although Gnollis appeared to no longer be a problem, the idea that Nevan might not want to marry her after all made her breath catch in her lungs. But she didn't want to coerce him into anything. "Look, about last night." She waved at the lane, keeping her eyes on the middle of his chest. "Gnollis seems to have given up. We don't have to... If you don't want—"

"Oh, I want." He reached out and took her hand. "Do you?"

Could it really be this easy? She lifted her eyes to meet his gaze. "Yes, please." As she said the words, a huge weight seemed to shift off her shoulders. She'd been so wrapped up in protecting her family, she hadn't realized that what she wanted and what she needed were the same thing. Him.

Cupping a hand against her cheek, he leaned down and gently pressed his lips against hers. The kiss was slow and sweet and full of promise.

Then a big blue head pressed between them.

"Starlight!" Nevan pushed the dragon away, but the smile on his face sent her heart soaring. "You promised to give me some privacy!"

"She did?" Franisa looked from Nevan to the dragon and the little pixie fluttering above her head. The dragon leaned in again, locking eyes with her.

Nevan gave Starlight's head another push, but she didn't budge. "Yes. We discussed it on the flight."

Franisa couldn't drag her gaze from the dragon's beautiful silvery eyes. "And does she mind? Me, I mean?"

"I like." The words seemed to ring in her head. *"You fly?"*

Franisa choked. "You want me to fly with you? In the air?" She pointed up. "On your back? Can you carry a passenger?"

"She gots lotsa power." Aislin fluttered closer, her sparkles falling and fading before hitting the little stone stoop on which they stood. "She good flyer. Flying is fun!" She buzzed around them, doing pixie aerobatics.

"I am not doing that." Franisa pointed a shaking finger at the looping pixie.

"No, we'll stay straight and true." Nevan's words seemed to refer to more than just the flight. "I brought you a belt. In case you wanted to come." He trailed off hopefully at the end, sounding more like the diffident boy she'd known for so many years.

She frowned up at him. "What—don't take this the wrong way. I am not opposed to confident Nevan. But what happened? I know you've been interested in me for a long time—" Seeing his cheeks redden, she broke off, reaching up to put a hand against his heated skin. "It's nothing to be ashamed of. But what made you brave enough to—"

"You." He put his hand against hers, holding it to his cheek. "Starlight. Everything over the last few days. The way you took control of that boat and sailed Sundri to FarPoint, even though you hadn't done it in years. The way you stood up to Gnollis just now. The way you looked at me when I—" He sighed, a happy, contented sound.

He squeezed her fingers. "And fighting that fire—I guess it gave me a boost. That I'm doing what I'm meant to do. That I'm worthy." The dragon's head swung over, and she tapped the top of his head with her nose. He turned and slid a hand up the beast's neck. "And Starlight said you'd say yes. Then Koni said—"

"Ah ha! I knew that elf had something to do with it!" She laughed and turned back toward the door, almost relieved to have broken the tension between them. It was a good tension, but too much—especially with an audience. Even if it was just a dragon and a pixie. "Let me get the basket."

She slipped into the kitchen, returning a moment later with her wrap and the food. "How are we going to carry this?" She couldn't believe she agreed to ride a dragon, but with Nevan and Starlight, the idea felt natural.

While she'd been inside, Nevan had retrieved some leather straps from somewhere. He held out a single belt that would easily wrap around her waist twice. Two more straps hung from it with elongated rings on the ends. He lifted one and ran a thumb along some zig-zagged cuts on one edge. "See these cuts? They allow the metal to flex."

He pressed the longer side above the cuts, and it bent inward, leaving a gap. Then he slipped that over the ring hanging from his own belt and released. The metal snapped back into place, and he tugged on the straps. "Locked. You try it."

She took the metal, still warm from his grip, and squeezed the side. The metal moved, but she didn't have the strength to open it wide enough. "I can't take it off."

His hand closed over hers, and he smiled down into her eyes. "That's all right. I'm here to do it for you." He unclipped the ring, then held the belt out again. "May I?"

Setting the basket aside, she nodded and lifted her hands. He reached around her, passing the belt behind her back, then buckling it securely around her waist. His nearness made her heart tremble, and she drew in a deep breath, then laughed. "Eloise is right. You do smell good."

Nevan pulled the long end of the belt snug and settled it, his hands warm against her hips. "I guess it's a good thing you like dragon." He pulled her a little closer.

She tilted her head up, inviting another kiss. He leaned in, his hands tightening as she slid hers up his chest. The second kiss was as sweet as the first.

And interrupted by the dragon again. *"Fly?"* Starlight tapped her nose against Nevan's shoulder, then flicked her tongue around Franisa's head and shoulders. *"Fly now?"*

"She's as subtle as a five-year-old." Franisa picked up the basket and nodded at the dragon. "Let's do this before I come to my senses."

Nevan paused as he reached for her hand. "You're talking about the flying, not—" He waved his hand between them.

She wrapped her fingers around his. "Yes, the flying. There's no question about the rest."

"It's a lot. You, me, the children, the dragon—" He chuckled a little. "It's a lot."

"It's perfect." She squeezed his hand. "Now, how do we do this?"

He pulled her closer to the dragon's side and released her hand to grasp her waist. He lifted her slowly, taking the time to kiss her on the way up. "Fling your leg over her neck."

Franisa lifted her leg, grateful she'd worn her work pants rather than a dress this morning. She slid it over the dragon's neck, scrambling to grip the leather harness fastened around the beast's shoulders as Nevan let go. He kept one hand on her hip, giving a little push until she was astride.

"Now I'm coming up." Using the dragon's back leg as a step, he gracefully climbed on behind Franisa. Their legs draped over the dragon's shoulders, tightly pressed together. Nevan used the straps and flexible rings hanging from her belt to attach her to the dragon's harness, then clicked his own on. "I added a second set of rings back here. For passengers." His arms slid around her waist, and he pulled her back against his chest.

Breathless, she gripped the basket handle tightly. "When did you do that?"

"Oh, weeks ago. I hoped I'd need them someday." His chest vibrated against her as he spoke.

"How many weeks ago?"

"Right after you told Gnollis I was your intended," he answered sheepishly.

Starlight swooped her head around on that long neck to look back at them, then tapped her nose against Franisa's leg. *"Fly?"*

Franisa settled the basket in her lap, holding it against Nevan's arms. She took a deep breath. "Fly."

CHAPTER TWENTY-EIGHT

Flying on Starlight's back was the best thing that had ever happened to Nevan. Until he flew *with Franisa* on Starlight's back. The three of them soaring together over the island was perfection.

Starlight had launched them into the air with a powerful leap, her wings beating down in the narrow space behind the bakery. Nevan's heart had squeezed in alarm—those translucent membranes looked so fragile and the building so solid. But as always, Starlight had judged perfectly, her wing tips skimming past the plaster and beams as they rose.

Franisa gasped, and he tightened his grip around her. The sturdy straps and rings would hold, but she seemed to relax as he held her close. The dragon's strong strokes ruffled the ends of the thatched roof, startling a family of birds who launched into the sky twittering angrily.

He laughed. "Poor birds."

"I've been trying to evict them from my roof for ages. They keep coming back," Franisa said breathlessly. "Maybe having a dragon taking off in my yard will help."

He looked back over his shoulder as they rose above the house.

"They don't look like they're going anywhere." He hummed in thought. "How would you feel about modifying the bakery?"

"What do you mean?" She leaned into him, resting her head against his chest.

Her presence made it hard to think clearly. Giving a little shake of his head, he nudged Starlight's neck with his leg. "Circle for a moment, will you?"

Starlight obediently banked, turning tightly over the square in front of the bakery. At another gasp from his betrothed, he pressed his arms firmly against her sides. "You're safe. But look. Maybe we could build a kind of perch for Starlight on the back of the house. And a door where that window is. Then we could come and go from the upper floor. Easier for her to take off."

"You want to live here after we—" Franisa broke off with an uncertain laugh.

"Did you want to give up the bakery?"

"No, of course not. That's my livelihood. And my children's legacy." She cast a swift look over her shoulder at him. "And not to cast aspersions on your manliness, but I'm not sure dragon riding is a very sustaining career."

He chuckled. "Don't worry, we've been having that discussion. Koni's tax will support the fire brigade, including all of us dragon riders. We can live at FarPoint if you prefer."

She squirmed a little. "I don't think there's room for all of us in the stables. And it's not exactly private."

He jiggled her a little with his arms. "I forgot, you haven't seen my new place. We'll stop by to visit Sundri, then you can decide. Starlight, let's head home."

As they'd been talking, the dragon had continued to fly a tight circle over the bakery and smithy. At Nevan's command, she tilted her wings, straightening their flight. But instead of taking the fastest route over the island, she soared toward the port. "Where are you going?"

"New flyer. See all." Starlight wiggled her wings a bit, tipping them left then right.

"I guess you're getting the tour." They flew over the town, gradually gaining altitude as they crisscrossed over the pub, then Cala's bookstore, out to the dairy and around the dwarven enclave. As they finally reached the port, Starlight banked gently, taking them across the bay well above the ships docked there. With a few more strong downbeats, they sailed along the shore, easily staying above the rising land as they approached the point at the end of the island.

"There's FarPoint!" Franisa relaxed enough to release one hand from the basket and point at the tiny-looking building. "We got here so fast!"

"Can fly faster!" Starlight's rhythm increased.

Nevan squeezed his legs gently against the dragon's neck. "We're going fast enough. There's no hurry today. Take us around the tower, then down to our aerie."

"Aerie? What do you mean?" Franisa asked as they looped around the landward side of the building. Finn bugled from his post atop the stone tower. Far below, Cala stood in the courtyard next to Nari. Shading her eyes with one hand, she looked up and waved. "Did she know we were coming?"

"I called her while you were in the house. And Starlight might have told them. The dragons speak to each other." He wasn't sure "speak" was the right word, but they definitely communicated. Only Starlight seemed to use words so far.

They dropped lower as they soared out over the sea. The cliff dropped away beneath them, earning another gasp from Franisa. Starlight banked, bringing them down and around in a spiral. Franisa squealed softly at the tight turns, but Nevan wasn't sure if she was scared or thrilled. As they curved toward the cliff, light glinted on something bright in his cliff-side retreat.

Starlight flared her wings and landed easily on the ledge, turning to give her passengers an easy dismount. As Nevan unclasped his straps, Tyge emerged from the cave, his hair mussed and his clothing wrinkled. His unreadable gaze passed over them, and he gave a stiff bow. Nevan fought his immediate flush of inferiority in the Verduunian's presence.

"He's sad. Worried." Starlight stretched her neck to taste the air

around the older dragon rider. The man absently reached up to pat the dragon's neck. That little act of kindness did much to soften Nevan's feelings toward him.

"Good afternoon, Tyge. How's the patient?" Imitating William's confident attitude, Nevan slid down Starlight's side. He reminded himself this was *his* home, and while Tyge might be one of the famous dragon riders of Verduun, he was a guest here. A supplicant even. Nevan wasn't going to let the man's arrogant attitude dent his newfound confidence.

"Nevan. Mistress baker." Tyge ran a hand through his greasy hair. "I'm sorry, I don't remember your name."

Franisa handed the basket down to Nevan, then waited. "I'm Franisa Hearthwell. We brought some bread and butter." She cast a questioning look at Nevan.

"Yes, help yourself to that." Nevan handed the basket to the other man.

"Nevan? Can you—" Franisa gestured at her belt.

"Oh, sorry! I'm not used to carrying passengers!" Instructing Starlight to crouch lower, he leaned around Franisa to unlatch her flying straps. He moved slowly, savoring the opportunity to be near her. When he'd gotten her unclipped, he reached up to grasp her by the waist and slowly lower her to the ground.

Tyge cleared his throat, and Nevan jumped, almost dropping Franisa. They turned, like guilty children facing an elder.

"Have you seen William?" Tyge's gaze flitted over and through them as if their presence was of no importance to him. Or perhaps his concern for his dragon kept him from focusing on the here and now. "I was hoping he'd come down to see Sundri today."

"I spoke with him this morning." Nevan put a hand on Franisa's back and urged her a little closer to the older man. "He said he'd bring the healer."

Tyge turned to the side and spat. "That cattle wizard?"

Still channeling his inner William, Nevan drew himself up to his full height—towering over the other man. "Wedreth is an exceptionally talented healer of both humans and animals. She's the best we've got right now. We've put out some feelers to attract someone with dragon experience, but protecting the island requires—"

"Yeah, I know. Your daft elf mayor won't let anyone come unless they have a pure heart and—"

"Which makes me wonder how you got here!" Franisa broke in.

A spurt of pride went through Nevan, and he pressed his hand more firmly against her back. He could feel her trembling, but her fierce glare hid her trepidation from Tyge. They scowled at each other for a long moment, then Starlight inserted her nose between the combatants. *"Fly?"*

Franisa jerked a little and glanced at the dragon with a small smile. Tyge merely pushed Starlight's nose away. Apparently the famous Verduunian dragon rider couldn't hear his little Starlight.

"True."

With a smirk he tried to hide, Nevan patted his dragon's neck, then gestured at the cave. "We just came down so I could show my betrothed what I've been working on. No need to disturb you or Sundri. I trust he is resting peacefully?"

Tyge's teeth ground together then he glanced over his shoulder at the bulk of scales glinting in the mild sunlight near the back of the shallow alcove. "As peacefully as he can with his wing stitched together like a quilt. He needs magic. Strong magic, not the little that war witch can provide."

"That *war witch* is your hostess." Franisa pushed Starlight's nose away as the dragon tried to stop her angry forward march. She stopped uncomfortably close to Tyge, standing on her toes to point a finger in his face. "And whatever magic she has expended on his behalf is more than *you* deserve. Why you think we owe you anything is beyond me."

Tyge stared her down for a long moment, then turned and stomped back into the cave. "I'll let you see yourselves out."

Franisa started after him, but Nevan caught her arm. "Don't. He's distraught, and dragons pick up emotions. Negative emotions can slow healing. We want him healthy as soon as possible." He didn't add that the man and dragon would both be evicted as soon as they could fly, but he could see she understood that sentiment.

Trying to reduce the emotional temperature in the cave, he gestured at the vertical beams marking off the wall that would be built across the front. "I'm putting in a lot of windows, so it's light inside. In the summer, the sun is high enough that the place stays cool. And I've already installed that little heater. Getting wood down here is a chore, but the canvas 'bucket' we used to carry Sundri can bring a week's load in a single flight."

He slid his arm around her and turned her toward the ledge. "And you can't beat the view."

They gazed out at the sea sparkling in the afternoon sunlight. Off in the distance, the wild dragons played in the sea. Franisa shaded her eyes with a hand and frowned at them. "Do you miss your siblings, Starlight?"

The dragon cocked her head at Franisa, as if she didn't understand the question.

"She plays with them most days. In fact, once she takes us back up, she can go." He slapped the dragon's side, then urged his betrothed closer to her.

"Can we walk up?" Franisa smiled hopefully at him. "I mean, if this is going to be your home, I'd hope there's a way I can come visit. And if you show me, Starlight can swim now."

"Swim?" Starlight bounced in place, eager to join her herd. School? Thunder?

"Let me get her harness off, then I can show you." He had Starlight turn so he could reach the buckles at the front, then caught the straps as she shook them from her front legs one by one. Looping the leather over his shoulder, he stepped back and waved at the sea. "Off you go!"

Starlight butted the top of her head against his chest and touched her nose gently against Franisa's cheek, then dove over the side of the cliff. They watched as she plummeted, pulling up just as she reached the sea and soaring across the waves, dipping her wingtips into the spray. Nevan beamed with pride at his partner's skillful flying.

"This way." He gestured to the path at the end of the ledge. "It's a bit narrow at the beginning, but I'm working on that." He turned as they reached the end of the ledge. "Oravai, Sundri. Tyge." Franisa echoed his words, but they got only a grunt in reply.

His betrothed leaned close to the stone face as she rounded the little outcropping, then visibly relaxed as the path widened. Although it was still narrow, it looked easy compared to that first bit. They ducked under the tree and came out on the landing beside the stairs to the beach.

"I should probably cut down that tree." Nevan jutted a thumb back at the plant, little more than a straggly bush clinging to a crack in the stone at head height. "But it worked so hard to grow there."

From the safety of the landing, Franisa looked past him. "I think it deserves to stay. And you're the only one who really has to duck." She reached up to pat his shoulder. "Besides, it provides a little privacy. No one would think to walk out there."

"No one will be on these stairs without Koni's magic." Nevan gestured to the stone treads cut into the living rock. "Both ends are hidden if you don't have one of his amulets. If we live there, I'll have to get you one."

"Oh, I'm not living there." Franisa looked over her shoulder as she started up the steps, her grin taking the sting from her words. "You and Starlight can keep it as a refuge from town, but I'm staying put in my bakery. I might come visit on occasion." She cast him one more flirty glance and headed up the steps.

He watched her hips sway as she climbed, his mind a pleasant buzzing blank, then hurried to catch up when she rounded a corner. "I guess we'll live at the bakery, then. Tyge can have the aerie."

"You think he'll stay?" She paused to catch her breath, turning to admire the view. "There's Starlight!"

The little dragon—easily recognizable by her smaller size—shot up into the sky then twisted and turned to dive into the sea, splashing the other dragons floating nearby.

Nevan basked in the warm pride in his betrothed's voice. She'd clearly adopted the dragon into her little clan. *Their* little clan. He slid an arm around her, and she leaned against him as they watched the dragons' antics for a while. Then he leaned down and kissed her.

After a long, delicious moment, a shadow passed overhead—Finn and William flying down to visit the invalid. Nevan and Franisa broke apart to wave, then resumed their climb. As they stopped at the top of the stairs to rest again, he remembered Franisa's question. "I'm not sure Tyge *can* leave. Verduun thinks Sundri is dead, so if he recovers, he can't return. And if he doesn't... I don't think he'll want to go back."

"Fantastic."

Her sour tone surprised him. Not that he disagreed, but it wasn't like Franisa to sound so negative. He took her hand and tugged gently, starting across the stony top of the peninsula toward the tower. "Maybe if—when Sundri recovers, he'll be more pleasant. And if not, we can just leave him alone in his little cave."

"But you put so much work into it already!" She leaned her shoulder against his arm as they walked. "It doesn't seem fair—"

He pulled her to a halt, turning to face her. "I'd rather have a healthy dragon. And you."

She laughed a little and stood on her toes to press a kiss against his jaw. "Good answer."

CHAPTER TWENTY-NINE

A week later, Sundri still lay in the aerie, stiff and silent. Wedreth, the healer from Valebra, had suggested the dragon might heal better if he could get some exercise, which was impossible in the little cave. When Tyge had suggested the healer should get exercise by jumping off the edge of the cliff, the woman threw up her hands and left.

"That isolation isn't good for Sundri." Cala poured ale for the Dragon Council—as they'd taken to calling themselves—the three dragon riders plus Koni and Franisa. After school, Koni had walked Franisa and her children out to FarPoint to discuss options.

"It's not good for Tyge either," William added. The others grumbled sourly—the Verduunian hadn't made any friends in his time in Safe Haven. William lifted a placating hand. "He wasn't so surly in Verduun."

"There weren't any *inferior* dragon riders in Verduun," Nevan muttered then gulped some ale.

"He didn't say that, did he?" Cala pushed her chair back from the table. "Because he and I will have words—"

"No. But I can tell what he's thinking." Nevan set his tankard down.

"And more to the point, so can Starlight. He doesn't hear her, but she can hear him."

"Are you sure?" William looked up in surprise. "She isn't reading your thoughts and applying them to him?"

"Oh, she probably is," Nevan said. "But she can definitely hear him too. She says he's worried about Sundri."

"We're all worried about Sundri." William waved dismissively. "Hence our discussion today."

"But Tyge thinks the old injury—the one from when he was here before—he thinks the scar tissue from that injury is preventing this one from healing."

"He hasn't mentioned that to me." William drummed his fingers on the table. "Has he discussed that with Wedreth?" Then he waved off their reactions. "Never mind. I withdraw the question. Of course he hasn't."

"If it were just him, I'd say let's toss him out." Cala wrinkled her nose. "But I'm not willing to abandon Sundri just because he's a—" She laughed a little. "Because he's a *Verduu*." She said the last word like a curse.

William snorted into his ale, then began coughing. Nevan pounded his back while Cala got him a glass of water. When the fit subsided, the older man wiped his eyes and sat back with a smirk. "That's what you used to call me, I'm betting."

"It's a common swear word in the Borgonne. Mostly applied to the vaunted dragon riders of course, but it's a multipurpose curse." She patted her husband's hand. "I don't like to use it now, but sometimes no other word will fit."

"As long as we agree I am not one anymore, you can use it as necessary." William squeezed her fingers and turned back to the uncharacteristically quiet council. "Koni, you haven't said a word."

The elf leaned his elbows on the table, steepling his fingers over his tankard. "I have little to add to the conversation at this point. I agree getting Sundri and his rider out of the aerie is a good idea. Healthier for both of them. Sir Tyge's sour attitude isn't helping with his dragon's recovery. Can we move them... elsewhere?" His gaze darted to the door leading into the entryway and thence to the stables.

"You want him to live with us?" Nevan's voice cracked a little. "I'm not sure that's going to be any better for Tyge's attitude. And it might be detrimental to mine and Starlight's."

Koni snickered. "I concur. Let him and his dragon have the stable. You can move down to the aerie. Or perhaps"—his gaze slid to Franisa—"to the bakery?"

Franisa blushed bright red and ducked her head. Koni smirked and sipped his ale.

Cala looked from Koni to the others, her brows coming down. "Is—did you—" She waved her hand at the two of them. "And you didn't tell us?!"

Nevan bit his lip, then nodded shyly at Cala. "Yes, your coaching worked. We're officially betrothed, for real." He reached for Franisa's hand and gripped it tightly. He wasn't sure why he hadn't admitted as much when it first happened, but something had kept him from speaking. Maybe he just needed time to let reality sink in.

"Finally!" Cala threw up her hands, then jumped from her chair. "This calls for a celebration!" She hugged Franisa then moved to the dresser at the end of the table and pulled out a bottle of mead which she set on the table.

Koni's hand curled around the bottle. "Where have you been hiding this?" He looked at the writing on the glass. "It isn't mine."

"No, I got that from the Dawn Trader. They had a shipment from Dorfmund. Not that your mead isn't delicious, but—"

"Lazyz is the gold standard." Koni interrupted her, gazing at the bottle with loving eyes. "The best mead in all the land. Or so I've been told. I tasted some, about decades ago. It was incredible. That was what inspired me to make my own. A pale imitation, I'm afraid." He peeled the wax seal from the cork.

Cala set some small glasses on the table beside the bottle. "I've been saving it for a special occasion. This seems appropriate. Will you do the honors? You'll notice I gave you a *small* glass."

Koni poured a couple of inches of amber liquid into each of the five glasses. “A small glass is all I need if this vintage is as good as they claim.”

William snorted. “I’ll believe that when I see it.” He took the glass Koni offered and raised it. “To Nevan and Franisa. May their union be as smooth as the flight of a dragon.”

“I’m not sure that’s—” Franisa started.

The others overrode his betrothed’s faint objection. “To Nevan and Franisa!” They all sipped their mead.

Nevan tried not to make a face. The beverage was far too sweet for his taste. Franisa took a tiny sip and set hers on the table too.

Koni’s bright gaze darted from their faces to their glasses and back. He took another sip and set his empty glass down. “When is this hand fasting to take place? I see no reason to put it off. You both have important things to do.”

“And you don’t want our marriage to get in the way of Sir William’s fire brigade?” Franisa suggested, her tone dry.

“Exactly.” Koni darted a glance at the half-full glasses again.

With a laugh, Cala pushed hers across the table to the elf. “This mead may be the best in the land, but I prefer your drier version any day, Koni. You’re welcome to finish mine.”

He took the glass with a smile of gratitude. “No reason to waste it on the untrained palate.”

Cala chuckled as she slapped his arm. “I paid you a compliment! And gave you a drink. No need to be rude.”

Koni did one of his complex hand gestures as he half-bowed. “I appreciate both the sentiment and the libation.” He lifted the glass in another toast. “And your ability to give honor where it is due at the expense of your own prestige.”

“If you’re saying I’m not ashamed to admit when I don’t like something that’s supposedly superior, you’re one hundred percent right. Life is too short to drink wine you don’t like. Or mead, for that matter.”

Nevan breathed out a sigh of relief and pushed his glass across the table to the elf. “I’d much rather have ale.”

Franisa followed suit. Nevan refilled their tankards and the two tapped them together. William finished off his mead, then held his ale out for a top off. "Some mead may be great, and some mead may be too sweet, but ale always starts at good."

At Nevan's confused frown, William smirked and held a hand above the table. "Ale starts at good." He lifted his hand higher. "And gets better. Never worse."

"I can drink to that." He clinked his stein against William's and drank.

"Now, back to business." William waved toward the garden. "How do we get them out of the aerie?"

~

TYGE STOOD IN FRONT OF HIS DRAGON, ARMS SPREAD. "YOU can't throw us out! Why bother rescuing Sundri if you're just going to toss us away like this!"

"We aren't throwing you out." William laid the bundle of canvas and leather on the floor of the cave. "We're moving you up into the stables, where it will be easier for the healer to visit. And you'll get a home-cooked meal every day. Or at least a pub-cooked one." He exchanged a laughing glance with Cala.

"A meal is all I'm promising. Better than subsisting on dried-out bread and warm cheese." Cala gestured at the basket sitting on the ground beside the remaining upright beam. "And a real roof over your heads instead of a cave with a half-built wall."

Nevan frowned at what was left of the wall he'd been building. Two of the uprights he'd wedged into place had disappeared since his last visit. Apparently, Sundri's tail had done some violent work. Nevan hated to think of the dragon being in pain, but he also remembered how much work it had taken to bring those heavy beams down to the aerie and put them into place. Perhaps it was a good thing he and Starlight had a new home.

"We're going to move Sundri the same way we brought him up here." William spread the canvas out beside the dragon. "Finn, Nari, and Starlight are fresh, so the lift should be relatively easy for them. We're more than halfway up the cliffside. Easy as fire."

Tyge blinked. “Easy as fire,” he repeated. “Although I’m not sure moving him again so soon is a good idea.”

“It’s been almost two weeks.” William put a hand on Tyge’s shoulder. “Is he any better?”

“Not really,” Tyge whispered.

“Then let’s get him somewhere he can heal.”

With a sullen grumble, Tyge helped William and Nevan spread out the canvas. “Why do you think moving him up there will help him?”

“He needs positive reinforcement from his peers.” Cala, who had been standing near Nari on the ledge, moved closer. “From what we’ve observed of the sea dragons, and what William has told us of the war dragons, they’re social creatures. Accustomed to living in a thunder. I learned a little healing magic at the academy, and the connection of emotion and body was paramount. A being—human, elf, orc, and, I dare say, dragon—can’t heal if they are in pain and fear. Having the others around him will strengthen his life force and health.”

“Sundri is a war dragon, not part of your sea thunder!” Tyge sneered and spit on the ground.

“You know, you’re making it really hard for us to want to help you.” Nevan dropped the leather strap he’d been holding and crossed his arms. “We’ve offered you a place here. A clan to take you in. A thunder for your dragon. And you offer us insults and anger.” Tyge started to say something, but Nevan flung up his hand, cutting him off. He stomped closer, looming over the other man. “If it weren’t for your dragon, I’d say we toss you on the first ship out of Safe Haven.”

“And at this point, I’d back him up.” William nodded decisively. “So how about you help us move Sundri to a location where he will have a chance at healing, and stop acting like a… a *Verduu*?”

Tyge gasped and reached for the sword he wasn’t wearing. “How dare you, William! Has that—” His words cut off as if cleaved by a knife. He gripped his throat.

Koni strolled around the outcropping and onto the ledge. “I came to see what was taking you so long. It’s a pity when childish prejudices get in the way of helping those we love.” His icy blue eyes seemed to glow with disdain.

Tyge's hands fell away from his neck, and his face went red. He gazed at the dragon for a moment, then bowed deeply to the group. "I apologize for my rash and hurtful words." It came out hoarse and tight but surprisingly sincere. "I beg that you will forgive me."

"For Sundri's sake." William dusted his hands together. "Now, let's move that dragon."

They rolled the dragon onto the canvas. He fought them, twisting and writhing in pain, even with Tyge whispering comfort. His tail swung and hit the last remaining beam with a thunderous crack, splintering the wood. Nevan winced but continued pushing the dragon's flank.

Once the fabric was under the beast, they fed the leather straps over him. Cala buckled it to the ring on Nari's harness, then directed the dragon to a perch just above their ledge. Finn came in to get his strap attached, then moved aside to let Starlight in. Then the three of them lifted off, their wings beating fast and hard. All three were used to dropping over the side then using their speed to rise, but they understood the need.

Slowly the dragons lifted their burdens. William, Koni, and Cala hurried up the path while Nevan and Tyge carefully guided the sling out of the cave. Once the dragons began rising, they followed the others up the steps as fast as they could. Nevan's long legs gave him an advantage, and he caught up to William as the older dragon rider reached the top. They ran across the stony promontory after Cala.

The dragons appeared over the top of the wall, their burden swinging gently beneath them. The three flew in a tight formation, their silver blue wings flapping in time as they slowly lowered Sundri into the courtyard. Tyge put on a burst of speed and passed Nevan, flying through the gate Cala had opened to be with his partner. The dragons settled on the wall, peering down at the injured beast.

"Well done, Starlight!" Nevan tried to think the words loudly as he ran into the courtyard. "You were perfect!"

Starlight dropped her head low so Nevan could stroke her ear ridges. *"Better here."*

"I know." He lowered his voice as he unbuckled the harness. "And you don't have to stay here if you don't want to."

"Starlight stay." She nuzzled him for a moment. *"For now. Sundri need."* She shook off the harness, then hopped down into the courtyard to crouch beside the war dragon.

THE SEA DRAGONS DIDN'T LEAVE SUNDRI ALONE FOR THE NEXT week. Whenever one left to fish, the other two remained. The humans tried to move the war dragon into the stable, but the sea dragons wouldn't allow it. Starlight told Nevan he needed rest more than he needed a roof over his head. "Dragons live outside."

"I'm not sure war dragons live outside. I think they have a guild house." Nevan sat on the ledge of their aerie while Starlight fished in the calm sea below. As he practiced speaking with Starlight, their range seemed to increase to the point he could reach her anywhere within sight.

"*House is for riders, not dragons.*" Starlight dove and caught a fish in her front claws. She swooped up out of the water, tossed the fish into the air, and caught it in her mouth as she rose. Then she circled to look for another target.

"How do you know? You've never been to Verduun." Nevan leaned back to lay flat on the warm stone of his ledge, staring up at the pale sky.

"*Sundri tells me.*"

He sat up in surprise. "But Tyge says war dragons don't talk."

"*Sundri talks. The rider not listen.*"

"Huh." He watched Starlight gulp down another fish. "Have you had enough?"

"*For now.*" She soared high overhead, then swooped down to land beside him. As Nevan scrambled to his feet, Starlight shook herself, splattering him with seawater. The dragon laughed silently, but Nevan could still hear it.

"You scamp." He pushed her head away with a surge of contentment. Then he sat up. "Surge. I think that's it. A surge of dragons."

CHAPTER THIRTY

The day of the hand fasting dawned bright and warm. A bubble of sweet anticipation filled Franisa's chest as she opened the window in the bedroom, letting in the fresh spring air. The weather had shifted from cool to pleasant, but with the big oven not in use this day, the house held a chill.

Franisa sat at the little table in her bedroom, watching in the mirror as Cala put the finishing touches on her hair. Her friend had braided the thick mass into an elegant upswept style, claiming it was how the war witches wore theirs for ceremonial occasions. She'd woven some ribbon flowers into the braids and secured it with a set of golden hair pins.

"They're ceremonial. I knew I'd have no need for them, but I couldn't bear to give them up." Cala tucked the last one in. "This seems a fitting occasion."

Franisa picked up the hand mirror and peered at her reflection in the larger one over the table. "That's beautiful! I had no idea war witches learned hair styling."

Cala laughed. "What else are a bunch of teen girls going to do when their studies are finished for the day? No, don't answer that. We got into all kinds of trouble. But we learned this too."

Franisa tied her mother's locket around her neck and stood. "How do I look?" She shook out the full skirts of her pale-yellow gown. It was the same dress she'd worn when she married Keldan, and despite ten years in a cedar chest, the dress still looked as good as the day it had been sewn. She had Cala's aunt Milli to thank for that. The old witch had been a genius with preservation charms.

Cala adjusted the locket. "You look beautiful."

"Mama, you look like an apprentice!" Eloise stood in the doorway, bouncing on her toes in the pink dress she'd worn to dinner at the smithy. Was it only a few weeks ago? So much had happened in that short time, Franisa felt it had been months.

"I think you mean princess, darling." Franisa smiled at her daughter.

"No, you're prettier than a princess." Eloise touched the fabric and took an experimental sniff. "And the dress doesn't smell of cedar anymore."

"Airing it out helped a lot." Franisa chuckled. "I thought you liked cedar."

"It's all right, but cardamom and oranges is better. And dragon." The little girl skipped around her mother then back out the door. "Lord Koni is here!"

They followed Eloise down the stairs to the kitchen. Koni stood by the door, resplendent in a white suit with gold trim and a flowing cape. He was flanked by two beautiful women. The brunette looked slightly familiar, but Franisa recognized Koni's redheaded wife immediately. "Delina! I haven't seen you in ages!" She hurried across the room for a hug.

"Sarai!" Cala cried, following Franisa to the trio. "What are you doing here?"

The dark-haired beauty embraced Cala. "Koni asked me to come. He said there's a dragon that needs healing. I haven't worked with dragons since I left Verduun, but the magical principles seem to be similar to what I learned in the Borgonne for all races."

"Franisa, this is William's sister, Sarai Lavigne." Koni indicated the woman with a flourish. "And you know my lovely wife. We'd best be on our way." He turned sharply, his cape swinging wide.

Delina put a hand on Koni's arm. "We aren't late. The hand fasting can't start without the bride. Don't rush her."

Koni swept a bow toward his wife. "I wouldn't dream of it. Franisa, are you ready to go, or do you require more time to complete your preparations?"

Franisa looked around the bakery, then patted her hair with one hand. "I think I'm ready."

"I regret that I have only two arms to escort so many lovely ladies." Koni offered his elbow to Franisa. "Let us commence."

They trailed out the door, Eloise shutting it behind them. The six of them strolled up the lane to the square where a huge group of residents cheered. Franisa blushed and waved, then let Koni lead her around the fountain. As they passed, villagers tossed flower petals before them, then fell in behind in a long procession.

"Will we walk the whole way?" Franisa asked Koni, her tone hesitant. She still felt a bit awed by the mayor. "Surely you can't take the whole village along the elven paths?"

"You won't walk." He stopped at the road leading out of the village. Gwardil stood there with the donkey, Winnie. The cart had been festooned with bright flowers and loaded with pillows. "You and Eloise will ride. The rest will walk. It won't hurt them to take a stroll." He picked up the little girl and tossed her into the cart. She squealed and landed with a little thud, shaking the rickety cart. Winnie looked over her shoulder and brayed loudly, as if she found Eloise's arrival amusing.

Koni assisted Franisa into the wagon in a more dignified manner, merely handing her up into the open back. She sat, facing backward, legs dangling, and gazed at the huge crowd that had gathered behind them. A hand fasting wasn't a frequent occurrence in Safe Haven, and the villagers intended to make the most of it. They all wore their best clothing, and many carried baskets and bundles, some giving off mouth-watering aromas. The entire town would contribute food to the party after the ceremony.

The walk to FarPoint took far less time than she expected. Had Koni used his magic to take the whole village along the elven path? Or maybe her happiness made the time fly. Whatever the case, the rhythm of the cart changed as they rolled up the rocky promontory on which the tower stood.

William, Enrich, Nevan, and his whole family waited in front of the tower. Franisa's heart leapt at the sight of her betrothed. Koni helped Franisa down from the cart and took her to the tall arched doorway leading to the courtyard. The three dragons perched on the wall, watching the unusual human activity. Franisa wondered what they thought of the event, then realized she could ask Nevan afterward. Or maybe even ask Starlight herself. They seemed interested and even Finn had come down from his tower perch to watch.

Nevan met them at the wide gate, falling in on Koni's other side as they walked together into the enclosed yard. The big doors to the stables were closed. Franisa wondered if Sundri was inside, but this didn't seem the time to ask.

A number of tables and benches filled the courtyard, save for an open space before the big doors. There, flowers had been hung on the lintel, and a dais had been set in place. Koni led them to the platform and helped Franisa up the low step. Then they turned to watch their well-wishers pour into the courtyard. Elspeth had set up a table at the back with a huge barrel of ale and a smaller one of mead. People deposited their bundles and baskets on another long table against the lower seaward wall, then took places on the benches.

Cala took her place next to Franisa, and William stood beside Nevan. Eloise and Enrich sat in chairs close to the dais next to Nevan's parents and Gebby.

When everyone had filed into the yard, Koni cleared his throat. "My friends! Welcome to the hand fasting of Nevan and Franisa. If there is anyone who has reason to dispute this union, speak now."

Franisa held her breath, uncertain why. Surely no one would object to their marriage. Koni waited for a long moment, then repeated the question.

Franisa frowned at him. "Isn't once enough?"

"Three times is traditional," the elf said in an uncharacteristically uncertain tone.

"Traditional where? Not here." Nevan leaned forward to peer at Franisa, then raised a brow at the mayor. "What's your game?"

Koni fidgeted for a moment, then called out a third time, "If there is anyone who has reason to dispute this union, speak now!"

Gnollis stomped into the courtyard with Philomena on his arm. He wore his usual rough garb, except he'd exchanged his red cap for a blue one. His wife was resplendent in a deep purple gown and a tiara made of silver metal and violet stones. The little dwarf glowered at the elf. "You were supposed to close the gate so I could fling it open! What's the point of a dramatic entrance if it isn't dramatic?"

Koni closed his eyes for an instant, then gestured to the dwarf. "My apologies. Would you like to go back out and try again?"

"No point now. Everyone knows we're here." Gnollis stomped up to the dais and favored Franisa with his usual sour glare. "You were a decent daughter in-law." He turned to Derwin and Lilabeth. "Your son couldn't do much better. This union has my blessing."

Cala drew in an indignant breath, but Franisa turned to put a hand on her friend's arm. She leaned close to whisper, "He means well." Then, raising her voice, she stepped closer to the little man. "Thank you."

He shrugged uncomfortably and stomped away. Philomena gave her a single once over, then nodded regally and sailed to a hastily vacated seat which she took like a queen.

"Is that Princess Philomena of Dorfmund?" Sarai whispered from somewhere beyond William. "I knew she'd married a dwarf, but no one seemed to know where they'd gone."

Franisa's jaw dropped as she stared at her mother-in-law. Philomena certainly had the bearing of royalty, but she'd never heard even a whisper that she might actually— "Wait a minute. Does that mean my children have royal blood?"

Koni waved a negligent hand. "That doesn't matter. We have more important things to do. Nevan, do you take Franisa to be your wife? To protect and to serve, to share burdens and pleasures, forsaking all others from now until eternity?"

Without the smallest pause, Nevan replied, "I do."

Koni turned to Franisa. "Do you take Nevan to be your husband? To protect and serve, to share burdens and pleasures, forsaking all others from now until eternity?"

Franisa took half a step forward so she could look around Koni to see her betrothed. He smiled at her, settling the nervous tremors in her stomach and setting her heart afire. How could she ever have had any doubts about this union? "I do."

"Excellent! Do you have rings or some other symbol of your fidelity?" Koni put out a hand.

Cala handed Franisa a gold chain with a circular pendant emblazoned with the stylized sun—the symbol of the One. She took the necklace and lowered it into Koni's hand next to the smaller one Nevan had placed there. Koni took both and showed them to the crowd, then deposited them in Nevan's palm. He took Franisa's hand and placed it over Nevan's and wrapped a red ribbon around them. "By the giving and receiving of these symbols, these two people affirm their pledge of fidelity. What the One has joined, let no one part." He unfurled the ribbon with a flourish.

Franisa took the larger of the two pendants and lifted it. Nevan leaned down so she could place it around his neck, then he put the other one over her head.

"By the power vested in me by the people of the island of Safe Haven, and in the name of the One, I now pronounce you married. Franisa, kiss the groom!"

Franisa's eyes went wide, and the crowd laughed at Koni's reversal of the usual ceremonial ending. When she met Nevan's shy gaze, she smiled, reached up to pull his head down, and kissed him soundly.

The crowd cheered. Eloise jumped up onto the platform and hugged Nevan's leg. The new couple broke apart and wrapped their arms around the little girl. "Enrich, get up here," Nevan called. "This is a celebration for the whole family."

Giving his grandfather a wide berth, Enrich climbed up and threw himself into his new father's arms.

AN ENDLESS LINE OF PEOPLE CAME PAST, CONGRATULATING the happy couple, then wandering away to partake of the wedding feast. And what a feast it was! Or so Franisa assumed, based on the heaped plates she saw go past. She and Nevan hadn't had a chance to even look at the heavily laden tables.

When Philomena deigned to approach, the whole line of people side-stepped away in a hilariously synchronized move. The little woman marched up to Franisa, the amethyst diadem on her head matching the rich purple of her silk gown. She blinked her hooded eyes at the couple, then nodded.

Before she could say anything, Franisa blurted out, "How could you not tell me you were royalty?!"

Philomena lifted her nose. "It didn't concern you."

"Many people would say my children's ancestry is my business."

The old princess waved a hand. "It's ancient history, and I renounced all claim to the throne, for myself and my progeny. It was Gnollis's sole condition."

Franisa felt her jaw drop and fought to close her mouth. "Gnollis insisted you give up your royal status? And you agreed?"

"Compromise is important in a marriage." Philomena turned to look at Nevan. "You turned out better than I expected. I remember when you almost set the smithy on fire."

"That wasn't me." Nevan's gaze darted away. "It was Pierr. I'm the one who let the horses out."

"Ah, my mistake. My statement stands. Congratulations." Franisa's former mother-in-law sailed away.

The people who had been waiting to speak with the couple had disappeared, perhaps unwilling to encounter Philomena's displeasure. For a brief moment, Nevan and Franisa stood alone in a shadowed corner of the darkening courtyard. They looked at each other, and someone's stomach growled. Franisa wasn't sure if it was hers, but her cheeks went hot anyway.

"Time for some food." Nevan glanced at the crowd filling the little space. "Maybe we should go this way." He pushed the door behind him open, then ushered Franisa into the dark stable. "We can sneak something from the kitchen and get a little respite."

A woman's voice rose sharply, coming from one of the curtained alcoves across the big room. "If you'd just make an effort to get him out into the sun, it would help immensely! Dragons, especially war dragons, need fresh air and sunlight!" From the odd accent, Franisa assumed the speaker was Sarai.

"What do you know about what dragons need?" Tyge roared. "You haven't seen a dragon in over ten years!"

"That's not true! I was here less than a year ago, and—"

"Let's get out of here." Nevan hurried Franisa across the stable and into the passage to the main house.

They made sandwiches in the kitchen, sitting at the big wooden table and enjoying the quiet. Franisa looked up from her food to see Nevan gazing fondly at her. Beyond him, through the big window, Starlight perched on the garden wall. Rather than watching the sea, she'd turned around to peer through the window at the couple.

A door slammed open, and Enrich and Eloise ran in. The little girl skidded to a stop beside Nevan. "Starlight said you wanted us."

The dragon nodded agreement from her perch. Nevan slid his arms around the children and beamed at his new wife. "Indeed I do. Now and forever."

ACKNOWLEDGMENTS

MARCH 2026

Thank you for reading Nevan and Franisa's story. I hope you enjoyed it —if you're still reading, I'm guessing you did. If you want to know when the next book comes out, join my newsletter. For sci fi and fantasy recommendations, you'll want to follow Julia. Sign up at her website, juliahuni.com. If you prefer romance and romantasy, you can join Lia at liahuni.com. Both newsletters get the same basic information, but different book recommendations from my author friends. On both, I'll email you every other week, and you can download my free short stories and bonus epilogues.

Oh, and I have a bunch of other books under both those names—I hope you'll check them out!

When I was in my late twenties, the US Air Force assigned me to a NATO unit at Sembach Air Base, Germany. While on paper I worked for a German colonel, who worked for a Belgian one-star, who worked for an American two-star, in reality I worked for the senior US officer, Colonel David P. Mott. He was a tall, gray-haired fighter-pilot with a stern face and a cranky attitude. People were terrified of him. Having survived 10 months as a POW at the end of the Vietnam War, he'd earned that.

But for some reason we clicked. My subconscious recognized that his bluster was a cover, and there was a good guy hidden behind the rough exterior. Very quickly, we developed a respectful grumpy-sunshine friendship. Thirty years later, we still exchange Christmas cards with him and his wife Liz.

As I was writing this book, I learned Col. Mott passed away last fall. I haven't seen him in over fifteen years, but I realized that while I didn't set out to write him, William Ordell has a lot of similarities to Dave Mott. And the relationship between Nevan and William is very similar to that between me and the colonel all those years ago.

So this book is for him. I added a few things to make William more Mott, like the bit about "ale starting at good." That's pure Col Mott.

Fair skies, Colonel.

The sea shell rolls in my story were inspired by a pastry made in the Sparrow Bakery in Bend, Oregon. Their Ocean Rolls are a croissant dough in a cinnamon roll shape, but with a cardamom filling. I love cardamom, but Franisa's version uses a sweet dough, like a brioche, instead of the laminated dough. I haven't tried making them in real life… yet. But I will.

In chapter 16, Nevan talks about how he can't see anything when he tries to visualize. A lot of authors talk about how their story unfolds like a movie in their mind, but I've never experienced that. It took me a long time to realize I'm like Nevan. I don't "see" anything. Or at least not much. Unlike Nevan, I haven't been trying to send pictures to a dragon, but understanding my brain works differently certainly helps me understand a lot of things about myself. Apparently this "condition" has a fancy name, but honestly, it's just how I am. And I'm doing fine—I don't need a diagnosis! But if I help someone else realize their brain works differently, and that there's nothing wrong with that, then my work here is done!

As you know, if you read author notes at the end of books, while we might do all of the writing in solitude, actually publishing a book can take the efforts of many people.

First of all, I'd like to thank my cover designer, the amazing Mariah Sinclair. As I mentioned in the first book, I've been wanting a Mariah Sinclair cover almost as long as I've been publishing, so having two of them (soon to be three!) is living the dream. Her work attracts so many readers—people who would never have read my words without her to catch their eye.

Thanks to my editor, Paula Lester. Although I try to learn the rules about commas in adjective strings and when to use lay vs lie, those rules don't seem to stick in my brain. Paula makes sure I follow them after the fact. Thank you Paula!

My deepest appreciation for my sister, sci fi author AM Scott (also known as romance author Anne M. Scott) for always being my first reader. She tells me when the story goes in the wrong direction, and helps bring me back around.

Thanks to my beta readers, Barb Collishaw, Jenny Avery, Paul Godtland, Larry Searing, Steve Twigg, and Simon Rosenberg. They catch the typos I add after Paula fixes things, and give me an emotional boost when they tell me I've written a good one!

Thanks to my sprint pals, AM, Paula, Marcus, and Hillary. Others may come and go, but this team has been with me since 2019. They're my sounding board when I'm not sure what to do and my cheering team when I need support. And they keep me coming back to the keyboard, day after day, to get the work done.

Thanks and love to the ever-shiny Dave the Support Husband who manages our marketing, remembers people's faces when I draw a blank, and pushes me to take a break once in a while. I love you!

And thank *you* for reading my book. Whether you've been with me since 2018 when I thought my sci fi was a cozy mystery, or joined me in the years since, I truly appreciate every one of you! Without you, there'd be no point in writing.

Finally, as always, thanks to the Big Guy who makes all things possible.

Also by Julia Huni

Space Janitor Series:

The Vacuum of Space

The Dust of Kaku

The Trouble with Tinsel

Orbital Operations

Glitter in the Stars

Sweeping S'Ride

Triana Moore, Space Janitor (the complete series)

Tales of a Former Space Janitor

The Rings of Grissom

Planetary Spin Cycle

Waxing the Moon of Lewei

Tales of a Former Space Janitor (books 1-3)

Changing the Speed of Light Bulbs

Sun Spot Remover

Warp, Rinse, Repeat

Friends of a Former Space Janitor

Dark Quasar Rising

Dark Quasar Ignites

Dark Quasar Reckoning

The Phoenix and Katie Li

Luna City Limited

Colonial Explorer Corps Series:

The Earth Concurrence

The Grissom Contention

The Saha Declination

CEC: The Academy Years (books 1-3)

The Darenti Paradox

The Romara Confrontation

The Gagarin Reiteration (2026)

Recycled World Series:

Recycled World

Reduced World

Krimson Empire:

Krimson Run

Krimson Spark

Krimson Surge

Krimson Flare

The Dragons of Safe Haven

A Dragon Rider's Guide to Retirement

A Blacksmith's Guide to Dragon Rearing

A Rider's Guide to Dragon Healing (2026)

Julia also writes earth-bound romantic comedy that won't steam your glasses under the not-so-secret pen name Lia Huni

Also by Lia Huni

When in Rotheberg

When You Bake with the Enemy

When You Get Stuck with your Famous Ex

When You Rescue your Celebrity Crush

When You Fake Date a Stranger

When You Fall For a Prince

When You Renovate a Grump

Sign up for my newsletter and get access to my free novella, *When You Dance at the Christmas Market*, and short story, *When You Find Christmas Magic.*

FOR MORE INFORMATION

Use this QR code to stay up-to-date on all my publishing, and get access to my free bonus stories:

www.ingramcontent.com/pod-product-compliance
Ingram Content Group UK Ltd.
Pitfield, Milton Keynes, MK11 3LW, UK
UKHW021937020626
12862UKWH00006B/811

9 798295 719585